MURDER ON THE BLUFF

MURDER ON THE BLUFF

ESTHER TYLER

COACHWHIP PUBLICATIONS
Greenville, Ohio

Murder on the Bluff, by Esther Tyler

First published 1936
Esther Tyler, 1911-1985
Cover: The Cliff House, Lake Minnewaska, N.Y. (LoC)
CoachwhipBooks.com

ISBN 1-61646-553-0
ISBN-13 978-1-61646-553-7

1

I met Michael at college, where I was busy spending more dollars than I like to think about learning that a Shakespeare is found once in many centuries, and Michael was busy spending more than that learning to wear my suits and shirts. Afterward we drifted together into a small apartment on West Eightieth Street and I settled down to writing bad fiction, while he massacred time in his own fashion.

This story proper begins on the February morning when the Skipper's note arrived. We were at breakfast, and the prospect of a fourth consecutive rainy day had lent the finishing touch to the excellent grouch I had been nursing for a week. Due to a long-awaited birthday check from his aunts, Michael's spirits were soaring.

"A swell day, old son," he observed, pinning the check down with the toast tray. My response was brief and to the point. I glanced morosely at the envelope labeled in Miss Farrington's careful hand and added, "There's a note. Aren't you going to read it?"

"You would," said Michael sadly. "Don't miss anything. Sometime when you— Damn it!"

His face fell sufficiently for my satisfaction. So I reached for the note.

"Dear Michael," it read. "Since it is your birthday, Barbara and I enclose this slight remembrance. We should be delighted if you could find it convenient to pay us a short visit next week, as Barbara is not too well and would be better for a little company. Pray ask James also, if he finds it convenient. I shall expect you Friday. Affectionately yours, Martha Farrington."

I glanced at Michael. His face was black and I promptly felt cheerful. "Well?" I said.

"Well, yourself!" he exploded. "Of all the lousy luck—"

I interrupted hastily. "There's another one. Here, I'll read it."

The second note was in the Skipper's scrawling hand.

> *Dear Mike,*
> *Martha has decided that I need company, and I'm afraid that nothing will do but that you and Jimmie pay your devotional in February. The choice this year is Jude Blinshop, but I have heard no talk on the subject. In any event, bring as many people as you like. I'll do what I can. Regards to Jimmie. Love,*
>
> *Aunt Bob.*

Michael, let me here announce, had more relatives than any three people of my acquaintance, but his immediate family consisted of two aunts with whom he had lived as a child. Being unable to tear himself away from the unquestionable swankiness of my suits and ties—as he so kindly informed me—his present residence at Farrington Bluff consisted of an annual visit there in my company. During college this custom had become a fixed one, and by the time of this yarn it was nothing short of an institution. We usually favored the Bluff in May or June when swimming, boating, and fishing were partial compensations. In February it was unthinkable. I glanced at Michael.

"We could," he ventured feebly, "have the measles. You could anyway, and—"

"No, we couldn't!" I felt rotten enough for anything that morning. "You can take care of your aunts for once in your life. And I warn you. If you drag Gay Palmer out there and explain her to M. Farrington as my fiancée, I'll break your neck!"

Gay Palmer was a young lady in whom Michael had been increasingly engrossed for some months past. A nice kid with red hair and freckles, a little inclined to break furniture when aroused and not too difficult to arouse. Michael, of course, enjoyed it. The deadlier the row, the wilder the reconciliation.

To get back to the story, I was fond of the Skipper. Having no aunts of my own, I had more or less adopted Michael's, particularly the younger one. Martha Farrington was small, stout and prudish—or at least as nearly so as her over-developed sense of breeding would allow. It was Mike's story—and I have never questioned it—that she presided over his cradle with Emily Post in one hand and the Social Directory in the other. Ever since I had known him, she had certainly presided over our annual visits, armed with an exceedingly eligible young lady to hurl at Michael's head. But the Skipper was different. If I had an aunt, I should like her to be like Barbara Farrington. Tall and square, even mannish in appearance, and possessed of a deep musical voice and a pair of tragic looking dark eyes. She wore mostly rough tweeds, could golf like a champion, had taught Mike all he knew about sailing and fishing, and spent her time diverting the attentions of her sister's yearly choices from his luckless head. Yes, I was extraordinarily fond of the Skipper.

And so we went. By *we* I mean Michael, Gay Palmer, and myself. Mike consigned me to the rumble-seat with the luggage, pointing out that I should have too much tact to break up the tender tête-à-tête in the front seat and kindly assuring me that if the cold got too bad I could yell at him to stop for coffee—or get under the suitcases where it was probably quite warm. I didn't argue much. Managing to get him to the Bluff in February was a feat not ruthlessly to be jeopardized by a mere four hours' freezing. Generally speaking, I can take it. So I did.

Farrington Bluff stands on a rocky little island connected with the mainland by a none too sturdy but extremely picturesque bridge. Perched directly on the bluff, it looks to the southward over miles of Long Island Sound and to the northward over a long sloping lawn, terminating in water and the bridge. East and west lie rocks, and below the rocks, the beaches. The pier and the boathouse stand on the western beach. Between them and the house are the tennis courts, and on the rocks to the east stand the stable and the garage. Over the entire estate towers a collection of beautiful old elms. In all, I should say, the island covers about half a mile of dry land.

In the proper season it is pleasant to whirl over the old bridge into the shade of the elms. After a four-hour ride in February it is hardly that. I swore so loudly and so well that Gay rapped applause on the window as we drew up to the house. But my fury was short-lived, for once inside the house I had something more important to think about. M. Farrington's vague remark about the Skipper was far from unfounded. She was not actually ill, but her hair had grayed appallingly and there were tense, strained lines in her face. I was startled and so, I could see, was Michael.

We were established in the library almost immediately. Before the numbness was fairly out of my hands and feet M. Farrington was systematically catechizing Michael about his fall and winter activities. With Gay's assistance he launched into a dramatic account of a debutante ball, and I was left to the Skipper, who stood gazing into the fire, the new silver in her hair glinting in the light and the knuckles of the brown hand resting on the mantel standing out livid, so tightly was it clenched. As I stared at her broad back, feeling more and more disturbed, she whirled and looked me full in the eyes.

"Skipper," I said, grabbing her hand, "what's wrong?"

She smiled. "Great Scott, Jim, do I look as bad as that?" Her voice was natural and easy in its booming cheerfulness. "Good Heavens, boy! You're half frozen. Mike, take this kid upstairs and pour something into him. He's cold. Time to dress, anyway."

Definitely uneasy, I mounted the stairs with Michael. In my room he parked himself in the best chair and fumbled for a cigarette.

"Jimmie?"

"Yeah?"

"What the devil do you suppose is wrong with the Skipper? Aunt Martha doesn't know. And—well, damn it, she looks rotten!"

"You're telling me!" I said. "Why the deuce can't you stay here and look after her?"

Michael lighted his cigarette and glared at the end of it.

"I should, that's a fact," he said. "If anything goes wrong with the Skipper, I'll never forgive myself."

And right there, just in case either of us had changed our opinion of the Bluff in February, a long, whistling shriek of wind seemed actually to shake the house. I thought of the ride back on Monday and shivered.

"Listen to that," growled Michael. "Enough to make anyone sick. And when I tried to talk her into going to Florida this winter, she told me to put on my long underwear if the climate bothered me."

I didn't point out that the Skipper had listened to that wind all her life and thrived on it. Instead I looked at my watch and observed, "If we don't get a move on, M. Farrington will explode. Scram, Mike!"

Still fuming, Michael scrammed.

True to the Skipper's hint, Jude Blinshop put in an appearance at dinner, but the meal was not much of a success. The atmosphere was peculiar. For one thing, the conversation was too free and easy for an M. Farrington function. Not once did Mike have occasion to kick my shins under the table as I hovered on the brink of a slip. Not once did M. Farrington edge him into an exclusive conversation with Jude Blinshop or suggest that he must show the child the conservatory directly after dinner. And not once did the Skipper so much as chuckle during the entire meal. It has since occurred to me that the disappointing flatness was due to the absence of the spirit of chase. We were keyed up for a contest that never transpired. I caught myself recalling M. Farrington's campaign for Tessie Appleton almost wistfully. That had been a week-end! And with Mary Gould— Well, certainly the old lady was losing her grip.

Jude Blinshop, by the way, deserves a word or two of description. Although I hadn't seen her in some time, she and I had been very fond of each other once in the dim, dark past. One of those sleek, slender girls for whom the collegiate world has coined the word smooth. Her hair was very dark, combed straight back and caught low on her neck. Her eyes were an amazing blue, matched exactly this evening by her gown. Her dark, clearcut profile gave a suggestion of aloofness and indifference. Beside her Gay Palmer looked pudgy, cherubic, and thoroughly insignificant. But not to Michael's way of thinking. Since his first pair of long pants, Mike had never succumbed to Jude's charms—a situation that had always been quite agreeable to me.

Coffee in the library proved an even more dismal affair. We had by that time pretty well exhausted our stock subjects of conversation—the respective healths of Mr. and Mrs. Palmer, Mr. and Mrs. Blinshop, M. Farrington's cat, and the Skipper's dogs—not to mention the severity of the winter and the spring repairs. We had also discussed Michael's social activities to date, the condition of my present novel, the reception of the previous one, Jude's opinion of Florida, and Gay's longing to live in England. The library did not share the dining-room's sheltered position, and the howl of the storm was painfully audible. Matters were decidedly at a standstill when Higgins appeared with the coffee.

Michael had taken possession of Christopher, the repulsive Persian cat that occupied the place of honor in the heart of Martha Farrington. Seating himself calmly on the fender, quite unmindful of Christopher's strenuous objections, he caused feline arias to mingle with the general uproar. Miss Farrington sat bolt upright at a discreet distance from the fire, while the two girls were arrayed on the davenport and the Skipper and I took our stand beside Michael. The stage was set, but the lines were sadly missing. Except for the wind and the cat, silence and plenty of it pervaded the Farrington library.

"Higgins," said Michael, manfully venturing into the void, "you don't look up to scratch. Getting lumbago?"

Everyone turned eagerly to Higgins. The man did look ill, as a matter of fact. That he should rattle a coffee cup was a situation in itself. We all braced ourselves for a good rousing discussion of his ailments, but Higgins had other plans.

"I feel very fit, Mr. Michael," he said, looking if anything a little worse, and promptly withdrew.

At this point the Skipper's foot hit the log a resounding whack and she began to chuckle.

"Give it up, Mike. Even Higgins can't stand the gaff. Take all these kids into the game-room and liven them up. Martha and I need a nap."

None of us hastened to point out that this was hardly the hour for napping. Michael rose with alacrity, releasing the exhausted Christopher.

"Skipper," he said, "you're always right." And informing Gay that she would mold if she sat there another moment, he steered her from the room, leaving me to follow with Jude. The arrangement suited me to the ground. The Skipper having yawned in my face and declared that she loathed both ping-pong and billiards, I said good night to M. Farrington and eagerly did my duty. My exhilaration was short-lived. The library door was scarcely shut behind us when Jude dropped my arm.

"Jimmie," she said in a low voice, "I want you to do me a favor."

I had once been in love with the girl and I could still feel my oats at the slightest provocation.

"Anything at all, Jude."

"Well, pigeonhole Gay for half an hour, will you? I must speak to Mike, and it's a little awkward for me—under the circumstances."

I might have mentioned that it would be more awkward for me, but I didn't.

"Why certainly. When? Right away?"

"If you don't mind. Thanks, Jim."

And we entered the game-room. Gay and Michael were already seated with their backs to us, and it took no keen eye to see that they were neither interested in ping-pong nor anxious for our company. I looked uncertainly at Jude, but she had turned away and was toying with a billiard cue. Well, I was playing marbles when my elders plowed through the Argonne, but I have my fighting instincts. I marched up to Gay and hauled her unceremoniously to her feet.

"Palmer," I announced, "unless I demonstrate to you immediately the glories of M. Farrington's roses, there will be fell consequences."

"Hey—" began Michael, but I yanked Gay through the door.

It is satisfying to carry off a situation, but I realized the moment we were in the hall that the situation had barely begun. Gay seated herself on the stairs.

"Well, Don Juan," she started, "I suppose there's some reason for this stupid stunt?"

Not a very good beginning. I didn't improve things any. Gay, it appeared, had heard of Jude Blinshop. She had also heard of M. Farrington's indoor sport, and Jude's evident attractions failed to soothe her. I was floundering badly and Gay's voice was somewhere along the coast of Labrador when to my infinite relief the Skipper suddenly came out of the library.

"What, no ping-pong?" said the Skipper.

Gay stood up. "No," she said without deigning me another look. "I have a snorting headache and I think I'll run up to bed if you don't mind."

"There's some aspirin in the drawer of the bedstand," offered the Skipper. "Probably this damned wind."

And there it was. I must have looked about as I felt, and that was not so good. She was a nice kid, Gay. Confound Jude anyway! The Skipper was chuckling.

"Jim, don't tell me Mike has fallen at last?"

Gay had marched up those stairs, her back like a ramrod. I nodded gloomily. "He's fallen about two thousand feet in the last two minutes," I said, "and he doesn't know it yet."

"Hmm." She went up one step and turned. "Jimmie, do me a favor?"

All things considered, I should have been cured, but I wasn't. "Sure."

"Don't let Mike drag any fool doctors around here, and for the love of Pete keep him away from Jude Blinshop!"

"Skipper!" I said. "Listen! What—"

"Please, Jim." She reached down and gave me a whack on the shoulder. "I count on you," she said and mounted the stairs.

Eventually I closed my mouth. In the course of a mere five minutes I had succeeded in precipitating a promising row between Michael and Gay and in checkmating my only reason for being at the Bluff at all—to get the Skipper to see a doctor. Concluding that there were no limits to my possibilities, I looked at my watch. It was nine-thirty exactly.

No sound from the game-room. The Skipper and Gay were definitely out of the picture. That left myself and M. Farrington. With some idea of doing penance for my sins by spending an hour with that worthy, I opened the library door. But the library was empty.

That left myself. Well, I picked up a book and tried to relax, but the wind wasn't conducive to relaxation. I sat down at the desk and tried to worry a plot that had been more or less on my mind for the past month. Again the wind had other notions. And the couple in the game-room showed no signs of coming to the rescue. At precisely ten o'clock I gave it up and went to bed.

Even there my woes did not subside immediately. The roar of the wind was terrific, and curiosity—not to mention a touch of jealousy—kept me busy speculating about the interview in progress downstairs. I had done considerable threshing by the time everything merged into a senseless hodge-podge in which I stood on the Farrington landing and watched Gay's furious face without any body glide slowly up ahead of me, while the voices of Jude, Michael, the Skipper, and M. Farrington hissed from below, "Do me a favor! Do me a favor!" Finally I roused enough to convince myself that the wind and not the household was doing the hissing, and then at last I slept.

I woke to a bright light in my eyes and someone shaking my shoulder. A loud siren seemed to be sounding in the room. There was a sudden thundering crash that shook the house. In one jump I landed out of that bed and smack into Michael, standing there fully dressed and dripping wet.

"The north chimney!" he shouted above the racket. It sounded more like the whole house. "For God's sake get into your clothes, Jim!" He was white as chalk and his hands were shaking. "There's hell to pay around here. Jude and the Skipper are missing!"

"Missing!" I echoed. "Where—"

"God knows. They're not in their rooms and they're not in the house. And the bridge is down."

I regarded him stupidly.

"Dammit all!" roared Michael. "*Will* you get dressed?"

Obediently I reached for my pants.

2

It didn't take me long to get into them. As I dashed into the hall after Michael, the entire house was a blaze of light. All up and down the hall doors stood open, but no voices were audible above the wailing of the storm.

They were all in the dining-room; there, I suppose, because the din was slightly muffled. M. Farrington in curlers and a hideous lavender robe. Gay, in fuzzy pyjamas, looking like a sleepy, startled Kewpie. Higgins in a genuine nightshirt, topped by a tail coat and finished off with red slippers. Behind Higgins, Cook in braids and an overcoat was trying to pacify the chambermaid, who looked hysterical and obviously desired to be administered to by William, thc chauffcur. It was a perfect scene, and it reached a climax as I entered.

Annie screamed. "I can't stand it any more," she wailed. "I'm going to faint!" Her second scream was a prize winner. But Cook had methods of her own. She landed a neat haymaker on Annie's chin before Michael could intervene.

"Shut up, both of you!" he ordered and there was comparative silence. "Now look," he continued, "there have been storms like this out here before. There's nothing to worry about. Miss Barbara and Miss Blinshop must have gone out for a walk and been caught in it. We'll have to find them. Higgins, you stay here and see to things. William, you can come with Mr. Wells and me. Better get a coat. Have you a flashlight?"

William had. As he vanished to get it, M. Farrington warmed into action.

"Why," she demanded, voicing the thought in all our minds, "would Barbara and Judith go out for a walk on a night like this—and at this hour? They must be in the house, Michael. Possibly—"

"They aren't," said Michael shortly.

Gay's voice, cool and crisp, joined the party. "I suppose you have reason to know?"

Michael turned to her. "I have. I was sitting here wondering about the storm and I suddenly got the idea that if the west chimney went, Jude and the Skipper wouldn't be any too safe. When I went up to suggest that they move down the hall, they weren't there. I thought the Skipper might be in with Aunt Martha, so I woke Aunt Martha up. And then I called Higgins and we looked all over. Then I went after Jim, and while he was getting his clothes on, the chimney went and you all came rushing down." He paused. "Why? What do you mean?"

Gay shrugged. "You're rather damp yourself," she said. "Do you take strolls in February, too?"

Right there I think it began to dawn on Michael that the course of true love can be lumpy. He stared at her.

"I went down to see if the bridge was all right."

"Without a coat?"

"In a top coat. It's raining. What the devil—"

But Gay turned her back on him and asked me for a cigarette. She didn't appear to enjoy asking me either, but she wasn't quite up to asking Higgins. My cigarettes, however, were in my coat and my coat was in my room. A few hours later I might have dashed outside clad only in my trousers, but at the moment I hadn't reached that stage. I made for the door, and my example was followed by

Higgins, Annie, and Cook. I took one fleeting glance over my shoulder as I went.

Gay was standing at the window, her back to Michael, and poor Mike was wearily trying to pacify M. Farrington. I took the stairs three at a time, one idea bouncing about in my head. Did Mike know anything about this performance, and did his knowledge in any way hinge on his talk with Jude? I remembered something that caused me to sit down hastily and hard—the Skipper standing on the stairs saying, "Keep him away from Jude Blinshop. I count on you."

Michael's voice cut short my ramblings. "Are you waiting for warm weather?"

At the foot of the stairs we found William in oilskins, armed with an enormous searchlight.

"Ready, sir," he said.

Michael looked at him. "Have you got a gun?

"A gun!" I echoed.

Michael snarled. "You've heard of them? Well?"

William's mouth closed with a snap.

"No, sir," he said. "Begging your pardon, we ain't likely to need it. However, Higgins—"

"Then get it," ordered Michael sharply.

As soon as the chauffeur's back was at a safe distance, I delivered myself of a few well chosen words.

"Look here, Mike, don't be a damn fool. There's nothing to get so worked up about. Probably—"

"Isn't there?" His voice was savage. "Well, this. Those two women didn't go out in this mess their health!"

I had an inspiration. "Maybe Jude got a call from home and asked the Skipper to run her into town."

"Nobody went anywhere. That bridge was down at ten o'clock, because I saw it."

Ten o'clock! "But you couldn't—"

"But I did," he said, very quietly.

"They might be in the cellar—"

"Sifting cinders? They're not. We looked."

William appeared, waving an efficient looking revolver.

"Higgins says, sir, that it ain't never shot wind yet, but it might if you was quick about it." William was grinning.

Michael pocketed the gun and opened the front door. A blast of icy wind and rain shrieked up to meet us.

"Keep the light ahead of you, William."

"Yes, sir. But don't you think if we was to stand on the steps here and flash it around, Miss Barbara might see it and sing out or head in this direction?"

"No," said Michael.

There was something in his tone that I didn't like, and neither did William. His, "Yes, sir," was surly.

We started down the drive. That night reminded me of one of my kid nightmares in which the world came to a sudden end with trees crashing, houses tumbling down, and souls in long white nightgowns shrieking all over. Aside from the chimney, the house gave no signs of tumbling and there were certainly no souls in evidence. But the old elms creaked and clashed horribly; the rain came in slashing torrents; and the roar of the wind was both deafening and breath-taking. The light was of little use, for it was impossible to see more than ten feet ahead of you. No, there was no contradicting Michael's statement that nobody had gone out for a casual stroll that night.

We went down the drive rapidly, fairly blown along by the wind at our backs. The light disclosed nothing but mud, water and broken branches. At the foot of the drive a roaring torrent of water had entirely effaced the little creek bed. The bridge was nowhere in sight. Only a few broken and twisted piles gave evidence that it had ever existed.

Michael cupped his hands and roared, "Boathouse!"

But getting there was no easy matter. Our way was up hill, over rocks, and against the wind. It was slippery and cold. Once William slipped and nearly lost the light altogether. When we reached the rocks overlooking the beach, I made an ineffectual effort to make myself heard above the din. The wet rocks sloped down smooth and slippery as glass. I seized Michael's arm.

"Go around!" I bellowed with every ounce of wind I had.

Michael's answer was to sit down on the rocks and start to slide. I say start because he sailed down the first dip, landed on his feet, staggered, and the next minute disappeared headlong into the darkness. Simultaneously William's huge paw descended upon my shoulder. He was dragging me toward the path and the steps, slipping and scrambling, more on our hands and knees than otherwise. A horrible picture of what might be lying at the foot of those rocks went with us. With the path came sure footing and we fairly tore along, but at the head of the boathouse steps we were stopped short. Water was beating against the top step.

Somewhere in that boiling mess was Michael—or what was left of him. And the Skipper— Something hard and heavy was thrust into my hand. The searchlight. William was peeling off his oilskins. I was hardly aware of what he was doing before he had again seized the light.

"Coat!" he yelled. "Off! Quick!"

I wrenched myself out of it and held the light for him. As fast as his wet fingers would move, they tied the coat and the oilskin together. Signaling me to follow, William began to edge himself out along the ledge of rock that ran above the boathouse. I followed him. Just beyond the boathouse he halted and signaled me to throw the light out over the water.

For a second only churning surf met our eyes and then something else, something dark and bulky. Even as I realized that it was Michael, William moved. He threw the coats, my heavy one on the end. Michael was yards to the right of us and the coats went straight out. But William's eye was good. In a flash Michael was washed toward us, and the coats were blown toward him. As they met I lent my free hand to the tug. In one surging swell he came in. We pulled like madmen. Headlong, Michael was tumbled onto the ledge.

He lay horribly still. Throwing the coats to me, William bent over. With one lunge he heaved Michael over his shoulder, and slowly, laboriously, we edged our way back to the path. Despite the care with which we laid him down, one arm was twisted under him. Blood was flowing from a gash on his head.

Luckily my hip pocket still contained the flask with which I had reconciled myself to that ride in the rumble-seat. I raised his head and forced a little whiskey into him. Possibly minutes ticked by. The roar of the blood in my ears drowned out the combined wind and surf. And then finally he moved. It was impossible to catch what he said. He insisted on getting to his feet and stood there, swaying, covered with blood, dripping wet, and altogether unpleasant to look at.

William roared, "Back to the house, sir!"

We thought Michael understood, for he started along the path before we could get the overcoat around him. As we came abreast of the tennis courts, Michael paused and signaled for the light. The backstop was down, a tangled jumble of wire, and the wet clay was a soft mush. In between the two courts, running straight toward the boathouse, a set of heavy footprints showed that someone had been too impatient to take the path. The Skipper? Michael was off like a shot.

At the drive we lost them. Too much water had poured over that gravel to leave any sign of anything. It seemed to me that wherever she was, the Skipper would agree that Michael needed attention at once. We were directly in front of the house. I grabbed him and shoved him, struggling and protesting, up the steps and into the house.

We were a mess, all three of us, dripping and coatless. William still wore rubber boots and a sou'wester. His trousers and his pyjama top were plastered against him as if by mucilage, and his lips were blue. But Michael was Exhibit A. His face was a pasty white, smeared with blood. His right arm hung useless at his side and his clothes were in shreds.

"Damn you!" His roar gathered volume as William closed the door behind us. "Let go of me. I'll—"

But he didn't do anything. A piercing scream from the dining-room announced that he had been discovered. M. Farrington bore down upon us, babbling as she came.

"Michael! Michael! My poor boy, what—?"

I caught a glimpse of Gay behind her and of Higgins behind Gay when Michael put an end to the scene. In her stress of feeling, M. Farrington clutched his bad arm and Michael crumpled quietly to the floor.

Then things began to happen. M. Farrington promptly went off into hysterics. Gay knelt beside Michael. Higgins stood wringing his hands, and William stared dumbly at the general proceedings.

"He fell on a rock," I said to Gay's mute white face. "Higgins, ring for Annie and take Miss Farrington to her room. Lend a hand here, William."

In spite of his aunt's protests we picked up Michael and started for the stairs.

"I'm going to call a doctor," said Gay at my elbow.

"He can't get through. The bridge is down."

"There are boats," she said quietly.

It was something of a job to get Michael upstairs. He's no featherweight, and below us M. Farrington was giving efficient proof of Higgins' lack of skill as a lady's-maid. We got him into his room and onto the bed, where a penknife made short work of what was left of his clothes. The gash in his head was wide, but not too deep. His knees and shins were merely scraped, but the arm was a different matter.

"It ain't broke, sir. I think it's his shoulder."

I nodded. We patched him up as well as we could and brought him around. It took him only a second to collect himself. His voice was hoarse.

"Did you find them?"

I shook my head. In the midst of our efforts to keep him in bed, Gay appeared behind me.

"The wire's down," she said dully.

Well, I had expected it. "Listen, Mike," I said. "You're staying right here. If you promise to do it, we go on hunting. If you don't, we'll stay right here and hold you down."

Once or twice a year I succeed in convincing him that I mean just what I say. I did it then. He stared at me for half a minute.

"All right. Only hurry, for God's sake!"

"I'll get them," I promised.

Downstairs, Annie and Cook between them had managed to remove M. Farrington to the library, whence the sound of her shrill sobs was distinctly audible. William and I climbed into dry coats and tested the Skipper's Scotch. It was good Scotch.

"I suggest, sir, that we go out the west door. If you was to go round the front and me round the back, we could cover quite a lot of ground, meet at the east side, and go on to the garage."

"O.K.," I said. "For God's sake don't fall off the bluff!"

So we parted. Either the gale was gathering force or we were losing it. Going was hard and thinking was worse.

Where the devil was the Skipper? And Jude! What was that girl up to anyway? I thought nothing of reaching the end of the house ahead of William. Going, I reasoned, would be harder for him on mushy sod with no protection against the wind. But by the time I had been there several minutes, it was beginning to get me. And then I heard something—a faint shout in the distance, calling my name.

It was coming from the direction of the bluff. I forgot the danger of dashing over the edge in the darkness. I forgot everything and began to run toward that voice. Long before I could see anybody I could see the light, and I bellowed at the top of my lungs as I came. William was standing not twenty feet from the edge of the bluff, and I was still some distance from him when he turned his light downward.

There, without hat or coat, face downward in the mud, lay Jude Blinshop, still clad in her bright blue dress and silver slippers. What the devil was William waiting for?

I shouted something unintelligible and flopped down on my knees. I tried to raise her. And then, as Jude's face came into the light, I knew. Her face and dress were streaked with something far brighter than mud. Through the middle of her forehead was a ragged, bleeding hole. Long before I found her pulse I knew that Jude Blinshop was dead.

There is no point in dwelling on what I went through in the next few minutes. It has no bearing on this story. Crouched in the mud, staring at that still, ghastly face, I was reliving a flickering succession of scenes with a girl who laughed, who danced, who— From a great distance and after a long time I became aware of the storm once more—of William's frantic grip on my shoulder and his voice rising meaninglessly above the uproar.

I moved without knowing what I was doing, raised her in my arms and started for the house without knowing where I was going. Mostly I was thinking of blue eyes, alive, laughing, and eager. I was feeling a girl's warm arms around my neck, feeling— Suddenly I was in the kitchen doorway with William hanging onto my arm.

"Don't you think, sir, we better leave her here until— I mean, Miss Farrington, sir. If she was to see us."

I stared at him. Dimly there came to me a recollection of M. Farrington and her hysterics, of the missing Skipper, of Michael and Gay upstairs. I nodded. William was helping me lay her on the kitchen table. Limp, sodden thing in a blue dress. Jude. Jude Blinshop! A blanket of some sort seemed to be over me. I couldn't think. I couldn't feel. There was empty space all around me and empty space inside of me. Then through that empty space a voice cut like a rifle shot. It was William's. And he was babbling something about murder!

Impossible! My stunned brain rejected the thought automatically, but even in the process it mulled over other facts. Dead. Shot! And the bridge was down. Suppose Jude had been shot? Then the person who shot her must be—

I opened my mouth, but the words never came, for just at that moment a sound from the door sent us both spinning wildly about to confront the Skipper standing calmly on the threshold.

3

The Skipper closed the door. "Well," she said in a perfectly natural voice, "what goes on here?" Just that. I tried to say something, but I was too late. The Skipper caught sight of the thing behind us. She stood stock still, gripping her sou'wester, and she looked old. Abruptly she staggered, but before I could reach her she was leaning against the door.

"My God!" she whispered. "Oh, my God!"

I forced myself to speak. "We were looking for you. We found Jude—on the bluff."

She passed a shaking hand over her eyes, and when she spoke her voice was flat and dead. "Where's Michael?"

William and I exchanged glances. "In bed," I said. "We—we haven't told anyone." Every inch of me howled to know where she had been, to ask her what had happened. But I couldn't seem to budge.

"Get something to cover—Miss Blinshop, William. Both of you get into dry clothes and meet me in the dining-room."

My "Right" was purely automatic. In the hall Higgins was hovering around the front door looking unhappy. When he caught sight of me he gave vent to a most un-Higginsish yelp of joy.

"We've found them," I managed. "Where is everybody?"

"Thank Heaven, sir!" Then with an obvious effort at control, "Miss Farrington is in her room. Cook and Annie are with her. With your permission, I'll tell her at once, sir. She's been—a bit difficult."

"Wait a minute, Higgins. How is Mr. Michael?"

"Resting quietly, sir. Miss Palmer is with him. I—"

I acted on impulse. I wanted time to get a grip on myself and to get things straightened out as much as possible before I faced M. Farrington.

"Then we'll wait a while before we tell them. You might be sure the outer cellar door is locked, Higgins. Then Miss Barbara wants you in the dining-room. I'll be down in a minute."

I was halfway up the stairs before he managed a bewildered, "Very good." He forgot to add the "sir."

Fortunately the doors of M. Farrington's and Michael's rooms were closed and the racket of the storm served as a good blanket to the sound of my steps. I was in no state to talk to either one of them. My brain was numb. Unspeakable things had happened and were about to happen, but it was important only that I dress and get back to the dining-room.

I did just that. The Skipper was at the sideboard, busy with a decanter. A roaring fire burned in the fireplace and before it sat William with a smoking drink in his hand. As I entered, Higgins appeared from the kitchen with another.

"Get in front of the fire and drink up, Jim," said the Skipper. I obeyed. It was all like a nightmare. A feeling of jangled nerves and a conviction that at any moment some unknown force would explode us all into atoms. But the heat and the drink did their work. At length out of the ghastly silence came the Skipper's voice.

"Sit down, Higgins—over here."

Higgins sat, hard, as if another moment on his feet would have finished him. The Skipper went on slowly and quietly.

"Diana—the collie bitch—was about due for a litter of pups. I was rather worried about her—nearly lost her last time. When I couldn't sleep in all this racket, I had her more or less on my mind. About ten-thirty I decided to go out and have a look at her. So I dressed and went out the back way to avoid a little of the storm. I've been out there ever since."

They were all waiting for me to speak. Desperately I plunged into my story, an anxious eye on the Skipper's face. But the Skipper was never hysterical. Aside from the color of her face and the slight twitching of her mouth, she might have been listening to a plot for a novel. After I had finished there was no sound in the room but the crackling of the fire. The Skipper recovered first.

"The first thing for us to do is to get hold of George Foster. He's the coroner—and a good doctor."

"We can't," I said dully. "The bridge is down—and the telephone wires."

Her grip on my shoulder tightened. "Are you sure?"

"Positive."

She drew a long breath.

"I see. Well, go up to Mike and tell him the best you can. I'll handle Martha. Higgins, you and William had better carry Ju—Miss Blinshop to her room. Wait until Mr. Wells and I get upstairs. I'll send Cook and Annie down right away."

At the foot of the stairs I stopped her.

"Skipper, wait a minute," I said. "There aren't any other servants here on the Bluff, are there?

"We're all here, Jim," she said evenly.

"Then it must have been a tramp on the grounds or some fool shooting to—to call for help!

We stared at each other. As plainly as any words could say it, her eyes said, "And Jude went out there for what?" God, but she looked haggard! Taking my arm, she started me up the stairs.

"We've got to bite on it, Jim," she said in a husky voice.

I left her at M. Farrington's door and walked on to Michael's. It took an effort to knock and turn the knob. Michael was asleep. Gay, still holding his hand, half rose from his side as I entered and closed the door behind me.

"How is he?" I whispered.

"Just fagged out, I think. Jimmie! You didn't find them!"

Her voice was low, but not low enough. Mike's eyes flew open and lighted on my face. He struggled up. "Jim! Where are they? You—"

"We found them, Mike," I said, "but—"

"But what?"

My lips were dry. I was obliged to moisten them before they would seem to move. "There's been an accident. The Skipper's all right, but we—we found Jude out on the bluff." I swallowed hard. "She's been shot, Mike. She's dead."

For one never-ending second they stared at me. Then Gay's hand flew to her throat. "No!" she cried sharply. "No!"

But Mike sat like a wooden Indian, a shred of coverlet tearing away in his clenched fingers.

"Skipper!" he said heavily. "Skipper! Oh, my God!"

I was riveted to the spot, too busy fighting back the implication of those words to do anything. But Gay moved blindly to him.

"Mickie!" she said. "Oh-oh—"

Michael's arm went around her, but the expression on his face never changed. I turned away to the mantel and left them that way. There were a few pictures in my own mind right then that were all I could deal with. In the end it was Michael who forced me to go on. Gay huddled beside him, her freckles standing out in startling relief against her chalky face, but Mike, propped up against the pillows, was ghastly. The hand that supported Gay was shaking.

"We found Jude on the bluff, Mike. And just as we got into the house the Skipper came in. She'd been with a sick dog in the stable. Jude must have gone out to look for her and been hit by a shot from a boat in distress—or—"

"Bunk!" said Michael curtly.

The bluff was a sheer drop of at least fifty feet to the water, and I knew it. There was a strained silence. Then Gay's voice, forced but level.

"There must be a tramp in the grounds somewhere."

More silence. A tramp coming to a place like the Bluff on such a night? Hardly. Burglars? That didn't make sense either. Jude would never have pursued a burglar into the storm. Would she have followed the Skipper without hat or coat? Was there someone else out there? My head was roaring with wild ideas.

"It wouldn't do any harm to see that the house is locked," I said. "That's one thing we can do." The look in his eyes was giving me the creeps. He was a sick man and, unless I missed my guess, he was going to be sicker. "And you're not going to do anything. You're going to sleep."

"Sleep!" said Michael violently. *"Sleep!"*

Gay's hysterical laugh agreed with him.

"Look here," I said, "you've been through enough for a good case of pneumonia. We're cut off from shore and will be until this sea stops running. And there's a lot of damned unpleasant figuring to do in the morning. If you don't sleep, you may die on our hands. Do you get me?"

He didn't, but Gay did and that was all I wanted. I left her to carry the point. The Skipper opened M. Farrington's door in answer to my knock, and just one glance told me that she had not been having an easy time of it.

"How is she?" I whispered.

The Skipper smiled, a rather twisted smile. "She'll live. How did Michael take it?"

"Hard." I hated to alarm her, but there seemed no help for it. "I'm afraid he's pretty sick, Skipper. Shock, cold water, and his shoulder."

She nodded. "Stay with Martha a minute. I want to have a look at him."

Of all things on earth that I did not want at that moment, a tête-à-tête with M. Farrington headed the list. It was difficult enough to answer her questions when the answers were obvious. Right then there were no answers and I was busy enough with questions of my own. But the Skipper didn't wait for a reply. For the first time in my life I entered M. Farrington's room.

It was like her. Stuffy little knick-knacks in glass cases jutted out all over the tables and stands. From the walls, morbid looking men in whiskers and pompadoured women in bustles simpered eternally. In an absurd bassinet beside the bed reposed Christopher, looking fat and disagreeable, and in the bed, pitifully white and shaken, lay Martha Farrington.

Something in her face got me as I crossed the room. For all her prudery and fussiness, I was fond of the old lady. I was suddenly keenly aware of all the innumerable little kindnesses she had done me. All the impossibilities of that impossible night seemed summed up in that picture of M. Farrington lying there helpless. I sat down beside her and took her hand.

"Aunt Barbara has just gone to say good night to Michael," I said. "You mustn't worry, Aunt Martha. It will all work out somehow." I realized how inadequate those words were but couldn't think of anything more impressive to add to them.

Her head moved fretfully from side to side. She scarcely seemed aware of my presence. "I thought it would all finish when you and Michael came," she said faintly.

My breath came in so hard that it seemed to crack my ribs. With all my might I was fighting back the horrible suspicion that was closing in on me like a monstrous octopus.

"You thought what would finish?" I prompted, loyalty to the Skipper lying like a ton of lead in my chest. There was no answer. M. Farrington was crying, not in the loud, ear-piercing hysteria that had greeted us earlier in the night, but weakly, pitifully, as if too worn out to do anything else.

"Don't cry, Aunt Martha," I said. "Try to rest. I'll take care of everything." Wild promise!

The hideous clock on the mantel ticked persistently over the sound of her weary sobbing. I strained to make my mind a blank—to forget the Skipper's stricken face, to forget Michael's words, above all to forget that picture of Judith lying in the light of William's torch. Every nerve in my body jangled to the sound of that clock and of that crying. And then slowly the sobbing diminished, paused for an instant, started again and stopped altogether. The clock and I were alone in a nightmare world. M. Farrington's voice recalled me to my senses.

"James, promise me something."

I rubbed my eyes dazedly. "Anything, Aunt Martha."

"Never repeat what I am going to tell you to anyone."

"You can trust me."

"I know I can." She hesitated. When she spoke again her voice was stronger, nearly normal. "Something has been troubling Barbara for months. She refuses to see a doctor. She can't seem to bring herself to confide in me. I sent for you and Michael because I was frightened."

I felt cold and clammy. "I know," I said.

"When I told her that I had invited Judith, she seemed terribly upset. I would have undone it if I could, but Judith had already accepted. And now—" Her grip on my hand tightened. "James, I left the bathroom door open when I went to bed. About half past nine I heard Barbara come up. She didn't go to bed apparently, for she didn't come in to say good night. I fell asleep and after a while I woke to hear her talking with—with Judith. After a few moments I heard them go downstairs together. James, I—" Her voice cracked and there was silence. We sat staring at each other, and the horror in her eyes was caused by the same thing that was creeping up and down my spine. I found my voice finally.

"But—what were they talking about?"

"I couldn't hear. I couldn't hear anything."

Again the clock obtruded itself upon my consciousness. I counted its ticks—one—two—three—four— And the Skipper came quietly in.

I rose clumsily to my feet to face her.

"Just dislocated, Jim. I think I got it," she said.

"That's great," I said dully.

The Skipper looked at me for a moment and I thought she winced. "Get to bed, Jim," she said. "Just leave the bathroom door open and keep an eye on Mike. We'll be all right."

It was risky to leave them alone like that. And yet, looking the Skipper square in the eye, it was impossible to think— I murmured a jumbled good night to M. Farrington and got to the door. There stood the Skipper. I kissed her and ran out of that room as fast as I could go.

For one moment after I had closed Michael's door the ticking of that infernal clock seemed to have followed me. There was Michael and there was Gay, both looking better and both looking a bit surprised.

"Where's the fire?" demanded the former with a faint smile. I hadn't seen one in many hours. "I won't run away—not after the manhandling I've just had. How's the Aunt?"

"Weepy, but still with us. Beat it, Gay, and take some more aspirin. This guy's going to sleep. If you want anything, bang on the wall and I'll come roaring, armed to the teeth. Scram!"

Gay laughed. Whatever I had been going through in that last half hour, it was evident that the Skipper had bolstered up those two very effectively.

"In that case, I won't bang." She kissed Michael, threw me a "see you later" look, and took herself off.

Over the weird arrangement of bandages, blankets, and pillows that surrounded him, Michael considered me.

"For once," he observed with a chuckle, "you'll admit that it would have been a good idea to have stayed in New York."

His chuckle reminded me of the Skipper.

I gave him what I considered enough aspirin to numb an elephant. My watch said 5:15 as I put out his light. The last thing in the world I had any intention of doing was sleeping. My program was all for action. I would merely wait until I was sure he had dozed off. As I flopped down on my bed, head in hands, I could hear Gay's restless footsteps in the next room. I meant to figure some things out before I joined her. I meant personally to inspect the locks on every door and window in the house. I meant to do a lot of things. And five minutes later I was stretched out "sawing wood" for all I was worth.

4

I have seen many a morning after, but never one like that. I woke with a pounding head and an unshaken conviction that if the powers that be were attending to their job, they would dispense with creation in general—speedily. But the powers must have been otherwise engaged. I was still sitting on the edge of my bed, holding my head on with both hands and experimentally stretching one stiff leg after another when Michael appeared in the bathroom door. As I considered his sling and the bandage on his head, dimly wondering where he got them, he burst into vehement speech.

"Perhaps you'll be through admiring my physique by lunch time and help me get on a shirt."

Memory did some effective dirty work that left me feeling like a combination tragic muse and jackass.

"How do you feel?" I hazarded.

"If I felt lousier, they'd fumigate me!"

All in all, I felt more like the jackass. I had slept—slept while an unknown killer— My thoughts weren't very pleasant. I cut myself shaving, burned myself in a scalding shower, and broke two shoe laces. By the time we were both dressed it was nine-thirty and I had exhausted an extensive vocabulary.

Michael, disdaining my suggestion that he might stay upstairs for a little while, marched down ahead of me, a bad case of grouch written in the set of his chin and the way his one good hand slapped the banister. Tragedy seemed to have taken a fling out the window that morning in favor of common, ordinary bad temper. We found the dining-room enveloped in forbidding silence.

The Skipper was at the table, absent-mindedly fiddling with some bacon, while Gay banged angrily among the coffee cups on the sideboard. The idea of the women being up and about while we calmly slept—well anyway, slept—annoyed me into speech.

"It is," I announced with finality, "a rotten morning."

"Think of your discovering that all by yourself!" said Gay, and spilt her coffee, to my infinite satisfaction.

The Skipper laughed. "How's your arm, Mike? Get any sleep?"

Michael's arm, as he had already explained to me with some violence, felt better and he had had more sleep than any of us. But he slumped into a chair, took the coffee Gay handed him, and growled "O.K." in a tone that made it quite clear that anyone who wanted to argue about anything would be accommodated immediately.

Lighting a cigarette, the Skipper contributed, "Martha's breakfasting upstairs. She'll be down later." And silence descended upon the dining-room.

For the space of about five minutes we crunched bacon and consumed coffee without incident. Higgins, looking rather seedy, appeared with fresh toast, opened his mouth to ask after Michael, discreetly closed it again, and took himself off. The Skipper smoked furiously, and the rest of us kept our eyes on our plates. Then, monotonously and with irritating force, Gay's fingers began a steady tattoo on the tablecloth. At least two sets of nerves promptly began to act up again. Michael's cup went down with a bang that bathed the surrounding territory in coffee.

"Damn it, Gay, quit that, can't you?"

Gay flared. "Don't be so touchy!"

Before I could get in my two cents' worth of sunshine, the Skipper interposed. "Easy, kids! Let's talk this over."

That being the one thing we all had in mind, we lapsed into silence. The Skipper smiled.

"We might as well look it in the face. These storms always last at least three days, which means that we must stick together or go mad. There's been a tragic accident which we must certainly explain to the satisfaction of everyone, if we're to keep from each other's throats—not to mention Jude's family or the local police."

Michael was breathing so fast and so heavily that I could distinctly hear him across the table. The Skipper waited for someone to speak. No one did. She sighed.

"Obviously there are two possibilities. Jude was killed either accidentally or intentionally, and in either case by some member of this household. If it was accidental, we should be able to establish that fact immediately. If it wasn't—"

Another pause, this time a breathless one.

Then "—we shall have to establish that fact too," concluded the Skipper.

Michael's voice was hoarse. "But what can we do?"

I answered him with more hope in my voice than conviction. "For one thing we can search the grounds. There must be a thug of some sort out there. It's the only logical answer."

Michael shot me a peculiar look. "Why not let it rest?" he demanded. "You know damn well that there's no one out there, Jim. We can't help Jude now. Old Foster would give us a fake certificate if the Skipper asked him, and we could say that she'd fallen off the bluff in the storm and—and forget about it."

I had known Michael since we were seventeen, but I had never heard him make such a proposal. Neither had Gay. She gasped in amazement. Once more the Skipper climbed into the breach.

"Michael, don't be ridiculous. Accidents don't need hushing up. And if it's not an accident, Jude's parents and we, her friends, have a right to know it. And no right to let a deliberate murderer remain at large."

Out of the numbness his speech had produced in my head came an idea. Mike thought the Skipper was guilty! Wild elephants could never have dragged that suggestion from him otherwise. And there she sat, insisting that we investigate. I grasped at a feeble straw.

"Mike! The footprints! The footprints on the tennis courts. There must be someone out there. We'd have noticed the clay on anyone's feet in the house."

Michael's eyes were far away. "Drop it, I say. For God's sake, Jim, what good will it do? I tell you there's no one there. It just keeps things boiling to pretend there is."

"There must be!" Gay was on her feet. "Mike, don't be a sap. These grounds must be searched, and if you won't go with Jimmie, I will and so will William."

"And so will I," said the Skipper, "and so will Michael!"

Michael looked at her, a long look that to save my neck I could not decipher. "All right, Skipper," he said at last.

We took all sorts of precautions. Heavy jackets, oilskins, boots, plenty of brandy, and Higgins' revolver. With the exception of Cook and Annie, we all assembled in the library and none of us looked cheerful. My own state of mind was a bad jumble. My thoughts were whirling from Jude and the past to the ghastly reality of the present, spurred on by a certain insistent suspicion that made my blood run cold. Action of any sort was a godsend. The probability of accomplishing anything was another matter. I should have preferred leaving both Gay and the Skipper in the house, but there was a glint in the former's eyes that invited no interference and I had never given the Skipper an order in my life. Furthermore, I wasn't counting on Michael for anything. M. Farrington voiced my feelings to the letter.

"It strikes me, Barbara, that you and Grace will be more in the way than anything else. And Michael has no business out of bed. I should think that James and William would get along much better alone."

Gay's chin came up with a jerk and I braced myself for the deluge, but the Skipper spoke before it could get started.

"Two people can't search these grounds, Martha. Gay and I can take care of ourselves, and I think Michael's mind will be easier if he goes. He's well wrapped up. Don't fuss."

"Barbara, I will not allow it." Her voice was rising. Unless I missed my guess, she was warming for a scene and it was going to be a corker. "I absolutely insist—"

But Michael's patience snapped. He whirled on M. Farrington.

"Rot, Aunt Martha! All the servants are here but William, and the doors and windows are locked."

His words were rude, and his manner was ruder. But M. Farrington amazed us. The explosion for which we breathlessly waited never came.

"Very well, my dear," she said quietly. I could have knocked Mike down with pleasure.

We went out the west door from the game-room, a wet, cold wind howling up to meet us. Since I had suggested the expedition, it was more or less up to me to engineer it. Accordingly, I stationed William halfway between the edge of the bluff and the house, with Michael and Gay at intervals along the drive. That left the grounds divided into four sections. I took the Skipper with me. Beginning at the edge of the bluff to the west, we went down toward the boathouse. In one way and one only were we better off than on the previous night. At least it was now possible to see more than ten feet ahead of you.

Water still lapped the former side of the boathouse steps. A large section of the pier had washed away and the boathouse was completely flooded. We went up along the path to the courts, which we scrutinized thoroughly. The footprints were still there. They ran clear across the courts to the drive, seeming to start from the rocks just above us. It was impossible to tell how large had been the foot that had left those prints or in what direction they had been heading. They were just shallow impressions in soft clay, rather like the marks left by walking across a melting sheet of ice.

The wind was still at our backs. Up the steep and slippery rocks we scrambled, the Skipper disdaining my help. The beaches below us were completely covered with thrashing water that boiled up into our faces. Silently I pointed to the scene of Michael's disaster and the Skipper nodded. We went down cautiously, separated at the foot of the rocks, and compassed the remaining section of the lawn between us. Nothing. A short distance up the drive stood Gay, looking like a drowned rat. She waved, but only half-heartedly.

We went up the drive toward the stable, the wind in our faces and the rain cutting like lashes of a whip. With every step the haunting thought that Jude might have lain for a long time wounded and still conscious in that fiendish whirlwind followed me. It was slow progress.

The east beach was completely flooded. By following the drive, we got a clear view both of the section of lawn between us and the house and of the section between us and the beach. I stationed the Skipper at the corner of the garage and went laboriously around both it and the stable, slipping and sliding along on my hands and knees most of the way. Rounding the corner of the stable in safety, I could see the solid figure of William far down the bluff where I had stationed him. And between us—nothing.

In front of the stable the Skipper joined me. Both it and the garage were securely padlocked. It seemed to me that to search either of those buildings would be a tacit admission of disbelief in her alibi. I hesitated, but not so the Skipper. Producing a key, she unlocked the stable. Without a word I followed her inside.

It had been years since horses had graced the premises of Farrington Bluff. The six large box stalls now enshrined the Skipper's various dogs. The stalls ran three on either side of the opening which reached to the rafters, and above them on both sides former haylofts bore discarded relics of Farrington carriages, harnesses, and boats.

The one thing that I wanted to look at in that building was Diana, the collie bitch, but I hadn't the nerve. I propped a ladder against one of the lofts and mounted it cautiously. Junk—the melancholy, once-valued possessions of a former generation, covered with dust, bedraggled, and horribly depressing. I scouted through it, sneezing into the remains of an old Victoria, barking my shins on the grinning skeleton of a battered dory, and sending a choking cloud of dust into the air as I bumped into a venerable horsehair sofa. There was no one in that loft and no sign of anyone having been there since the time of old Michael Farrington. One glance at the film of dust in the other loft told the same story. I went back down the ladder.

The Skipper was kneeling in the stall at the foot of it—Diana's. On an old plaid blanket lay the collie and beside her—puppies. I felt much better than I had for two days.

"Meet Toby," said the Skipper. "Look at his ears, Jim."

But I'm afraid my interest in Toby was purely perfunctory. The Skipper gently deposited him on the plaid.

"Come on," she said, "let's finish this business."

The plan of the garage was very simple. It was a two-story rectangle, facing the drive and wide enough to run three cars into it easily. There were just three in it then—Mike's, the Skipper's, and M. Farrington's. The Skipper's was nearest to us, and I noticed with a start that it was splashed with mud. Had she used it since the rain started? I pointed silently, but she had already noticed.

"That's odd, Jimmie."

I said, "Yeah," and I didn't say it very enthusiastically. There was nothing in any of the cars, but spreading in confusion from the door of the Skipper's all over the floor of the garage were smudges of the red clay of the tennis courts. The Skipper's eyes were very large and very dark as I stared into them.

"Skipper," I said, "get into the big car and lie down on the floor of it—quick!" I had Higgins' revolver out. I had remembered something. There was a room over that garage where William slept in the summertime.

"I'm going with you," said the Skipper. "Behind you if you insist, but I'm going!"

There was no time to argue. "I do insist," I said, and started for the stairs.

I suppose that if my life depended on it, I might possibly hit the broad side of a barn with a double-barrel shotgun at five paces. With a pistol at the same distance and with the same target, my expectation of life would be very slight. I thought of that as I went up those stairs. I thought of Jude on the bluff and Michael on the rocks. The roar of the wind was in my ears. The Skipper's stiff oilskins were brushing mine and her breath was warm on the back of my neck. Gripping the revolver until my fingers ached, I pushed open the door at the head of the stairs.

To all intents and purposes the room and the tiny bathroom beyond it were empty. My eyes swept it rapidly—dresser, book rack, chairs, bed. And then I jammed myself into the doorway in a wild attempt at shielding the Skipper. That bed had been slept in— recently. Was someone under it? I dared not stoop to look, for in the far corner of the room stood a large, old-fashioned wardrobe and in that wardrobe—what? I made a quick decision. Kneeling swiftly, with my gun still trained on the wardrobe, I took one quick, desperate look under that bed. Nothing.

I got to my feet. "Get outside, Skipper," I said, and my voice was ridiculously near to cracking. "You, in the wardrobe! Come out or I'll shoot!" No answer. Only a nervous chuckle from the Skipper behind me. For a fraction of a second I hesitated. Then I pulled the trigger and fired point blank into that wardrobe door. The report of the gun was like the crack of doom.

Deafened, hardly breathing, we waited. No movement from behind that door. I walked across the room and jerked it open. Hanging inside were one pair of dark trousers and a chauffeur's cap. The bullet had pierced the cap neatly in the middle.

5

Only once in my life have I ever experienced another sensation like that one. Some idiot had put me in charge at a dinner party, and in my fuss and flurry I found myself introducing the guest of honor and his wife to one another. Standing with that wardrobe door in my hand, I relived that memorable sensation. Dully I waited for the Skipper's laugh. But it didn't come.

"Jimmie," her voice was hoarse, "let's get back to the house."

I was too grateful for the absence of that laugh to protest. Without a word I followed her down the stairs and out of the garage. While I was fumbling with the lock, I could see her signaling to Gay, far down the drive, that the hunt was over. As we turned toward the house, the wind from straight off the bluff was terrific, and the torrents of rain once again assured us that if there had been any traces of red clay on the drive, they had long since been obliterated. From the corner of the house, we gestured to William and made our way to the front door. Higgins had already admitted Gay and Michael by the time we got there.

M. Farrington was alone in the hall—for once without any questions. She favored us with one quick look and took decisive action.

"Don't wait to talk about it, Barbara," she said. "I've sent the others up to change, too. Take a hot bath, both of you."

We went gratefully, parting in silence in the upper hall. In my room, Michael was sprawled on the bed, waiting. He had managed to get out of the oilskins, but the feet stretched in front of him were still encased in hip boots.

"Well?" he said jerkily.

"Nothing," after a moment's hesitation.

He straightened up to study my face. Whatever he saw there appeared to satisfy him. He stretched out gingerly on the bed.

"I told you so," his voice was tired. "Get me out of this stuff, will you?"

Only once did I speak to him during the long, tedious process of getting the two of us ready for M. Farrington's lunch table. I couldn't stand the tight lines around his mouth.

"Mike," I said, "the Skipper is square. You know it."

He turned away, picking up a comb. When his voice came it was perfectly steady. "I know it."

I didn't try again. With fiendish intensity, I concentrated on soap, towels, collar-buttons—anything. The lunch bell rang while I was struggling with Michael's tie.

M. Farrington was worth her weight in gold at that lunch table. Right there she made amends for every Farrington state dinner I have ever endured.

"We'll eat first and discuss this afterward," she stated.

No one argued. Gay was white and shaken, the Skipper abstracted, Michael silent and morose. But M. Farrington and I talked. We talked about the deplorable condition of the drama, if I remember correctly. And when I gave out, Gay took it up. Not until Higgins withdrew at the end of the meal, was there silence. M. Farrington took a deep breath and plunged in.

"I surmise," she said, "that you are all satisfied that no one is lurking in the grounds?"

No answer.

"Then I think that all the steps we may take, can be taken right here with a little thought and a little cooperation from each one of us."

More silence. Michael's lighter flared.

"I fail to see," he observed, "any necessity for taking steps. There has been an accident. Very well. As soon as we get in touch with the mainland, the police can do everything that is necessary."

We all stared at him. There was that alternative, of course. Any sort of story might be bluffed through. William and Higgins were to be counted on. And the police would have no reason to question it. Gay made up her mind first.

"I don't like that, Mike."

"Why not? We might as well face it. The chances are that the person who shot Jude is sitting at this table. Do you think anyone here would shoot her intentionally?"

M. Farrington spoke briskly. "Michael, if you are right, we can end this situation here and now. We are all friends. If one of us was so unfortunate as to—cause this accident—that person should speak out now for the sake of all of us."

We waited for an interval that seemed like several centuries. The Skipper sat motionless, her eyes on the table, and her right hand clenched in front of her. M. Farrington, a trifle pale, was studying Michael's face. It was absolutely expressionless, but the hand that held his cigarette shook slightly. Gay's frightened eyes caught and held mine. There was a question in them that puzzled me. M. Farrington's hard, dry voice cut through the silence.

"Very well. The police will be here by tomorrow or the next day at the latest. If we wait for that, things will be very unpleasant. I am of the opinion that an organized investigation will be much happier than an individual and furtive one."

It was only common sense. We all realized that, but no one encouraged the idea.

M. Farrington smiled grimly. "At all events, it would be more successful and it might spare us the ordeal of a public police investigation."

Police! At Farrington Bluff! But of course there would have to be police. For the first time the matter ceased to be personal. Gay's hand gripped my knee convulsively.

"Oh, surely—" she began.

"Very surely," said M. Farrington. "Someone must take charge. I should prefer it to be neither a woman nor a servant. Since Michael has seen fit to go bathing in February, obviously not Michael. James, I am afraid you will be obliged to offer your services."

Without warning, laughter engulfed me, shrill, meaningless gusts of it.

"Well," said M. Farrington's sardonic voice, "is that an acceptance or otherwise?"

Michael answered for me, eyes narrowed, a peculiar expression on his face.

"Jim's your sleuth, Aunt Martha. He'll love it. An authority on the subject, in fact."

There was something in that remark that I didn't like, and a great deal about the whole proposition that I liked even less. I glared at him.

"Well?" impatiently from M. Farrington.

"All right," I said stiffly. I was to trap Jude's murderer. I! And if it should turn out to be— I didn't dare finish the thought.

"Thank you," pursued M. Farrington dryly. "James, there is, of course, the possibility that you are conducting an investigation against yourself. But we shall have to run that risk. It is understood that we are all pledged to help you in every way. Proceed, if you please."

I, the creator of Billington Traithswaite, sleuth extraordinary, surveyed the members of that party. No blasé quip rose to my lips. Neither did my steel-gray eyes glint mennacingly. Rather I gaped foolishly for a full minute before I could so much as blurt, "I'll have to think. You— I wish you'd all go to your rooms and stay there."

Michael snorted at the feeble attempt. I heard M. Farrington's, "Come, Barbara," felt the reassuring pressure of Gay's hand, and suddenly found myself alone in the room with the Skipper.

"I'm sorry about all this, Jim, sorry that it had to happen at all and particularly sorry that you were dragged into it. But, believe me, Martha is right. It's better this way than in the hands of the police. Don't blink at anything. We leave it to you."

Then I was alone in the dining-room. They were both right, of course. And yet— I poured myself a stiff drink and gulped it down. I rang for Higgins. The man looked sick.

"Higgins," I said, "at Miss Farrington's request I am taking charge here until we can get in touch with shore. I wish you would so inform the servants."

"Very good, sir."

"I have asked everyone to go to his or her room for a short time—and remain there. I should be greatly obliged if you would keep a careful check on all the servants. And if you should see any of them outside of the quarters between now and the time I call you, notify me immediately."

He blinked. The man was, I thought, on the verge of saying something, but changed his mind. He bowed automatically and withdrew.

I took myself into the living-room. The impossibility of the situation no longer interested me. I was beginning to appreciate to the full the shortcomings of my own attempts at fiction. The thought of my remarkable Billington infuriated me.

I finally sat down at a desk and located pencil and paper. I decided to go carefully over the whole confounded visit and jot down every peculiar incident. It was no easy task. At the end of an hour I had a list that read something like this:

1. *Something is wrong with the Skipper—something that prompted M. Farrington to send for us in the middle of winter, diverted her from trying to marry off Mike, and has even upset Higgins in some way. He was certainly off his feed last night.*
2. *Why is the Skipper so averse to seeing a doctor?*
3. *Did she want to keep Mike away from Jude for the obvious reason? She put it a little strongly for that.*
4. *What did Jude tell Mike and when did they separate?*
5. *What did Mike expect to find in the boathouse that prompted him to jump over the cliff?*
6. *Did Jude walk or was she carried to the spot where we found her? If she walked, for whom or what was she looking? Obviously she went in a great hurry. No hat or coat.*
7. *Where was Mike up until the time he called us? Outdoors, apparently. He was soaking wet. He said he saw the bridge down at ten o'clock, just the time I went to bed. What was he doing out there? Why did he later head so determinedly for the boathouse?*

8. *Where was the Skipper? The puppies are there all right, but did they come last night or before that? Would even the Skipper spend such a night in a stable with a sick dog? Why didn't she tell M. Farrington where she was going? Why did she object to Jude? What were she and Jude talking about when M. Farrington heard them? Where did they go? Was the Skipper the last person to see Jude alive?*
9. *Why doesn't Mike want a search or investigation of any kind?*
10. *Whose footprints are on the tennis courts and in the garage? Who slept in the garage last night? Who tried to leave the Bluff in the Skipper's car?*

At last I put down the pencil. Wearily I read over that paper. Who? What? Why? It occurred to me that it is much easier to solve imaginary problems than real ones, and this was all too real. I helped myself to another drink.

On a fresh piece of paper I wrote *MOTIVE* in large capitals and considered. M. Farrington? Obviously not. Jude was M. Farrington's choice of the year for Michael. If the old lady had any conceivable reason for wishing Jude out of the way, why send for us to swell the number of state's witnesses? The Skipper? She had certainly asked me to keep Mike away from Jude for some reason. That she would go to the length of murder to gain her obscure end, I was not prepared to believe. Michael? He had never lost his head over Jude, but that was hardly a suspicious circumstance.

Again that tête-à-tête in the game-room loomed before me. I discounted it altogether. Jude and Mike had been friends all their lives. There were a million things they might have talked about. Gay? She had certainly been in a rage, but that was nothing unusual. The furniture might suffer from Gay's disposition, but the idea of murder was preposterous.

The servants? I ticked them off on my fingers—Higgins (ridiculous), William (pointless), Cook (more pointless), Annie (absurd).

Such was my state of mind that I gravely considered any possible motive of my own before I fully realized what I was doing. I left a blank after the word *MOTIVE* and wrote *WEAPON* also in large letters.

Again I was at a standstill. I wrote, "Revolver in the possession of Higgins. All the regular household aware of it." Sitting back, I reviewed my handiwork. Then I rang for Higgins.

"Have you kept careful watch of the servants?"

"I have, sir. They are all together in the kitchen."

"Good. Rouse the rest of the house and tell them I'd like to see them right away."

It occurred to me as I listened to his slow shuffle up the stairs that I was probably making a mistake in questioning them in one another's hearing. And yet I was beginning to feel that the best way to protect that unhappy party was to keep its members all together. I would have more luck with Michael anyway if the Skipper were present. He would never lie to her. But if he were shielding her? Suddenly I decided to recall Higgins and to approach the whole thing from a different angle. Too late. The door opened and Gay walked in.

"Good Lord, Jim, don't do that again!"

"Do what?"

"Leave us all caged up like that and go prowling around in the hall. It's amusing to read about, but right now it's not so darned funny."

I stared at her. "You heard someone in the hall?"

"Certainly. Do you think I'm deaf? I heard you come up and I heard you go down. You ought to give a Hallowe'en party some time. The guests would be carried out in dozens."

"They're always carried out when he gets started," said Michael from the door. "What's the big idea? Some fancy third-degreeing, or what?"

I tried not to look as if I had just seen a King Cobra.

"Oh," I said, "you heard something, too?"

"Sherlock!" from Michael.

The Skipper and M. Farrington coming in together saved us from another argument. They both looked tired and worried. I didn't wait for comments.

"Were any of you outside of your rooms after you went upstairs?" I demanded.

M. Farrington answered promptly. "Yes, I've been in Barbara's room all along. I was nervous."

"Did you go through the hall?"

"Why, no. Did you want—?"

The Skipper interrupted. "What's the matter, Jim?"

"Nothing," I snapped and once more rang for Higgins. The silence was charged with many things. I am afraid I was a little disappointed when he finally did appear.

"Higgins, were you in the upper hall at any time after I instructed you to watch the servants?"

"Why, yes, sir. Just now when you requested me—"

"I know. But were you there at any other time—or could any of the servants have been there?"

"No, sir. I'm positive."

I digested that slowly. "Aunt Martha—Skipper, did either of you hear anything unusual while you were upstairs?"

Their negatives were prompt. Someone then must have come up those stairs and gone down the hall toward the east end of the house, since Mike had heard it and the aunts had not. Gay's room was opposite the head of the stairs. I whirled on her.

"You heard this person come up and go down?"

She shrugged impatiently. "Really, Jim, you're too obvious. You could be heard from here to the mainland—slow, creeping steps as when the maniac is about to grab the heroine by the hair. You should have shrieked occasionally for local color."

It is one thing to have your fictitious hero suspected by every person present. It is quite another to be suspected yourself by your own roommate and his fiancée.

"Look here," I said, "you can believe me or not, just as you like, but I haven't been up those stairs since lunch time."

She didn't believe me. I could see it in her face and I could see it in Michael's.

"Higgins here will tell you—" I began hotly, but Gay interrupted.

"Oh, don't perjure Higgins. It would have worked better if you'd only had sense enough to—"

From somewhere in the rear of the house a full-throated scream rang horribly through the hall.

6

Into the startled silence that followed that frightful sound, came a low, hysterical giggle. The hair on my neck was beginning to prickle. I could see Higgins' bulging eyes. It was M. Farrington, collapsed in a chair, her head in her hands, rocking spasmodically back and forth. Michael moved mechanically.

"Stop it! Stop it!" With his good arm he seized her shoulder and shook it roughly.

"Quiet!" the Skipper said. The effect was instantaneous. At off hours when I have had one drink too many I can still see that scene. Michael half bent over his aunt's chair, Gay stiffly erect, and myself gripping the edge of the desk, while all eyes were riveted on the Skipper's haggard face. Half turned away from us, she stood staring toward the hall door. Waiting. Waiting for what?

I didn't walk across that room. I bolted for the door. If the devil himself had been in that hall, I would rather have encountered him than endure that waiting another minute.

The devil, fortunately or otherwise, was not in the hall. Nor was anyone else. The scream had come from the kitchen and in that direction I galloped as fast as my legs would carry me. The door of the servants' dining-room crashed open to my hand.

In the half light from the hall I could see that the room was empty, but I could also see the swinging door leading into the kitchen moving, as if someone had just gone through it. Beyond that door I could hear the sound of heavy footsteps coming, seemingly, from a point halfway between the floor and the ceiling. One moment only I hesitated to see Higgins following me in a labored dog-trot. Then I went through that door.

Directly against the nearest wall ran the staircase to the servants' quarters and halfway up it stood William in his shirt-sleeves, one half of his face covered with lather and a razor in his hand. He was breathing heavily and his starting eyes were fixed on something on the floor, hidden from my sight by the kitchen table. Our eyes met for the fraction of a second.

"Christ!" said William hoarsely.

Almost I had ceased to feel. Certainly I walked around that table with as few qualms as I might have stepped to it for a cigarette. Lying in a grotesque heap on the floor was the mammoth figure of Cook. Her arms were sprawled horribly and blood was flowing from a huge gash on her forehead. As I knelt beside her, William came heavily down the stairs and Higgins panted through the dining-room. I felt for her heart.

"Water," I ordered. "Cold—with ice if there is any. Quick!"

It was Higgins who moved to obey me. William stood there staring down at her. Over and over beneath his breath he was muttering, "My Gawd! My Gawd!" The monotony of it wasn't particularly helpful. I told him to get bandages.

"Bandages?" he repeated blankly and lumbered toward the stairs. I was glad to be rid of him.

Cook was bleeding profusely—too profusely to make my handkerchief very effective as a bandage. By the time

Higgins plopped a basin of water at my elbow, the handkerchief was saturated. Whatever other ailments she might have, Cook was not anaemic. Between us, Higgins and I staunched the wound and bound it up with the bandages silently offered by the still dazed William. Michael and Gay had joined the party long before I rose from my knees.

Neither of them had anything to say. Apparently the pictures their imaginations had been able to conjure up in the other room made the actual sight seem negative. Here at least there was no question about the weapon of attack. All over the floor and even on the table were scattered broken bits of a common, ordinary flower pot. Cook stirred at last. Her lips moved and her eyes fairly flew open.

"The eyes!" she cried wildly. "The eyes! Get them, I'm telling you! Get them before they get you!"

Higgins tried to calm her. "Be quiet a little," he said, rather ineffectually.

Michael finally asked her what happened. That provoked the explosion.

"Happened? Mother of God! I should have known better than to stay in this Godforsaken place! I sent that good-for-nothing Annie out here for my glasses, and when she didn't come back, thinks I 'I'll just teach that young fool a lesson.' I had a good notion she'd sneaked off upstairs. So I go into my kitchen, meaning to get the glasses myself and accuse her of swipin' 'em. And I'd no sooner got to the drawer they was in—" here Cook's lip began to tremble—"than I could feel the eyes borin' into my back!"

Michael sniffed impatiently.

Cook glared at him. "Rot, is it, you think? And I suppose it's rot I've got on my head?" Strangely enough, no one laughed. Cook was gathering momentum. "I felt them, I'm tellin' you. Cold, they was. I turned quick to scare them off and—there—they—was!" Her freckled hand was pointing to the outer door. "Like pieces of fire. Before I'd had time to so much as give a decent yell, they stabbed me!" Her voice rose higher and higher and ended in a bloodcurdling whoop.

I seized a ragged bit of pottery from the table. "Cook," I said sternly, "be quiet! Someone came in that door. You saw the reflection of the light in his eyes. You weren't stabbed by anything. You were hit with a flower pot. Look here."

But Cook was too far gone for flower pots. "It's the devil, I'm telling you!" she shrieked. "And that Annie—"

"Great Scott!" cried Michael. "Where is Annie? She couldn't help hearing this!"

William's face was white. "She ain't upstairs, sir. I just went in her room after the bandages."

"Perhaps," Gay was talking to convince herself, "perhaps she's cleaning or something upstairs."

Higgins frowned. "I doubt it, Miss. When Mr. James told me, I left explicit orders that they wasn't to go no place outside of the quarters. Annie's a good girl. She does as she's told."

That was too much for Cook. She struggled to her feet.

"Good?" she shrilled. "Good? Why, that dirty little—"

"That will do, Cook." The Skipper stood grim and determined behind us. "We've had enough of this nonsense. Michael, go stay with your aunt. Don't stand there gaping."

Michael went, the Skipper shutting the door deliberately on his back.

"Jim, that girl is in this house—be quiet, Cook—and we're going to find her, if we have to tear the rotten place apart! Is that door locked?"

She referred to the back door. I stepped to it eagerly, but it was locked and the key was on the inside.

"Higgins and I will take the lower floor. You and William take the upper one. Hurry!"

There was a bread-knife in the midst of the mess on the table. I picked it up and started for the stairs with William at my heels. But we didn't get very far. For distinctly through the silence came a sound—a vague, shuffling noise, indescribable and rather horrible.

For a split second we stood listening, spellbound. Then the Skipper moved. She sprang to the back door, turned the key, and threw the door open. On the floor at her feet lay Annie, bound hand and foot with a piece of clothesline and gagged with a white handkerchief.

For myself, I could have continued standing there indefinitely like a decorative mummy. But a harsh, inarticulate roar boiled from William's lips. Roughly he brushed past the Skipper and knelt beside the girl. His large, capable fingers had the handkerchief off in a moment and were at the knots in the rope before Annie's preliminary screams split the silence and stirred us to life.

The girl was hysterical and in no half-hearted fashion. There was no piecing together her jerky words. Removed to the sofa in the dining-room and treated with cold water, smelling salts, and aromatics, she continued to send scream after scream echoing through the house. The Skipper shook and even slapped her. Cook, a terrifying spectacle in her bandages, added to the general uproar by favoring us with a vigorous description of her feelings toward Annie.

"Beg pardon, sir," said William in my ear. "I think if you was all to leave her to me for a minute, I could quiet her."

We filed into the kitchen thankfully. In the same room with the girl the racket was unthinkable, but from behind closed doors it was still bad.

"Your party, Jim," said the Skipper.

I said, "Thanks," bitterly. They were all looking at me—waiting. I glared desperately back at them, and my eye fell first of all on Cook.

"Did you hear anything at all in here after Annie left you?" I demanded.

"I did not!" her retort was spirited. "You won't be hearing the Old Nick. He's—"

"Just answer my questions, please. How long had Annie been gone before you went after her?"

"How would I know? I didn't time her. A couple of minutes, maybe. She's that lazy, I never thought—"

"What did you do while you waited for her?"

Cook looked uneasy. "Well, now, I was lyin' there on the sofy and I maybe took a couple of winks. I wouldn't know for sure."

And that was that. For all the value of her evidence she might just as well have been at the South Pole. I tried another tack.

"Where were you when I rang, Higgins?" Did I imagine it, or did he look frightened?

"In the library, sir. I was looking through one of the upper shelves for a volume of Goethe which Miss Farrington has been unable to find, sir."

Very pat. A little too pat. Higgins had been asked to keep an eye on the other servants.

"You hadn't been in the servants' quarters since I had spoken to you?"

"Oh, yes, sir. I went directly there after leaving you. I delivered my message, and then it occurred to me that this volume—"

I threw caution to the winds. "Just why did you tell me that they were all waiting in this room?"

"I told them all to wait, sir." He spoke without an instant's hesitation. "I assumed that they had."

It wasn't the sort of remark one would expect of Higgins. For a moment it rather stumped me. I turned to Cook again.

"When did William go upstairs?"

"Just a little while after Mr. Higgins left us—right away practically."

In a way it all pieced together. Someone might have come into the kitchen through the back door, banged Annie over the head, and put her in the entry, only to discover Cook in the next room. It was quite possible that the commotion had aroused Cook from her nap. She had played directly into the hand of the intruder by going into the kitchen. Perhaps he had intended to handle her as he had handled Annie, but she had whirled around and surprised him. If Annie had been struck by a flower pot, it was probable that her assailant would start on his second exploit with the same missile in his hand. Unexpectedly confronted by his victim, he would have hurled it involuntarily. And then— My eye fell once more on the swinging door.

Cook might have been the person who had set it in motion. But the back door was locked from the inside. Our quarry must have turned the key himself and gotten out of the room before we came rushing into it. It was only a step to the game-room from which, after our mad rush en masse into the kitchen, he could proceed wherever he chose. The intruder must be in the house!

I advanced upon Cook. "*Who* did you see in that doorway?" I shouted, pointing theatrically.

The effect was tremendous. Gay screamed. The Skipper half rose from her chair. Higgins backed toward the wall. But Cook glared back at me, fascinated.

"So help me," she whispered. "I saw the eyes!"

Either she was a magnificent actress or the dim light had actually protected the person she had seen in the doorway. There was no way of telling which. But—the prowler in the upper hall!

"Do you sleep lightly?"

"Sleep?" Her mighty voice rose again. "I'll never sleep again, and God's my witness! Till this day I could lay me down and sleep with the best of them—"

Simultaneously with the Skipper's short laugh, William opened the door. His face was still anxious.

"She's all right now, sir."

"Good," I said crisply. "Come in here, William, and keep an eye on everybody in this room. I want to talk to Annie." Of all the people on the Bluff right then, I most trusted and most relied upon the chauffeur. He advanced into the room reluctantly.

"Very good, sir." I watched him settle onto the table before I closed the door.

Annie still lay on the couch in the servants' hall. She looked limp and pathetic. In a vacuous way, her tear-streaked face was pretty. I spoke as gently as I could.

"All right now, Annie?"

"Yes, sir."

"You'll have no more trouble. We'll see to that. You went out to get Cook's glasses, didn't you?"

"Yes." Her eyes were terrified.

"Just what happened?"

The girl shivered. "I don't know, Mr. Wells. I started to open the table drawer and something—hit me. I'm—I'm scared! Why should anyone want to hit me? I—I—"

"We'll take care of everything," I said with more conviction than I felt. "Don't worry. How long were you in the entry as nearly as you can figure?"

I was afraid that she would go off into hysterics again at any moment. She was shaking from head to foot and her eyes glistened dangerously. But her face screwed in thought, and at last she said earnestly, "About four hours."

I stared at her dumbfounded. Then and there I began to appreciate the difficulty of extracting the truth from the most well meaning people.

"I suppose it must have seemed that long. Who was in the kitchen when you went into it?"

"Nobody. Honest! I didn't see nobody from the time I left Cook till Miss Barbara opened the door. Gosh! It was awful! I couldn't get up and I couldn't say nothin' and—I was scared. Suppose nobody had heard me and the guy who put me there had—"

"How do you know a man put you there?" I snapped.

"I don't. I didn't say no man—"

"All right." I felt a bit foolish. "I was just wondering. Look here, can you stand up? I think it would be a good idea for this party to stick together."

She could stand up, and she did. She could also talk, but her conversation was not particularly illuminating. It intimately concerned her sensations upon wakening to find a gag in her mouth and her opinion of some person or persons unknown. I steered her into the kitchen quickly. Two things demanded immediate attention. There was an unknown person at large in the house, and a second night was practically upon us before I, as investigator, had had a chance to question the suspects about the events of the first. It seemed to me that our prowler deserved first consideration.

"I wish you'd all go into the library," I said. "I mean everyone but William and myself. I'm going to search the house, and I want to feel sure that you're all together. Each one of you is responsible for seeing that no one leaves the room until we get back. Skipper, will you ring when everybody is there—including Michael and Aunt Martha?"

Alone with William, a sense of normal being came upon me. In that household of quasi-lunatics, he seemed as steady and sane as a rock.

"Better wipe off your face," I suggested.

William grinned from beneath the caked lather on his face. At the dish towel rack, he followed my suggestion.

Then from a drawer beside the sink he produced a flashlight.

"All set, sir. Shall we look around a bit here?"

My eyes swept the room. Broken pottery all about, but otherwise normal. One drawer in the table still stood open, and Cook's glasses were in plain sight. If our visitor had come from the muddy drive outside, he must have flown across the kitchen linoleum. There was no sign of footprints. We went through the two pantries thoroughly. We examined all the closets and table drawers. As a parting shot, I stepped to the back door and opened it.

In the light of William's torch, the entry, scene of Annie's incarceration, revealed two startling facts. Just outside the door stood a double stack of flower pots, and all over the floor were smears of red clay—the clay of the tennis courts. Annie's bonds and gag still lay where William had dropped them. Mechanically I stooped and picked them up. An ordinary piece of clothesline, one end of it freshly cut, and a handkerchief of fine white linen, embroidered and handmade. The sort of thing a man's maiden aunt might give him, I thought with a chuckle. But the laugh froze on my lips.

Daintily stitched in one corner of that handkerchief was the name, "Michael Farrington." As I stared in horror at the thing, the bell in the kitchen sounded the Skipper's signal.

7

William's voice called me from my trance. "Nothing out here, sir."

I'm afraid my "No" was rather weak. I was trying to think—trying to forget that I was dealing with Michael and his family—trying to function as if I were merely considering fiction for a grisly-minded public. Would it have been possible for Michael to have caused that mess in the kitchen? Anyone in the party, Cook, Annie and myself excepted, could have been the prowler in the upper hall. Any one of them could have sneaked down the servants' staircase and handled Annie. The handkerchief pointed to Michael.

But the affair with Cook was peculiar. If logic had anything to do with it, Cook must have screamed just before the flower pot struck her. And when we heard that scream, every member of the party but William and the victims had been in the room with me. One glance at William assured me that he really had been shaving. Part of his face glistened like an apple, and the rest was encased in a brief but decided stubble. It flashed across my mind that in fiction William would most certainly be guilty. The most innocent seeming and the most helpful is any author's villain. But I wrote that sort of thing; I didn't believe it. Still, it was possible that the lather might have been applied and partially removed while Cook was slumbering peacefully on her "sofy."

Suddenly I rejected my original plan of allowing William to search the first floor while I searched the second. I was just embarking on the most trying experience of that week-end—the experience of suspecting every person in the house. If there was an intruder inside, I reasoned, our search would be reduced to a simple game of hide-and-seek with the odds decidedly in favor of the hider. And if William could not be counted on— For a moment I considered organizing the entire household into a searching party, but only for a moment. M. Farrington, Cook, Annie, and Michael were in no condition to be relied upon. Mike should have been in bed, and the other three showed signs of becoming problem cases on the least provocation. That left William, Higgins, the Skipper, Gay, and myself. Five of us. Two of them women and one an old man. If we were to go together, we were possibly turning the murderer loose to roam the house at will with the invalids unprotected. If we divided into parties of two and three, it was just possible that the murderer was being sent off into the empty house alone with another unsuspecting victim. The risk was unthinkable. I am not defending my action. I am merely explaining how it seemed to me at the moment logical.

I stuffed the rope and Michael's handkerchief into my pocket.

"William, I've changed my mind. I think I'll have a little talk with the rest before we go on with this."

"Hell, sir, you can't do that! We can't go sitting around talking while some bloody devil—"

My grip on myself wasn't very good, and it was slipping with every uncertain minute. "I can do whatever I see fit," I said curtly. "Come on!"

"All right, but I ain't in favor of it!"

"So what?" I growled. But I did glance into every room as we went down the hall—the game-room, the living-room, the dining-room, and even the conservatory. They were all empty. If they hadn't been, perhaps I might have realized my mistake, but I was appallingly sure that the person I sought was at that moment conversing glibly in the library.

They all turned at the opening of the door—all except Michael who had been saying something. His doubled fist still rested on the desk and his face was very red. The atmosphere of the room as reflected on their faces was tense.

"You were saying, Mike?" I said.

For half a second he held the pose. Then, "You're damned right I was saying that we'd better let bad enough alone."

"Michael," said the Skipper, "sit down and shut up. Now!"

I doubt if her words would have had any effect, but she accompanied them with a forceful shove. Michael sat. I motioned to William to park himself somewhere.

"Have you found anything, James?" quavered M. Farrington.

"Yes," I said to William's evident astonishment,

"I've found all I was looking for. I'm going to ask questions, and if you aren't particularly enjoying this, I'd advise you to answer them as carefully as possible. Gay, get a pencil and paper and write down every word of it."

There was a pause. After a moment Gay walked to the desk and picked up a pencil.

"Aunt Martha, I will begin with you. Your inviting us here at this time of year was unusual. This party was your idea?"

"It was."

"Will you tell us why?" I was being callous and I knew it without looking at Michael's black face.

"Certainly. Barbara seemed unwell and depressed. As I wrote you, I thought she would be better for a little company. And I hoped that—that she might bring herself to confide in you or Michael more readily than myself."

M. Farrington's lips were a thin, straight line. In her eyes at that moment gleamed the light which usually presaged a laying low of the nearest available victim. But I went on.

"Had you any reason for thinking so?"

"I had not." The eerie voice of the storm seemed to mock both of us.

"Had you any particular purpose in inviting Judith here?"

She stiffened, but she had the grace to blush.

"I thought she might make pleasant company for you and Michael."

In spite of the tension, a general smile greeted that.

"Naturally," I said, the thought of the still figure upstairs wiping the smile from my lips with a vengeance. "Now, about last night. At what time did you go upstairs?"

"Directly after you left us. I didn't notice the exact hour. I went straight to bed, if that is what interests you."

"Did you sleep immediately?"

M. Farrington drew herself up. "The next thing I was aware of," she stated deliberately, "was Michael standing beside me with the information that Judith and Barbara were not in the house."

I felt as if cold water had unexpectedly been dashed in my face. And then the realization of my own colossal stupidity struck me. *Never repeat what I am going to tell you to anyone!* And there I stood before the Skipper expecting to hear it voluntarily repeated. My face burned furiously.

"Did anything unusual happen while we were out in the grounds either last night or this morning?"

"Nothing."

"You heard no footsteps in the hall upstairs this afternoon?"

"I did not."

I thanked her and met the Skipper's inscrutable eyes fixed on my face. I took a long breath.

"Skipper," I said, "you asked me to do this. What had been troubling you?"

She reached for a cigarette and lighted it with a steady hand. "I'm fifty-two, Jimmie. When you reach that age it's not so easy to be consistently cheerful. That's all there is to it."

"You didn't go upstairs with Aunt Martha last night?" Stupid question. I had seen her go upstairs. She laughed softly.

"My dear boy, after you left us I smoked a cigarette, bored myself stiff, and went to bed. I think you were the last person I saw en route. Martha was asleep. So I didn't wake her. I lay awake till the thought of that dog got me. Then I dressed and went out to her. That's all there is, Jim—except that I heard nothing in the hall."

I cleared my throat. "Why didn't you tell Aunt Martha where you were going?"

"It would have worried her."

"You went directly to the stable?"

"I did and I came directly back. I didn't hear anything but wind."

I braced myself and let the next question fly. "What did you mean last night when you told me to keep Jude away from Michael?"

The Skipper flicked ash from her cigarette coolly. "I meant that if Mike wants to marry Gay, I see no reason why he shouldn't have a clear field." Gay's pencil snapped.

Should I or should I not ask her point-blank what she and Jude had been talking about when M. Farrington heard them? I decided not to. To all intents and purposes that interview had already been denied. I should be giving away my knowledge and gaining nothing. I turned to Michael.

"What did Jude talk to you about in the game-room?"

His shoulders were hunched. "That," he said, "is none of your damned business."

I know now that in that one moment I lost the opportunity of saving us all from what followed. My anger prevented me from seeing the effect that question and its answer had on anyone in that room. Mike's attitude through that entire day had been getting increasingly in my hair. At the demand of the entire party I had accepted a responsibility as distasteful to me as I was inadequate for it. And it was becoming increasingly evident that my inadequacy might prove disastrous.

I tried to keep my temper.

"What did Jude tell you, Mike?"

Michael looked at me—a long look and a strange one. His face was set, and I knew before he opened his mouth that he was lying. Well, they had all lied.

"She told me that she thought the chimneys were in bad shape and this storm might make them dangerous. She didn't want to alarm anyone else."

It was a feeble attempt, but I knew that a second question would be just so much wasted breath. That much was evident from the set of his chin. Behind me, Gay snorted indignantly.

"All right," I said wearily. "How long did it take her to tell you that?" He was eyeing me cautiously—trying to anticipate my thoughts.

"About five minutes."

It had been nine-thirty by my watch when the Skipper went upstairs. That sprightly conversation in the hall might have taken five minutes, but probably less. And in any case, according to Michael, the conference in the game-room must have ended shortly after I went into the library.

"And just why didn't you rejoin the party?"

Michael swallowed. "Jude had a letter to write and I decided to go out and have a look at things—the chimneys and bridge and all that."

I could have wrung his neck. If he had to lie to me, why in hell couldn't he lie plausibly? My hand came down on the desk with a whack.

"If you're all guilty, there's no point in my going on with this. If you're not, you might be decent enough to tell the truth!"

M. Farrington's voice broke the deadly silence.

"You feel that someone has been untruthful, James?"

"Untruthful!" I fairly howled. "You're lying, every damned one of you! Do you expect me to read your minds?"

The atmosphere was charged with something I could not place, something unhappy and a little eerie. There was no answer, even from M. Farrington. I should have done anything but what I did do, which was nothing more nor less than to lose my head completely. Feverishly I hurled questions at the rest of them—at Gay, at William, at Annie, at Higgins, at Cook. I wasted just that much breath. They knew nothing, any of them. They had gone to bed at hours varying from Cook's nine o'clock to Higgins' eleven. Gay had taken aspirin and gone to sleep. Cook had slept naturally. William, Annie, and Higgins admitted to not sleeping, but had heard absolutely nothing but the storm.

"And no one here went into the kitchen at any other time?" My sense of futility increased with every second of that pause. I whirled on Michael.

His chin came up aggressively. "No!"

My next gesture was even more foolhardy. I reached in my pocket.

"Then how did this get into the kitchen?" I demanded, and threw in front of him the handkerchief I had found in the entry.

They all stared. All except M. Farrington, I think, realized what it was. Slowly the red mounted in Mike's face. He reached for the thing, and I thought that he started as his eye caught the daintily executed name in one corner. His voice was the voice of a man who has been hit on the head.

"I don't know." His fingers played absently with the thing. "I don't know." He sat down slowly.

"But it's yours?"

He passed a hand vaguely over his eyes. "I don't— Yes. It must be." He went on staring at it, fascinated.

"But there is nothing to indicate that Michael took it to the kitchen." That was M. Farrington, bristling like a mother hen. "Surely one's handkerchief case is not under lock and key. It would be a simple matter for anyone to—"

For the first time in my life I interrupted M. Farrington, and I did it rudely. "Yes, I know," I said. "But it rather conclusively proves that the person who hurled that pot at Cook has been in the house long enough to be either borrowing or stealing handkerchiefs."

I should have had sense enough to realize the danger of putting all my cards on the table, but it was blurted out beyond recall. And in characteristic ways every person in the room reacted to the statement. M. Farrington's hand flew to her throat with a quavering "Oh!" The Skipper sat suddenly bolt upright, her face stern. Instinctively Gay clutched Mike's arm, and they huddled together. Beyond them I caught a glimpse of Higgins' face and of William, rigidly motionless. Annie and Cook began to jabber meaninglessly. With an almost mechanical rhythm we eyed each other—you—you—you? It was horrible. Had a board creaked or a window rattled, I firmly believe that we should all have dived for shelter under the nearest pieces of furniture. But nothing creaked.

You? You? You?

The Skipper broke the spell. She pushed back her chair with a clatter. "This is ridiculous! Why should anyone in this room strike Cook or Annie? Any one of us could go into the kitchen for a dozen reasons. There's someone else in this house, Jim. And a person who forced his way through locked doors would have no difficulty in finding a handkerchief."

"I was merely supposing," I said. "I'm in a nasty spot, and I'm not trying to wriggle out of it. I'm simply putting it up to you. The murderer is either in this room or at large in the house. If he or she is here, a search would provide a good opportunity for more deviltry. If not, and we fail to search, we are leaving ourselves at the mercy of somebody who has already killed one of us. I'm leaving it up to you. I won't take the responsibility. What shall we do?"

"Search," said the Skipper promptly.

"Does anyone have a different opinion?" I said. Breathless silence.

"Very well. We'll all go. There are nine of us." I did some rapid arithmetic. Four men—one along in years and one incapacitated. Of the five women, Gay alone looked capable of walking across a room without staggering. In my coat pocket my fingers brushed the revolver with which I had disgraced myself earlier in the day.

"Higgins," I said, "take this revolver and stand on the landing. If anyone you don't know shows up in either hall, you are to shoot, do you understand? And shoot straight. William—Miss Palmer, Mr. Michael, and Miss Farrington are to go with you. Keep check on every member of your party, and be sure that Higgins is at his post as you come out of every room. We'll search this room now. Then you wait in the hall and give Higgins moral support. When we finish the first room upstairs, we'll signal Higgins and you can go through the next one down here, and so on. Make sure of all the doors and—"

From the hall came a sound—a low agonized whimper that cut short my orders as if by the push of a button. It came from the hall and with it came another sound—a slow, soft shuffling. It was coming nearer—nearer! The hair on my neck was prickling. Nearer—nearer— It was in the room! For a moment I could not see a thing, but one step brought me within full range of the open door. Through it was coming the mangled remains of Christopher, the cat. His lower jaw dangled inches below where it should have been. His fur was matted with blood, and he was dragging himself along painfully on his belly, mute, appealing eyes on his mistress' face.

Like the crack of a rifle came M. Farrington's scream!

8

Close on that scream came a strangled curse from the Skipper. The revolver was jerked from my hand. There was a sudden flash and a thunderous report, and Christopher lay still.

"What did you do that for?" Michael's voice was dazed.

The Skipper placed the gun on the table deliberately.

"He was suffering," she said. Would she have acted that rapidly if she had been dealing with a person? Would—

"William," she said, "take it and—"

But I interrupted. "Wait. Just cover it and put it in a closet. I think this party had better stick together."

"No!" It was M. Farrington on her feet, hands clenched to her temples, eyes bulging, her voice verging on a scream. "We can't stay here! I won't! I—I—"

Before either Gay or I could stop him, Michael was at her savagely, had her by the shoulders, and was shaking her like a bag of flour.

The Skipper's voice stopped it before I could. "Michael!" she snapped, and he halted. Then after a ghastly pause, "Martha, sit down."

None of us expected it, but M. Farrington sat, and in another moment Michael had himself in hand.

"Sorry, Aunt Martha," he mumbled thickly. "Lost my head."

"Now then," said the Skipper briskly, "let's have no more of this. Whatever is roaming around this house can't be half as dangerous as the very special kind of hell a little mob hysteria will turn loose. Michael, give your aunt some brandy."

We all watched him pour it, one thought uppermost in every mind. Was it safe to drink it? Was it safe to do anything in this horrible house? Reluctantly M. Farrington took the glass he handed her, hesitated, and finally drank. We waited for several seconds. Nothing happened. Gay seized my arm.

"Let's search this room—*now,* Jimmie! We're wasting time."

We searched it carefully, from end to end. We moved furniture, tore up the carpet, even yanked out books. None of us knew exactly why, except that it would leave us one spot that we could be sure of. There was nothing there that might not have been there always, nothing that I had not seen a dozen times myself.

"A blank," said William, surveying me suspiciously. "Don't you think you might get on with it *now,* sir?"

Coupled with my own growing conviction that I should have searched the house immediately, his vague insinuation rankled.

"I'm in charge of this," I growled. "Do as you're told and leave the rest to me."

His "Yes, sir," was venomous.

We left William and his party standing in the hall just outside the library door, M. Farrington quiet, Michael very black, and Gay tense and silent. William's alert, suspicious face was the last thing I saw as I rounded the landing. There we left Higgins, and it is remarkable that several of us were not killed on the spot, so badly was the revolver shaking in his hand.

The upper hall was a blaze of light. It seemed to me that the prowler, if he were human, would have switched those lights off. The thought was in no way reassuring. Gay's room lay directly opposite the head of the stairs. With one wave of encouragement to Higgins, I pushed open the door. The room was empty. Closet, bath, under tables, chairs, and bed—nothing.

The Skipper paused with her hand on Gay's suitcase.

"Look here, Jimmie, hadn't we better leave the search for clues until later on? If there's someone in the house, we're giving him plenty of time to get out of it when we go browsing around this way."

Cook roused to speech. "But if there's somethin' here we ain't supposed to see, we'll be leavin' plenty of time for someone," with a significant leer, "to be gettin' it out of the way."

I decided quickly. A lost clue dwindled into nothingness beside that prowler.

"You're right, Skipper," I said to Cook's indignant face. "Let's go."

Higgins still stood on the landing, but he was huddled into a corner, half-crouching, his face screwed into a mask of terror.

"How was it?" he demanded hoarsely.

"Nothing," said the Skipper. "Are the others all there?"

"Please, Miss Barbara," his voice was shrill, "I don't like this, do you see? I'm in the middle. Whichever way the killer comes, he can get me. I ain't staying here. I don't like it."

"Don't be a fool," I said sharply. "You're in plain sight of four persons all the while. You have a revolver."

He drew a long, shuddering breath. "I ain't yellow, Mr. Jimmie. Nobody ain't never said that of me. But a devil of a lot of good it'll do me, being in plain sight of four people when I get mine. Begging your pardon, Miss Barbara, I ain't staying here!"

I knew how he felt.

"Gay," I called, "come up here and stand with Higgins, will you?"

Gay's voice answered at once. "O.K., Jim. Coming." We could hear Michael protesting, but she appeared.

"Any luck, sailor?" she demanded.

I waggled my head. "You watch the upper hall and Higgins the lower one. That makes it all right, doesn't it, Higgins?"

"Yes, sir," rather shamefacedly.

"All right, William," I shouted. "Go ahead."

Before we had been in that hall twenty seconds, we could understand Higgins' state of mind more fully. To stand in an empty corridor, every nerve strained for a sound from the party below, waiting for someone or something unknown to appear, was not a pleasant experience even with three companions in the brilliantly lighted hall. Alone in the dimness of the landing with only empty space beyond, it must have been insupportable. The silence seemed to be wrapped around us in layers, penetrated only by the sound of our own breathing. And then came a sound from below—a door closing and William's voice.

"All right in the living-room, sir."

There was no light in M. Farrington's room, and I concluded that at least one person had been where she claimed to have been during my wild performance downstairs.

"I'll get it," said the Skipper behind me. There was a click and the room was flooded with light. I promptly reexperienced the sensations of my first ride on a roller coaster.

The room might have been struck by a cyclone. M. Farrington's cherished bits of shell and china were scattered in ruins all over the floor. Chairs and tables were overturned, bedclothes thrown wildly in all directions. Even the drapes had been ripped from the windows. Christopher's bassinet was on its side, some six feet from its former position. The bedstead and floor beside it were smeared with blood. One look at the bed made quite clear the manner in which the poor animal had met his fate. He had been savagely bashed against the mahogany. Great, wet splotches of blood went in a wavering line toward the door where he had evidently dragged himself.

I leapt to the closet door and flung it open. Clothes, Nothing else. Through the connecting door of the bathroom came the Skipper's voice.

"Nothing here, either."

Simultaneously Annie's shrill sobs broke forth, reenforced by a deeply rumbled prayer to all the saints from Cook.

I shouted something and started to herd them ahead of me out of the room. "Skipper! Are you there? Are you—"

The Skipper turned from an inspection of her closet, her face drawn and set.

"Empty," she whispered. "Good Lord! What *can* we do?"

I dragged her into the hall after the others. Annie and Cook were pretty far gone. Higgins crouched with his back to the wall and the revolver waving frantically before him. As we emerged through that ghastly door, William, his face like chalk, dashed wildly past them and up the stairs.

Uproar on the stairs heralded the approach of Michael and his aunt. The thought of the latter seeing that room galvanized me into action. "Skipper—" I began over my shoulder. But for once there was no response. The Skipper was leaning against the wall, her eyes closed and her hands clenched at her sides. As I spoke, she swayed and William caught her as she fell.

I think I helped William carry the Skipper into Gay's room, but I'm not sure. I distinctly remember pouring out a liberal dose of mouth wash, and being prevented by main force from administering it to her. It went on for eternities. When it was finally stilled, the Skipper was sitting up. M. Farrington lay sobbing in a big chair, supported by both Michael and Higgins. William stood at the door, his arm around Annie and a stern eye upon Cook who was seated ignominiously upon the floor at his feet, her eyes staring into space. I stood by the bed, holding up Gay who seemed on the point of falling. No one spoke for a long time. Then William in a hushed voice:

"I think, sir, that this just about does up our searching party."

I said in a voice intended to be steady. "We are all absolutely safe here as long as we stay together. We have a revolver. That bathroom door can be bolted. The windows are out of reach from the ground and there is absolutely no danger. William and I are going to leave you here for a few moments while we look around. You can lock the door the minute we go. And don't unlock it until we tell you to!"

"No!" cried Annie. "Oh, please—"

But William turned to the door. "Let's go!" he said.

Michael never could take orders. "Look here," he exploded, "I'm not staying here while you do the dirty work. What do you think I am? I brought you here, and I'll take the risks. You and William stay where you belong."

M. Farrington's voice rose in horror. "James, don't think of allowing it. He's weak! He has fever! He—"

"He's staying right here," I said bluntly.

"The hell I am! I'm—"

"Shut up!" I snapped. "Any more out of you and I'll push your face in. Someone has to stay with the women. They're your responsibility. See to it, for once."

I didn't give him time to answer. I strode out the door with William at my heels. We could hear a click on the other side as someone shot the bolt home.

One room remained to be searched on the west end of the hall—Jude Blinshop's. Before that door I hesitated. It was quiet. All the mad excitement oozed out of me. The one reality of the whole wild, gruesome nightmare—Jude was dead. I would have given something just to lean against that door and blubber like a two-year-old.

William spoke softly in my ear. "I'll go in, sir, if you'd rather not."

"Thanks," I mumbled. "I'd rather. Watch the hall."

I'm afraid I didn't notice for several minutes whether or not the room was occupied. A low lamp burned beside the bed. The figure under the sheet was very still. William's cough in the hall finally roused me. I didn't move the sheet. The memory of that disfigured face was too strong. It took a definite effort to stir myself to the point of crossing to the closet and making sure it was empty. Looking under the furniture was a little worse. I closed Jude's door behind me very softly.

"That finishes this end of the hall, William."

"Yes, sir. It might be a lot easier if we could lock up these rooms that we're sure of. Shut the—the—him out!"

I liked the idea. On the inside of the three doors, we found keys, and we locked them all. I pocketed the keys.

The Farrington hall is perfectly straight and rather wide. On the north side, just beyond the head of the stairs, was my room, and, next to it, Michael's. Opposite them a swinging door opened into the narrow corridor of the servants' quarters. My room was just as I had left it. Standing in the hall, I sent William through into Michael's.

"All right here, sir," he said from the door. A swift glance over his shoulder verified the statement.

We were now confronted with a serious problem. In order to search the servants' quarters properly without risking the approach of someone from downstairs, we had to cover two staircases and two corridors, the smaller one running at direct right angles to the main one. There seemed nothing for it but to station one person at the junction of the two halls and let the other one search. It left a very definite risk for the sentry, should his eye be even momentarily distracted from either staircase. It also involved a complete mutual trust on the part of the searchers. William, I knew, had his suspicions of me, and suddenly I began to distrust him.

"I'll match you for position," I said.

"I'd rather keep watch, if you don't mind, sir." Immediately I jumped to a rash conclusion. "No," I decided. "You know the ground better. You hunt and I'll watch here."

I think some inkling of my idea dawned upon him, for he eyed me queerly. "If you say so, sir. I'd rather look myself, if I was you."

I shook my head vigorously.

His only comment was, "Well—Higgins' room," and he opened the door on our right.

The sensation of waiting before was nothing to these new ones. I tried to keep my eye on the hall with its grim staircase—on the dim narrow corridor at my elbow with its three closed doors and dark flight of stairs—on the faint splotch of light that was the open doorway of Higgins' room. I could see one end of a small iron bed and beyond it a small clothes press. I could hear the wind outside and William's heavy footsteps. Once I thought I heard something else from the direction of the back stairs, but either I was mistaken or it was not repeated.

"All in order, sir."

"Try the next one."

He vanished across the hall. Slowly an idea was beginning to dawn on me. William! William could have brained Annie, dashed upstairs and smeared soap on his face, shaved off half of it, heard Cook stirring, dashed down the stairs, and—

"Nothing here."

"Whose room is it?"

"Annie's.

"All right. Go ahead."

He walked to the next door on the left. "This is Cook's," he said, disappearing into it.

Could it be that I was on a wild goose chase, searching the house *with* the murderer *for* the murderer? William could have smashed Christopher before he brained Cook. The animal might have been stunned and unable to crawl down to us at first. William had been upstairs. He would have had ample time to—

"O.K." His voice coming at me suddenly out of the darkness reminded me that I had almost relaxed my vigil. William's own room remained. It was at the end of the corridor and on the opposite side from where I stood. I thought I should be able to see it quite clearly when the door was opened.

"Good," I said, striving to make my voice sound natural. "Go ahead."

If anything was on his conscience as he opened the door, he didn't show it. He pushed it open confidently and switched on a light. As much as I could see of it, his room was the exact replica of Higgins'. Same bed and tiny closet. Small stand by the bed. I could see no farther. If William was the murderer, he might be up to almost anything beyond my range of sight.

There was, I admit, no sense in my action. I gave one hasty look up and down the main hall and threw caution to the winds. Very quietly I let the swinging door between the passages go. Then slowly, inch by inch, I edged myself down the corridor in the direction of the beam of light coming from his room. I kept my back well against the wall in which his door stood. Almost it seemed that the man would hear my breathing. Just outside the beam of light, I halted. I could see most of the room, but no William.

A disconcerting thought struck me. After all, should my bright idea be entirely wrong and William find me not only deserting my post but also sneaking down a dark corridor toward a spot to which I myself had sent him, my position might need a lot of explaining. He certainly didn't consider me above suspicion in the first place. He had heard me order the others to keep their door locked until I told them to open it. He had watched me lock every door upstairs and pocket the keys. His case would be rather better than mine, if he ever had reason to present one. Nevertheless, I drew a deep breath and stepped into the beam of light.

Crouched in the doorway stood William, his face a mask of rage and hate. He held a golf club in his hand, and as I sprang at him roaring, "You dirty devil!" darkness descended over me like a tent.

9

How long I was unconscious I have never been able to determine. I came to lying in darkness, strapped down to something that I presumed to be William's bed, my hands bound under me, a gag tied in my mouth, and pain playing an Anvil Chorus in my head. It was a long time before I could summon enough interest to flavor the full horror of my position.

William was the murderer and William was roaming the house, unobserved and unsuspected! I thrashed about wildly. But it was no good. The straps that bound me held. After a while I gave up the attempt, exhausted.

It seemed incredible that I could have hesitated over William's guilt. My doubts about Michael and the Skipper were forgotten and I lay there impotently cursing my own stupidity. If anything more should happen before that night was over, I thought, I could blame myself. My bright ideas had huddled a bunch of women into a room with an invalid and an old man and left them there unprotected. Worse than that, I had managed to avert their suspicions from the guilty party and had instructed them to open the door to him immediately. Fool! Shortsighted, doddering idiot! Was William insane? My flesh crept at the thought of M. Farrington's dismantled room and the mangled cat. Not the work of a sane man. Not as I figured sanity.

He was mad, then. And what a crafty madness! I thought of his hefty shoulders and level, steely eyes. Why in the name of all that was holy would he kill Jude Blinshop? It was ridiculous, but—it had happened. Again I tried wriggling my legs, but the circulation had gone out of them. I tried to move my hands. No go.

Well, sooner or later he would come back for me, I supposed. It was strange that he hadn't finished me on the spot and made a clean job of it. Time possibly. Perhaps it was more expedient for him to get the revolver first, finish off the others, and then—and then— The gag in my mouth seemed to be strangling me. I roared and twisted and raged myself quiet. Wondering dully what time it was, I realized that I was hungry. Lunch seemed several generations removed and the recollection of it was torture. I longed desperately for a cigarette. Michael! It was all up to Michael. If only he could show a little more intelligence than I had, we might still have a chance. If—

There was a sound from the direction of the corridor, soft but unmistakable. William—or someone else? I lay very still, straining my ears to catch it again. Perhaps William had finished his job and come back for me! The noise came again, a little louder. Someone was talking in a low, careful murmur just outside the door. A deeper voice answered. Mike! I was sure of it.

With a desperate effort I wrenched at the straps holding my shoulders. They gave a little, and I wrenched again. My head hit something hard—the iron bed post. Gritting my teeth, I pounded my head on that iron. It seemed to me that the noise would have wakened the dead. But there was no sound from the hall. I tried again, frantically, but my straining ears caught only the sound of receding footsteps and a door closing softly.

I have had my share of disappointments, I suppose, but I have never had another like that one. Black despair swept me. Then suddenly a blinding ray of light shown full on my face. In breathless, motionless horror, I lay there waiting.

"Good God!" said Michael's voice from the darkness. In another second the room was filled with light.

Gay was with him. They were at me in a twinkling. The trunk straps that held me were on the floor and the gag was out of my mouth. Michael's vigorous slaps sent the blood flowing into my arms and legs. My tongue felt like a balloon. My eyes ached in the sudden light. It was a full ten minutes before I could either move or speak and more than that before I did either. Mike worked with a sort of determined fury, Gay nervously, stiff with fear.

"William?" I managed at last. "Where's William?"

"At the foot of the back stairs with a lump the size of a house on his bean," said Michael. "What happened, Jim? What happened?

At the foot of— Wires were crossing again.

"William," I said, "hid in this doorway and crowned me with a golf club as I came through."

There was a long silence.

"But—" said Gay slowly, "but—"

She didn't need to finish it. If William struck me—and I was positive that he did—who the devil struck William? And why? I stared at Michael.

"Could he have fallen?" I demanded.

Mike's face was screwed in thought. "Sure, but— Good Lord, he was clouted first! He has an awful head. Must have been hit with something sharp and heavy."

"Such as a golf club?"

"Yeah. There are pieces of one at the head of the stairs." He offered me a cigarette with shaking fingers.

As the match flared, Gay's voice quavered, "Are—are you sure—it was William?"

I inhaled furiously. "Why, it must have been. He—" But was it? William had gone through the door. I had seen him, and I had not seen him come out. I tried to recall the twisted face that had confronted me. I had assumed that it was he, but—

"I don't know," I mumbled in bewilderment. "I thought it was, but— I don't know."

"Think!" urged Michael. "You must have seen him. Think!"

"Why, he came in here—and—and— Damn it! I suspected him all of a sudden. I sneaked after him. He was standing in the door with a golf club, and he—got me."

"You did see him, then," Michael muttered. "William! It's cockeyed!"

My head was aching with the effort to make sense. "I saw him. Yes. I thought it was William, but—" There was no dodging the implication. "It might have been someone else."

Mike rose slowly from his knees. "I think," he said, "that in either case we'd better get back to the others."

The others! I had forgotten them completely.

"Where are they?" I demanded.

"Down the hall. We came out to look for you and found William. He couldn't seem to make sense, so we took him back to the rest and came after you."

As I stepped out of that horrible little room, I locked the door after me, and, slipping the key into my pocket, realized that the other keys were still there. Whoever had brained me could not have known that I had them. With those keys in his hands, we should have been at his mercy. It was odd that he should have left William's door unlocked and the key for us to find.

The narrow corridor was in complete darkness. We made our way along it slowly with the aid of Mike's flashlight. In the main hall full lights still blazed. The silence was oppressive. As rapidly as my stiff legs and aching head would allow, we crossed to Gay's door, where Mike knocked sharply.

"Michael?" came the Skipper's voice from within.

"O.K., Skipper." And the door was opened.

Inside, the room was blue with cigarette smoke. M. Farrington was still in the big chair, one pudgy hand hanging on to Higgins for dear life. William was sitting on the bed with Annie on one side of him and Cook on the other. The man looked as if his last call had sounded.

"Jim's all right," said Michael quickly. "Just a little shaken up. How are you now, William?"

"Not so good, sir." The chauffeur was glaring at me accusingly. "It's a nasty thing to be hit on the head from behind—nasty."

Gay shoved a chair at me and I flopped into it, hardly aware of what I was doing.

"William," I said, "what's the big idea—knocking me out and tying me to your bed?"

Someone screamed—M. Farrington, I think—and William sprang to his feet, shaking with fury. "You dirty bastard," he said and started for me.

Mike intercepted him. "William!" he shouted. "Are you crazy?" His left arm shot out, and William spun across the room. "We found Mr. Wells in your room just now—gagged and tied to the bed."

"What?" In spite of myself I pitied him. "Gagged and tied—" His eyes were those of a suffering dog. "Then—who—hit—me?"

"I didn't!" I said. "What happened to you? Can't you see that time is important? What happened?"

He turned to me like a man walking in his sleep. "I went into my room like you told me," his voice was dazed, "and you hit me when I went through the door. Only—you—didn't—hit—" Suddenly his voice rose in a bellow. "I'm getting out of here! I'll swim out. We're going to be murdered—murdered in the dark! Let me go!" Mike and I were hanging on to his arms. "Let me go! I can't do no more! I—" All the strength Mike had left went into that punch. William crumpled to the floor.

"Be quiet!" Cook was shaking Annie furiously. "Start any fuss now and I'll warm you proper!"

Over William's body, I stared at Michael's grim face. "It wasn't William, I guess," I said through dry lips.

"No. And the rest of us were all here."

The Skipper was kneeling beside William, and Gay was bringing water from the bathroom.

"Then," said Michael at last, "there *is* someone else in the house—someone none of us know about."

There seemed to be no other explanation. Which meant that no one in that room was a murderer. None of us had crept stealthily into the storm after a friend, and—I could have whooped with relief.

William moaned and opened his eyes.

"Better?" asked the Skipper. "You were a bit excited and they quieted you."

"Here," Mike was oozing good spirits, "let me help you. Stretch out on the bed a while. You'll be all right."

We helped him to the bed, Annie escaping from Cook and fluttering to his assistance. M. Farrington brought us back to the problem at hand.

"You really think there is someone else in the house?"

"Not a doubt in the world, Aunt Martha," said Michael. "And that makes everything all right."

"Does it?" the Farrington eyebrows went up. "Now I should say, Michael, that it makes everything very much wrong. You don't seriously intend to sit here idle while an unknown criminal roams the house—a criminal who has murdered one of your guests?"

M. Farrington had a knack for putting things unpleasantly. I had been considering doing just that, and so, I could see from his face, had Michael. Compared to the sensation of suspecting your best friends of an unspeakable crime, the feeling of merely being pursued by a thug was a pleasurable one. Michael reddened.

"It's this way, Aunt Martha," I ventured. "We can't do much in the dark, and he can't get away. And—er—well, we're a little done up. I think the most sensible thing for us to do is to make ourselves as comfortable as possible right here until morning."

M. Farrington needed no words to make you feel like something that crawls. The Skipper came to my rescue.

"The most sensible thing any of us can do right now is to eat. Do any of you realize what time it is?"

Incredulously we compared watches. It was after one o'clock.

"Twelve hours since lunch," continued the Skipper. "I propose a kitchen delegation to handle the crisis."

There followed something of an argument. The natural thing was to send the servants all downstairs together. There were four of them, William in no worse condition than I was and not half so bad as Michael. Higgins still had his revolver. But Cook had other ideas. She would never go back into that kitchen, not for all the gold in China, as she put it. The Skipper had no objections to taking Cook's place, but Higgins had never heard of such a thing and so assured us. Annie agreed with him and William agreed with Annie. M. Farrington, quite herself again, settled it.

"Cook," she said sternly, "stop your nonsense. Naturally you will go down to the kitchen. The others will all be with you. There is absolutely no danger. In fact," with sudden decision, "I think the rest of us would be more comfortable in the library."

Gay, who had never really seen M. Farrington in action, stared open-mouthed. "But," she objected, "there's someone down there. I mean—"

M. Farrington smiled thinly. "Of course there is someone down there, my dear. Therefore we shall drive him upstairs where all the doors and windows are locked and he can neither do any damage nor escape."

"Well, then, come along with you, Higgins," said Cook. It was settled.

We gained the library without incident. Wherever our prowler might be, he was neither in the halls, the dining-room, the library, nor—to judge by the silence from the other end of the house—the servants' quarters. Chaos of our own making was the only thing that confronted us in the library. M. Farrington, switching on the dining-room lights, stood the connecting door ajar.

"Sit down, Barbara," she ordered, seating herself on the divan. "James, make up a fire. Michael, you and Grace might put some of these books back where they belong."

After the high melodrama of the last twenty-four hours, I thoroughly enjoyed that reconstruction program. I fell to work on the fire eagerly, while Gay mounted the ladder and put up the books Michael handed her. The Skipper stood in the dining-room doorway, smoking, her back toward us, and M. Farrington's incessant prattle filled me with long lost, delightful laughter.

"This," she commenced in her best state dinner manner, "is what comes of their allowing such unemployment to continue. People are not safe in their beds. What I am to say to Judith's mother I do not know. It is the fault of the system. No one is safe anywhere. Michael, *don't* put Schiller on the top shelf. Barbara, I do wish you would sit down."

"Why?" said the Skipper brusquely, without turning.

"Because it is primarily important that no one should watch that front staircase." Everyone turned at that. "The man cannot go up the back way because of the servants. If he is not allowed to go up the front way, we shall have him quite near us. Aside from the fact that the thought is unpleasant, it will be more difficult to trap him down here."

"I'll be damned!" said Michael softly. The Skipper sat down.

"My only fear," continued the amazing old lady, "is that the servants may interrupt him."

But the servants didn't. It was fully twenty minutes before the rattle of silver announced the arrival of Higgins and Annie in the dining-room. They had seen no one, and none of them had ventured into the hall. Incredible as it seemed after such an experience, we were all ravenous. I think that even M. Farrington forgot to make conversation. In any case, no one listened to find out. At the Skipper's suggestion, Higgins retired in search of his own supper, and we were left to eat in peace.

But food, far from reviving us, produced a lethargy of contentment. I was struggling with a cup of black coffee when I realized with a start that we had all been drowsing at the table and that M. Farrington's pressing the bell and the subsequent appearance of Higgins were the only things that saved us from lapsing into a comatose state.

"Higgins," said M. Farrington, "you may tell Cook that we shall all remain downstairs until she has finished cleaning up. Then I think we may as well retire. You may let us know as soon as you are ready."

"Very good, madam," said Higgins and departed.

"Oh, Lord!" said Gay sleepily. "What time is it?"

Michael glanced at his watch. "Twenty minutes of three." Abruptly a startling thought aroused me. None of us happened to be a murderer, but one of our number had been killed hardly more than twenty-four hours ago, and we had every reason to believe that a crafty and homicidal maniac lurked somewhere in the house even yet.

"Look here," I said sharply, "we can't fall asleep! It's dangerous!"

They blinked at me. We had had very little sleep the night before and the past twenty-four hours had been cruelly exhausting. Nothing but action and considerable will power would keep us going for the few hours until daylight.

"Jimmie's right," said the Skipper; but her voice was very thick and her eyes were bleary. I poured more coffee.

"Tell you what," I said. "The back stairs are well blocked off. All the servants are probably in the kitchen. We are sure of this room and the library. He can't get anywhere upstairs except in the halls. Well, half of us can cover the lower hall while the other half goes through the living-room, game-room, and conservatory. Then, if he isn't in either of those, we can all go up the front stairs. The servants can go up the back stairs, and we'll have him."

They were still blinking at me. I could see that I was talking to empty space. My own voice alternately receded from me and bounced back in waves. I dashed my hand on the table.

"We can't sleep! Don't you realize that Jude is dead—that we'll all be dead if we sleep?"

Michael staggered to his feet. "You're right, I suppose," he mumbled, "but—can't seem to feel much."

I played my last trump. Dousing my napkin in ice-water, I slapped him on the back of his neck. It worked. His eyes flew open in a flash. With the aid of more ice-water and plenty of coffee, our party roused itself, but it was not a pleasant awakening. An atmosphere of tortured nerves shrieking for rest pervaded the room. I don't think I ever felt less like moving. My brain was singing, "Jude—killer—can't sleep!" but it attached little or no significance to the words.

We left Mike and Gay at the end of the hall, where they commanded a clear view of the main hall and of the small one leading to the library. The library windows and the hall door and windows were all securely locked. Except for the usual paraphernalia the hall closet was empty. The Skipper, M. Farrington, and I explored the living-room carefully. The windows were still fastened. Nothing but the scent of roses from the adjacent conservatory. "Can't sleep—can't sleep!" went the refrain in my head.

We stepped into the game-room. The billiard cues still lay where Jude and Michael had left them. The fire had been dead for hours. Mechanically examining doors and windows, I was seeing Jude—good Heavens! only last night—here in this room. I could feel the pressure of her hand on my arm—see— I let the bolt on the door back into place with a thud.

"On to the kill," said the Skipper, and winced, following the association of her own haphazard words.

Gay and Michael still waited in the hall, half asleep. I stepped quickly into the servants' dining-room through the swinging door.

They were all sitting around the kitchen table and they turned rather guiltily at the sound of my voice. Unwashed dishes were scattered over the room, and both rooms were fully lighted, with the window shades drawn.

What the devil had they been talking about? I could not have been eyed more strangely if I had walked in that door for my own funeral.

"We've searched all the other rooms downstairs again," I said. "Our visitor must have gone up through the front hall. All the doors up there are locked. You people go up the back stairs while we go up the front, and we'll have him. Are you a good shot, Higgins?"

The old man's face twitched. "I don't know, sir. I've never—fired the revolver, sir."

"William?"

He hesitated for a second. "Yes."

"Then you take the revolver. Shoot quickly and shoot low—and for God's sake don't miss!" William took the revolver reluctantly. "I'll call when we're ready," I said.

All of my party were waiting for me at the foot of the stairs, Gay and Michael awake at last, their eyes bright with excitement. The Skipper was talking to M. Farrington in a low voice.

"All right," I said. "Now we'll end this damned foolishness for good and all. William has the gun. Mike, you and I will go first. The rest of you stay well behind us, and don't leave the stairs until it's over. Everybody all right?"

The assents were a little hoarse.

"Here we go, William!" I bellowed, and pelted up those steps as fast as I could go. Ridiculous how interminable that short climb seemed! M. Farrington was puffing behind me and Mike was at my side. He panted, "Should have kept the gun yourself!" "Can't shoot and neither can you!" I hissed just as the first view of the hall came into sight. At the head of the stairs we drew up with a jerk. Nothing! The hall was empty. Seven closed doors stared us in the face, and the key to each one of them lay in my own pocket. We stood straining our ears for sounds of a struggle in the other corridor. Then the door of the servants' quarters began to swing slowly toward us.

10

I have never seen a door move so slowly. Through it tiptoed William, revolver in hand, and behind him came Higgins. Someone on the stairs gasped and then there was silence. I moved.

"The doors," I said. "Try them."

People were rushing up from the stairs, in from the corridor. Frantically we were tugging on locked doors, expecting them to open. None of them did. I tried them all myself, from one end of the hall to the other and even out into the smaller corridor. Locked, every one of them.

It was William who had one last gleam of hope. "Your keys, sir," he jerked. "Have you got 'em *all?*"

I drew the keys out and counted them. Ten. I counted the bedrooms. Six and four more in the servant's hall. One by one I unlocked those rooms and searched them. The light still burned beside Jude Blinshop's bed, but aside from the still figure under the sheet there was nothing there. I relocked that door last and went back into the hall.

"It's impossible!" I said. "Someone certainly struck me. It might have been William, but I couldn't have struck William, and—and someone did."

"The cellar," Gay said suddenly, "There must be a cellar."

There was, but it was inconceivable that Jude's murderer was down there—not unless he was a magician—and then some. Nevertheless, I rushed down the narrow stairs again. At the foot of them, a sudden idea pulled me up short. The cellar door at the Bluff is outside the house in the little entryway off the kitchen where I had picked up Michael's handkerchief. I myself had locked the door leading from that entry into the kitchen. In one bound I was at that door. It was locked and the key was where I had left it—on the inside of the door. Turning the key, I threw the door open on an empty entryway. The cellar door was bolted. I whirled back into the kitchen, relocking the door.

"Skipper," I said, "think carefully. Is there any other entrance from the cellar into the house?"

Her answer was prompt. "No. The only other entrance to the cellar is the outer one at the side of the house."

Michael spoke from behind Gay. "Then our man is still loose somewhere in the house."

I nodded. No one else had anything to offer. Over and over in the back of my head I was mulling the chances of William's having thrown himself down the stairs as a blind to start us hunting for a nonexistent marauder. Possible, of course. Probable? From the direction of the main hall, we could hear muffled sounds of the servants on the front stairs.

In the living-room I sank uncomfortably into a deep chair and studied a section of the rug pattern.

"The only trouble, Jim," said the Skipper quietly, "is that our friend is *not* in the cellar. The cat was all right when Martha and I came downstairs. He couldn't have been touched much before Cook screamed. And no one had time to mutilate that cat and make his exit down the back stairs before we got to the kitchen. No one went out the front door—unless he bolted it after him on the *inside!*"

"But, Skipper—" I began, when a warning look from her stopped me. Gay, Michael, and M. Farrington came slowly in. Their general aspect was gloomy.

"Perhaps," said Gay, after a long interval of staring at her own feet, "we had better hold a séance. It's done in all the best thrillers."

Mike's face was worried. "Rot!" he said sharply. "Don't get silly, for God's sake!"

Her laugh was shaky. "Why not? People are killed and slugged and tied up by empty air. There must be a ghost! We owe it to ourselves not to miss anything."

"Stop it!" Michael crossed to her swiftly. "Stop it! Get a grip on yourself! Don't—" Too late. She collapsed against him in a wild fit of tears.

That evening had pretty well exhausted my stock of sympathy. I stepped into the conservatory. But its heavy scent of roses reminded me of nothing so much as of a funeral. I thought of Jude Blinshop's funeral. I selected a casket for Jude—not a heavy one—blue, deep blue. No roses. Just— The realization of what I was doing struck me as a revolting shock. My foot sent a pot of American Beauties crashing to the floor.

I swore frantically.

"Exactly," said M. Farrington's voice at my elbow.

"Must have brushed against it, Aunt Martha," I mumbled, stooping for the roses.

"With your foot," said the dry voice. "James, you are not to lose your head. Sit down, please."

I sat dismally under an appalling rubber plant. I wished that I were dead, recollected that I might very shortly get my wish, shivered, and brought my wavering attention back to M. Farrington. She was speaking in her dry, precise little voice.

"The greatest danger of all, my dear boy, is that we may allow our imaginations to run away with us. Our predicament is unpleasant in the extreme and entirely unexpected. The thought of the supernatural in connection with these strange occurrences is inevitable, but thoroughly absurd. If we force ourselves to think—"

From behind the rubber plant, I gaped at her. The supernatural! M. Farrington *arguing* about the supernatural! Were we all going crazy?

"Don't worry, Aunt Martha," I said. "Cook of course would think banshees were after her if a match blew out. But I'm sure the rest of us are too—"

The picture of Gay in hysterics in the next room stopped me. I groped impatiently for a cigarette.

"Grace is not herself, James." Confound the woman! Did she think me deaf as well as dumb? "In our present overwrought condition, we tend to reduce perfectly normal happenings to the basis of superstitious phenomena. We must retain self-control. I advise you to provide immediate physical action for everyone. This waiting is—unpleasant."

I exploded. "But damn it!" I roared. "We can't keep pussyfooting around the house playing hide-and-seek. We've done enough searching for ten houses! What the devil *can* we do?"

"How do you usually amuse yourself?" She was laughing at me. Her lips never moved, but she was laughing. I got to my feet and lunged into the living-room.

Higgins' back was just retreating through the hall door. In a far corner of the room Michael was bending over Gay with a glass of something in his hand. The Skipper glanced round from the window, but returned immediately to her survey of the darkness outside.

"How about bed?" I meant to say it cheerfully.

Mike straightened up. "Don't be fantastic."

"All right." My voice started out jauntily and ended in a ghastly croak. "Then let's do something to amuse ourselves. Bridge? Billiards?"

"Dominoes?" Michael jeered.

"Anything," Gay's voice was shrill and shaky. "We can't just sit here. Let's *do* something!"

And so we tried it. I dragged out a table, located some cards, drew up chairs. M. Farrington, Gay, Mike, and myself played. The Skipper refused to leave her window. In spite of her incessant smoking, she seemed the only thoroughly collected person in the room. We let her stay there.

The horrible farce went on for hours—or seemed to. We overbid wildly and underbid foolishly. It was difficult to remember trumps. Scoring was erratic. In spite of all pretense, every ear in the room was straining to catch sounds from the silent house. Nerves twitched to the soughing of trees and the rattling of blinds. Most emphatically, the ruse was not a success. Finally Michael threw down his cards.

"This is the worst idea you've had yet!" he snorted, moving toward the brandy bottle.

"Let's try billiards." My own voice was barely recognizable. "You *move* playing billiards."

The Skipper and M. Farrington remained in the living-room, the latter patiently trying to read a book, the former still motionless at the window. We left the connecting door open, and Gay, Michael, and I went into the room where the whole ghastly mess seemed to have started. Our attempt was very brief. Not forty-eight hours ago Jude Blinshop had stood right where I was standing, holding that very same cue, waiting for me to leave her alone with Mike. I dropped the cue as if it had burnt my hand.

"Oh, hell!" I groaned in desperation.

Gay seated herself on the table, her foot swinging rapidly.

"Mike," she said, "it isn't just curiosity. I—I *must* know. You ought to trust me enough to tell me why you went outdoors last night."

We were right back at the beginning. What possible difference could it make now? What possible use in dragging it up again? Diversion. Damned grisly diversion! I started for the door, but Mike blocked me off.

"Stay right here, Jim!" Then, very patiently, "I've told you a dozen times, Gay, that it had nothing to do with all this. I went out to look at the bridge."

"You're lying!" At the fury in her voice the sickening whirl in my head began to tighten—tighten as if in another minute my skull would crack. There was no stopping her. "What did you go outdoors for? You were out there at ten o'clock. You said so. Mike, if you don't—"

I had had enough of it. Pushing Michael out of my way, I barged into the living-room, banging the door behind me. The Skipper turned from the window.

"It's nearly daylight," she said. "Thank God. What time is it?"

I blinked at my watch. "Ten minutes of seven." On the davenport, M. Farrington was fast asleep. With all my heart I envied her.

"What's going on in there?"

I tried to smile. "Oh—curiosity—nerves. No telling."

"Yes." She was switching off lights. "Listen, Jimmie, I'm going to take Martha upstairs with me. It's me for a cold shower. Tell Higgins to start some breakfast—and break up that Donnybrook Fair in there. It's daylight and we're civilized—supposedly. Have you our keys?"

In the game-room Michael stood at a window, his back stiff. On a bench in front of the fireplace with her back toward him, Gay was persistently bouncing a ping-pong ball. The atmosphere was arctic.

"It's daylight," I announced triumphantly.

"How cozy," from the window. No response from the bench.

I fumbled through the mess of keys, selected theirs, and handed them out. "Breakfast in half an hour. We'll have to shake a leg."

"Or a neck." Mike strode into the hall, slamming the door after him.

I walked over and removed the ping-pong apparatus from Gay's hand. "You're a good egg, Gay. I've always liked you. But you're digging yourself into a hole that you won't be able to climb out of. Mike is all right. Go take a shower and forget about it."

She got to her feet at that. "Mike," she said furiously, "is a lying skunk! I've just told him so, and now I'm telling you." And she was out of the room.

"Gay!" I shouted, rushing after her. But she flew up the stairs without looking back.

"Good morning, Mr. Jimmie."

I spun around to find Higgins beside me, freshly dressed, brushed, and combed. How much had he heard?

"How's everything below decks?" I said, a bit weakly.

"Fair to middling, sir. Cook— But she means well, sir."

"I'm sure she does. Can you manage breakfast in half an hour?"

"Yes, sir."

I left him there. I had no desire to talk to anybody. Mike's door was closed, and I didn't open it. Did Gay seriously think— The whole idea was ridiculous. I shaved, tubbed, and dressed in a stupor. Just as I was climbing into a shirt, there came a low, insistent knocking on my door.

It was the Skipper's voice. "Jimmie, can you come out here a second?"

I moved to the door. "Hullo, Skipper. What is it? Is—"

"Don't make so much noise." She was beckoning me down the hall in the direction of her own room. "Come—quickly!"

I went on the run. The Skipper paused before Jude Blinshop's door, pointing, and my eyes followed the direction of her finger. Jude's door had been forced open. The lock was still on it, but the woodwork had been torn by terrific pressure. We must have all of us come down the hall without noticing. I pushed open the door.

In the dismal half-light of the winter morning, the small bed lamp still burned, lending a ghostly unreality to the whole scene. A sheet lay on the floor just at my feet. The bed was empty! I took one half-hearted look under it. One glance into that closet and I was back in the hall. I must have been jabbering like a monkey.

The Skipper started for the door, and I flung myself in her way.

"Don't go in there!" I was roaring. "Don't—"

She shoved me aside and disappeared through the door. I should have followed her, but I didn't. I leaned against the wall with my head in my hands. "She was dead." I was saying it to the empty hall. "I saw her. I felt her heart. She was dead!"

"Jimmie, quick!"

I couldn't seem to make my legs move. It seemed a century before I reached the Skipper, who was standing in front of Jude's closet, her face reflecting the terror that held me paralyzed.

She was pointing to something long, lumpy, and shapeless that lay upon the shelf of the closet. Something that vaguely resembled a stack of blankets, but was not a stack of blankets. I seized the uppermost blanket and pulled.

A cold, limp hand was at my throat and something soft and heavy was rolling over me. My head struck the floor with a sickening thud. Even then I didn't appreciate the full horror of it. I was on the floor, struggling furiously with something that was wrapped around me like a vise. I was twisting, pounding, roaring. The world was tumbling in a thundering, blinding wreck about my head. And then I was on my feet, the Skipper in my arms, and both of us were staring down at a huddled mass on the floor—a blotch of eerie blue in that ghostly light. The dead, white face of Jude Blinshop was staring up at us.

I don't know what I did exactly. After a while I tried to quiet the Skipper.

What had been on that bed when I stood alone beside it earlier in the evening? What if I had reached down and moved that sheet? What— I finally managed to move—to lift the body to the bed, cover it with the discarded sheet, and turn out the useless light. When I finished, the Skipper was standing by the door.

"I might have known," she was saying over and over. "I might have known."

I took her arm. "Known what?"

She started, like a person suddenly waking up.

"Quickly, Jim," she said. "We must hurry."

Before I caught up with her, she was halfway down the hall.

"Wait, Skipper," I pleaded. "You can't stand any more of this. I'll call Mike and William."

"No!" in horror. "Good Lord, no!"

I followed her with no idea of where she was going. So the killer had evaded us by cramming Jude's body onto that shelf, taking its place on the bed, and forcing his way out of the room at his leisure. We could have had him twice. Twice! The Skipper was going down the front stairs and straight to the front door, where she paused, pointing jerkily. The heavy bolt had been drawn aside and the key was on the floor. Our man had escaped.

The Skipper flung open the door and dashed out to the steps. Wind whooped around us in fiendish welcome, but the rain had stopped. The Skipper was away—running for dear life toward the end of the house in the direction of the tennis courts. In an instant I was after her, shouting, "Skipper! Skipper! Wait!"

She never turned. At the corner of the house, she disappeared. At top speed I followed. Once I thought I would catch her as she paused for half a second at the path leading from the game-room to the boathouse, but she was off again before I had gained a dozen paces, running straight for the bluff.

That bluff was a sheer drop of fifty feet onto sand or rocks and— My eye caught the boiling, roaring surf beyond, and I remembered Michael's experience by the boathouse. It seemed as if my legs would drop under me.

She was nearly there. Desperately I mastered an impulse to close my eyes and avoid seeing it happen. And just at that moment she stopped short, on the very edge of the bluff. Another gasping leap and I was beside her. I had my hands on her, and I meant to keep them there. Then I, too, was staring into the abyss below us—staring at the body of a man lying face downward on a jut of sand in the middle of the bluff, just out of reach of the howling fury of the sea.

11

We climbed down only part of the way. He was dead. I realized that before we reached him. From the way his head was bent to one side, it seemed as if his neck must be broken. A deep blot of red stained his heavy white hair and was gradually spreading into the sand. Higgins' hair was gray and very thin. Whoever this poor devil was, he was not the butler.

I shouted above the noise of the wind, "We'll have to get help. Can't reach him without a rope!"

She nodded dully. Without a word, she allowed me to draw her back and in the direction of the house. I think she would have fallen had it not been for my arm. The side door was still bolted. We were obliged to make a circuit of the house and enter as we had left it.

From the dining-room, a low babble of voices indicated that breakfast was already under way. I steered the Skipper into the living-room, administered a dose of brandy, and ordered her to stay where she was. Once again the bearer of bad news, I entered the dining-room.

They were all there, being served by Higgins. M. Farrington paused in the midst of an announcement concerning the weather to eye me worriedly.

"Well," growled Michael, "now what?"

"We have found something on the beach," I said. "Higgins, I want you and William and a rope. Hurry!" Higgins gave me one horrified look and rushed toward the kitchen.

Gay was on her feet—"What—have you—found?"

It seemed to me to be the kindest thing to end the suspense of the last three or four hours.

"We've found the body of a man lying halfway down the bluff," I told them. "Our prowler is—through. We'll have to get him before the tide turns or we'll be too late. The surf's pretty heavy."

There was a tinkle of glass, and I caught M. Farrington as she capsized. Neither of the others moved.

"Oh," began Gay, repentant eyes on Michael's face; "oh—"

But we had no time for the sex motif just then.

"Come on, Mike!" I said curtly. "Gay, look after Aunt Martha, will you?"

Armed with a long coil of tow rope, the servants were waiting in the hall. From the side door, we made our way to the bluff. The body lay just as we had left it, the surf mounting steadily higher. There was no time to lose.

"Higgins, you're the lightest. Tie this rope around your waist. Can you tie a decent knot?"

"I don't know, sir." The old man's lips were gray.

I seized the rope and tied it around him. "Were going to lower you down," I said. "Then you untie the rope and put it around him this way. There's no danger. Are you all right?"

"Yes, sir."

We lowered him slowly. The roar of the water was loud in our ears as we waited for his signal. It came, and we hauled. The ground was wet and slippery. There seemed considerable danger of all three of us tumbling to our own destruction before we could bring our gruesome burden within arm's reach. Between us, William and I managed the last stage of the job. In another two minutes, Higgins was back beside us, wet and trembling but uninjured.

He was staring as if hypnotized at the body, which he had rolled over on his back. Slowly my eyes followed his. Except for the heavy white hair, the man lying at our feet might have been Michael Farrington! William knelt down beside the sodden heap.

"Dead, all right. Who is he?"

Whatever his name, that man was a Farrington. He had Michael's black brows, passionate mouth and chin—Mike's slim hips and broad shoulders. The dark eyes were now glassy and horrible, but they were like Michael's—and the Skipper's. With two servants in the midst of it, we had certainly uncovered a family skeleton. I was obliged to shove Mike violently to move him.

During that short journey back across the soggy lawn, a dozen wild thoughts were teeming in my head. Who? That was uppermost. Michael's brother? A cousin? An uncle? Who? Had Mike known him—his whereabouts—his motives? Mike had been shielding someone. There was no doubt of that. But I would have sworn that the look he bent on that pathetic figure had been one of blank amazement.

Had the Skipper known? She had been hiding something, too. She had suspected something. She had rushed from the house as if she knew just where to go. She—Great God! Was this bundle in our arms the reason for the sudden change in the Skipper? Had this man's hand moved Jude's body? Had he been lying, alert, waiting, under that sheet until—

"Where to, sir?" We were at the side entrance.

I looked at Michael, but his back offered no suggestions.

"The game-room, William," I said.

We deposited our burden on the billiard table. Michael gave us no assistance. His mute, vacant stare only intensified an already unbearable situation. To send the servants away would be to insure the rapid spreading of the news in all directions, but it was unthinkable to keep them there. William's eyes were glowing with excitement, his cheeks flushed. Relieved, I thought, relieved that it's over. But he'll talk— Lord, how he'll talk!

"I'll get a cover for him, sir."

I turned to Higgins. The old man's lips were twitching so badly that I had grave misgivings for the fate of his false teeth. Higgins knew, then, whatever it was that Mike and I did not know, and the story was safe with him. In all the terrors of the last two nights, he had not revealed it. I remembered the coffee cups rattling in his hand that first night, and Michael chirping, "Higgins, you don't look up to scratch."

"Will that be all, sir?" William, I could see, was in a hurry to get out to the kitchen with the news.

"Not quite, William. Keep your mouth shut. Understand? It will only get the women excited."

"Very good, sir."

It probably wouldn't work, but in any event there was nothing more I could do.

"All right," I said. And Michael and I were alone.

I have never in my life so heartily wished myself elsewhere. The fuss and fury were over and I was uncomfortably aware of the fact that I was stranded in another man's house where a terrific family scene was impending. Worse than that, my nose was irretrievably thrust into the middle of it.

"Well, Mike," I said clumsily, laying an awkward hand on his shoulder, "what can I do?"

For a moment I thought that he wasn't going to answer. Then, "Get the Skipper. Never mind the rest of them. I've got to talk to the Skipper."

I left him standing there, staring into space. If the Skipper had joined the others, how could I possibly get her without bringing the whole hornets' nest down on his ears? But the Skipper had not joined the others. She was sitting in the very spot where I had left her, her head in her hands, and she didn't seem to hear me come in. It took an effort to cross the room.

"Skipper," I said as gently as I could, "will you come into the game-room?"

She raised her head and looked at me. I would have given something for a poker face.

"Yes," she said at length very slowly. "Yes, of course."

At the game-room door I tried to get away, but she hung onto me. "Come in here, too, Jim—if you don't mind."

I did mind, very much. But I did as I was told, closing the door carefully after me. Mike came toward her, but she ignored him and stepped to the table, where she stood a long time staring at the dead face. I turned to the window blindly. The silence was beastly. I counted broken branches and small sticks scattered on the lawn, dully noted several pieces of brick missing on the terrace, observed that the surf was already washing above the bluff in a fine gray mist.

"Skipper," said Michael's voice. "Is—was—this Norman Farrington?"

Michael's father! But he had died when Michael was a baby!

"Yes."

Silence, a thick blanket of it. Was the hammering of surf actually in the room, or was all that noise in my own head?

"He was insane?"

"Yes."

I thought, "I could open this window and get out of here! Out of here—"

That queer, flat voice again, "How long?"

The other dull voice, "Ever since you were a baby." I slipped the spring lock on the French window and started to step onto the terrace. A deep cry stopped me.

"Michael! Stop! You must listen to me! You *must—*"

My eyes were dragged back to that room, to Michael wrenching himself from her grasp.

Automatically I closed the window as the door slammed behind him.

"Jimmie," said the Skipper hoarsely, "get him back here. I must talk to him."

I put an arm around her. "Better wait, Skipper," I said.

We both whirled at the opening of the door. It was only Higgins, bearing a covering for the body on the table. Without a word he stepped to the table and performed his errand. Turning, he walked over to the Skipper.

"Don't fret, miss," he said. "It's better so," and was gone.

After a while I shook the Skipper gently. "What do you want me to do?" I said. "Shall I tell the others?"

Her sudden grip on my arm made me wince. "No! No; wait until this rotten storm is over and—and help comes."

"But won't they wonder?" I objected. "I told them—"

She was almost shouting, "I know what I'm doing!" Her voice fell. "Sorry. You see, I particularly want to keep Martha from knowing this until—things are more normal. She was—very fond of Norman. Tell Gay anything you like, but keep the servants quiet, and leave Martha to me."

I opened my mouth to say that it would be pretty hard to fool M. Farrington after my announcement in the dining-room, but something in the Skipper's face made me close it again. After all, it was none of my business. I could only hope that William would keep his word, and I could keep an eye on Mike.

"Lock both these doors, Jimmie," said the Skipper, "and then we'll—we'll eat breakfast."

Breakfast! The word set my teeth on edge; and yet, crossing the room to do as I was told, I was aware of a hollow feeling in the region of my belt.

The dining-room was deserted. Voices beyond the closed door of the library indicated that M. Farrington and Gay Palmer still kept unhappy vigil against the return of the rescue party. It seemed brutal to leave them in such suspense, but the Skipper was pouring coffee with a steady hand. And its aroma was too much for me. I was famished. Whatever happened, apparently, I could eat and I did so. Higgins served us in silence. Not until my fourth cup of coffee did I turn to the Skipper.

"Well?"

"Your move now, Casabianca," she said with the ghost of a smile. "I'm taking Martha upstairs. From now on you and Gay will have to amuse yourselves. The entertainment," with a twisted grin, "is over."

I waited in the dining-room as long as I possibly could. I was in no mood for a rousing scene with M. Farrington. Dismally crumbling toast, I reflected that the storm couldn't last much longer. The rain had stopped. There should be boats from the mainland by the next day at the very latest. And then—police—inquests—reporters—the Blinshop family to be faced. What about Mike? What if he were to discover that his father's disease had been hereditary? Lord! What an awful situation for Gay Palmer!

I spilled a last despairing handful of crumbs on the tablecloth and wandered aimlessly to the sideboard. Would I ever be rid of the ghastly memory of that huddled bundle on the closet shelf?

Nine-thirty. Should I look up Gay? I wondered what the Skipper had told her. Perhaps it would be better to leave the kid alone. In her place, I—

"Jimmie," Gay's voice startled me from the door. "What the deuce are you doing? Come on in here, can't you?"

I went reluctantly. Apparently she had been pacing around in there alone for some time. Her face was very red, and her hands were jerking nervously.

"Look here, what the devil is going on? One minute you rush in howling that you've found a dead man on the beach, and the next the Skipper comes waltzing in with the bright remark that it was all a mistake. What is this anyway?"

"This," I said curtly, "is a damn mess."

"That's not an answer." She snapped a cigarette from the case in her none-too-steady hand. "I want to know what's going on, and I'm going to know. Where's Mike?"

"In his room."

She almost got to the door before I did.

"Now listen, Gay, you can't see him just now. Sit down. I've got to talk to you." I took her arm and led her, struggling, to a chair. "You and I have a lot of thinking to do, and we're going to make ourselves pretty scarce."

"What do you mean?" She sat under protest.

"Just this. The Skipper is trying to keep M. Farrington in the dark to save us from some messy scenes. There was a body on the beach. It's in the game-room now."

Her face tightened. "Who is it?"

I summoned every ounce of deception I could find.

"I've never seen him before."

She didn't relax. "Then it was a tramp after all. How—funny."

I left it at that. Let Mike handle it in his own way. There was nothing more for me to do but wait, wait for the first boatload of gaping natives from the mainland.

"What are the Blinshops like?"

"I've only met them once or twice. Nice enough people. They've been friends of the Farringtons for ages."

And so we rambled on for at least an hour. It was a horrible morning. Gradually we dropped all pretense of conversation. We tried to read. We tried to play Double Canfield. We paced and we fidgeted. The world as such seemed to have ceased existence for us beyond the limits of that week-end on the Bluff. Try as we would, our thoughts couldn't seem to get into the past beyond the Friday of our arrival or into the future beyond the arrival of a boat from shore. There were two of us alone with the weary task of enduring one another indefinitely.

Sleep was the logical thing. We both needed it desperately, but we had passed that stage of fatigue where sleep is possible. Every nerve and every muscle ached, and there was no way of resting them. At a rough guess I should have placed our tenancy of the library at ten years by the time Michael appeared.

And he was no cheering spectacle. His hair stood wildly on end. His clothes were crumpled and messy. His eyes had a nasty, glowing intensity that brought me to my feet in a jerk.

"Where's everybody?" he inquired thickly, crossing the room with a labored, weaving motion. He was drunk—roaringly drunk.

"Upstairs—" I began, but it was no use. Gay was at him like a shot.

"You've got a nerve! Where do you think you are?"

I had a fleeting desire to knock their heads together.

Michael waved a pompous hand. "Where? Home, my pet—at Farrington Bluff on beauteous, bounteous Long Island in the bosom of my family." Something in the remark appeared to amuse him. He roared with drunken gusto, holding weakly to the edge of the table.

Gay advanced on him, eyes flashing. "You filthy little rat!" she said. "You yellow, drunken lout, listen to me! You think you'll quit on your aunts now because the going is getting tough. Well, you won't! Either of those old girls is worth more than a dozen of you on one platter, do you hear? And if Jimmie doesn't whale the booze out of you right now, I will!"

Michael stared at her stupidly, steadying himself against the table.

"You can get this, too!" Her voice was rising shrilly. "After what I've seen of you in the last few days, I don't want to see any more. Is that clear?"

Possibly his silence irritated her more than anything else. Suddenly her hand shot out. There was a hearty smack, and a dull white streak glistened on Michael's red face—glistened, turned pink, and stood out a welt of red.

Then, like a streak, Mike moved. His hand seized her wrist and sent her hurtling into a table covered with glasses and decanters. There was a tinkling crash. I leapt across that room and had him by the throat. I shook him until my head roared and my breath was gone. Then I flung him violently into a chair.

For a long time none of us spoke. None of us could. Mike moved first, lumbering heavily to his feet. All the liquor had gone out of him, but there was something in its place—something that made me catch my labored breath in a painful gasp. He spoke very slowly.

"I'm drunk. All right. I meant to be drunk, and I mean to be drunk from now on. Can't you see that I'm safest that way? I've killed a person. Do you understand that? I've killed a person!"

12

I climbed out of the hideous silence like a drowning man coming up for the last time.

"Stop it!" I roared; and my voice struck weirdly on my own ears. "Stop it! Are you crazy?"

He whirled on me. "Yes. Do you finally get it? Crazy! Mad! Insane!"

I was struggling desperately with the horrible doubts in my own mind. "You're drunk," I said. "You're drunk. There's nothing else wrong with you. You're imagining things."

He moved away from my restraining hand, leaving me with the words still in my throat. "Nice going," he said, and stood grinning at me foolishly.

His unexpected calm frightened me more than his raving. Was it possible that he *had* inherited—something? Could it have been Michael, and not that wretched bundle on the pool table, who had—?

"Mike," I said. "Mike, listen—" and we all turned to face the Skipper surveying us grimly from the door. She was looking beyond me, straight at Michael.

"Well," she said at last. "Now what?"

Mike's voice was thick and deliberately blurred, it seemed to me. "Notta thing," he asserted with loud geniality. "C'mon in, Skipper, and make Jimmie keep quiet."

What the devil was he up to? There had been no liquor in him a minute ago. Putting on an act for the Skipper. Why? I glared at him.

"Skip it!" I growled. "How's Aunt Martha, Skipper?"

The Skipper had gotten the point as thoroughly as any one of us, but she never blinked.

"Sleeping. I dosed her well. Incidentally, that's a good prescription for all of us—sleep."

Mike chuckled drunkenly, too damned drunkenly to be convincing.

For a split second he and the Skipper looked at one another, the Skipper's frown enigmatical, Mike's eyes soberly defiant. Then he turned and reeled out of the room.

Gay broke the awkward pause.

"No guts," she said.

"Would you mind," the Skipper's voice was quizzical, "telling us what leads you to that conclusion?"

Gay hesitated. Then slowly, "Nothing. Nerves of my own, maybe."

She turned to the mess on the floor, stooped, and began to pick up broken bits of glass. After a moment, I moved to help her. Righting the table, I deposited the debris upon it. There was no blinking the fact that with the actual danger gone and a good eighteen hours of waiting before release could possibly come, our nerves were going to play the devil with us. Mike was drunk, worn out, and suffering from a series of nasty shocks. Upon thinking it over, I put no credence in his wild announcement. It was merely a sample of what we might expect unless we all got a grip on ourselves. Did Gay believe him? Her face was forbidding. Certainly their continual rows had at last gone beyond the joke stage. Our task was finished without comment from the Skipper, who sat on the divan smoking, her eyes on the floor. Gay, I think, was wishing herself out of that room quite as heartily as I was.

"I think," said the Skipper, "that we'd better clear up a few things right now."

Very decidedly I did not want to hear that explanation. "Why not wait?" I ventured.

The Skipper shook her head. "There's been too much waiting. I want you to tell this to Michael at once." She was leaning forward, not looking at either of us, her words coming with slow precision. "Norman Farrington was my half-brother—Martha's brother. She was very fond of him. Shortly after Michael was born, his father contracted some kind of jungle fever in South America. He never recovered—mentally. He has been in private asylums ever since. Mike never knew it. There seemed no reason why he should. It had ruined Martha's life and that was enough. The condition was incurable." She paused to draw heavily on her cigarette.

I said eagerly, "It isn't hereditary?"

"Obviously not." She blew a long, steady stream of smoke into the already clouded room. "Several months ago Norman somehow managed to get away from Dr. Crane. Martha used to visit him regularly and I imagine that she slipped him some money. At any rate, he got hold of some, and bribed two of the guards. The place is only ten miles from here. Half an hour after he got out, he arrived here in a taxi. Unfortunately he was enjoying a temporarily lucid interval, and I had trouble with Martha. His stories of the life in that place were—pitiful. Nothing I could say would convince her that he was not permanently cured."

I poured her some brandy, but she didn't taste it.

"Martha worshiped him. And I—well, he was my brother. Between them, they convinced me against my better judgment to allow him to stay here. No one knew about it but Higgins. Fortunately none of the other servants had seen him arrive. And Higgins was—Higgins. We kept him in Mike's room, locked in most of the time. Once or twice we brought him downstairs at night when the other servants were out of the way and it seemed quite safe. Higgins managed his meals and his laundry, and he used some of Mike's clothes. The asylum was constantly in touch with us, but we lied like troopers. He really did seem to be all right. That was eight weeks ago.

"I suppose the strain began to tell on me, and Martha began to worry. She wanted me to see a doctor, and so on. The last thing I wanted in this house was a doctor. I might have gone into town just to satisfy her, but I couldn't risk leaving her here alone with Norman. In the end, she sent for Michael and Jude. Her plan worked, of course. I didn't dare allow that girl to come here without some man in the house to look after her. I was criminally negligent. I allowed you all to come—even asked you myself."

Quietly she drained her brandy glass.

"We transferred Norman to Higgins' room. While we were at dinner Friday night, he escaped. I said nothing to Martha. Her heart is bad. I went out to look for him myself, and when I got back things had happened. I kept quiet because I knew we could get no outside help. We were as much on guard as we could be, and the idea of a roaming, homicidal maniac wouldn't have cheered any of you up.

"Martha is childish in some respects. She will never believe that Norman had anything to do with all this. I'm glad of it. All things considered, his falling over the bluff was the best thing that could have happened. It ends the damned mess anyway. I wish you'd tell this to Mike before he drinks himself into thinking that he's John Wilkes Booth."

She rose slowly to her feet. "I think I'll lie down now for a bit, if you don't mind."

I watched her go up the stairs, head and shoulders very straight and the hand resting on the railing limp and weary. Gay was standing stiffly at the window when I finally turned around.

"Well?" I said awkwardly.

She turned with a twisted smile. "I haven't been exactly True Blue Lou, have I, Jim?"

I muttered inanely, "None of us are covered with blue ribbons. Anyone gets off his oats."

She began an aimless ramble about the room, fingering knick-knacks without interest. "That doesn't help things much. We'd been thinking of a wedding in the spring, Jim. I don't think we'll bother now."

"That's stupid!" I said it all the more loudly because I knew that I lied. "The best thing for you to do is to forget that whole damned fuss. It's all over. Why keep it alive?"

"We won't be able to help it. Every time we lose our heads a little, we'll remember that we let each other down. We'll be flinging it at each other."

I had no answer ready for that one. Gay seized the poker and began to beat monotonously on the fender.

"It's been rather a costly week-end for me."

"Look here," I said roughly, "what do you think it's been for Jude? Or the Skipper?"

The annoying rapping continued. "The Skipper deserved it in a way. She brought it on herself." She was deliberately working herself up. More nerves.

"Bunk!" I snapped, heading for the door. "I'm going to talk to Mike. There's nothing for you to worry about. Why don't you go to bed?"

"There's a lot to worry about," doggedly. "The more I think—"

But I walked out and left her to her thoughts. Higgins was in the hall, arranging some roses.

"Storm's over, Higgins," I said. "Everything will be all right by morning."

"Mr. Jimmie—" He stopped me on the stairs. "Could I— That is, would you have time to—"

I had never heard the man stutter before in all my life.

"What's the matter, Higgins?" He was still white.

"I'd like to talk to you a minute, sir. Somewhere where we can't be heard."

I stared at him. "What about? There's no one to hear us, Higgins. What's on your mind?"

"Would you come into the living-room, sir?"

Reflecting that the poor old boy probably wanted to relieve his mind by telling me his version of the story, I followed him into the living-room.

"Well, what is it, Higgins?"

"Mr. Jimmie, the Farringtons have always been almost like my own family, as you might say. The old gentleman was very good to me when I was just a boy, sir, and alone in this country, if you see what I mean."

I smiled at him reassuringly. "I see what you mean. They've been pretty swell to me, too." What the deuce ailed him? If he trusted me enough to tell me the story, why all the preliminaries?

"This affair has been most unfortunate, sir."

My patience was getting a bit thin. I had many things to say to Michael, and I wanted to say them before he had soaked himself into a complete stupor. I frowned.

I said sharply, "What's on your mind?"

"Mr. Jimmie," he stepped closer to me and spoke in a hoarse whisper, "the danger's not over. There's—"

He stopped suddenly, and an amazing thing happened. His eyes, fixed on the window behind me, seemed about to pop from his head and under my very nose the man seemed to shrivel up. I wheeled toward that window. There was no one there, and my patience snapped.

"Higgins, what the devil are you looking at? What are you talking about?"

He passed a trembling hand over his eyes. "I—I don't know. Possibly, sir, I—I have been imagining things. Please forget it, sir." With a certain dignity he straightened himself.

Exasperated beyond all endurance, I fairly roared at him to speak his piece.

"Nothing, sir. I have been forgetting myself. Please excuse me."

I made a wild lunge, but he got to the door before I did. Crossing to the window, I leaned against it, staring out at the dismal lawn, my brain in an uproar.

"The danger's not over!" What did that remark have to do with the depressing secret of Farrington Bluff? What—? My eyes had fallen to the tiling on the porch floor just outside the window. There, clearly defined in rapidly hardening mud, was the imprint of a rubber boot. Higgins *had* seen someone at that window—someone who might or might not have heard what he was starting to say! The wild thought crossed my mind that maybe he was right—that there was more trouble to come, but I rejected it impatiently. What a hair-trigger state we had all gotten into! I went off in search of Michael.

He was not in his room. A disorderly confusion of clothes, books, and papers gave mute testimony to his state of mind, and a nearly empty decanter of brandy told me that the Skipper's fears for him were justified. I thought first of the bootprint outside the living-room window and then of Norman Farrington lying halfway down the bluff. Farrington Bluff was no place for a drunken man—particularly a drunken man in Michael's frame of mind.

In a vain hope of finding him, I rushed through the bathroom into my own room. He wasn't there. And I was reasonably certain that he wasn't downstairs. There were only two possibilities. Either he must be in talking to the Skipper or he must be outside. I rushed into the hall and raced with all my might to the Skipper's door. Without waiting to knock, I flung it open. The Skipper's oilskins lay on the bed and her boots on the floor beside them, but there was no one in the room. I had barely time to realize that fact, when a deafening report of a gun shook the entire house.

For a second I was too petrified to move. The sound had seemed to come from the direction of the next room—M. Farrington's. I dove through the joining bathroom and pulled up with a bang.

M. Farrington lay face downward on the floor beside the dressing table, one arm thrown out at her side. As I dazedly knelt to turn her over, the hall door flew open to disclose Michael, his eyes red and bleary, blinking at me in amazement. We stared at each other.

"She's hurt. Get some water!" I managed finally through stiff lips.

He hesitated, and I sensed more distrust in that pause than I could see on his incredulous face. His eyes fell and he moved unsteadily toward the bathroom. I wrenched my attention from my own appalling predicament to the old lady. She was alive. A bullet had torn through her left shoulder. Mechanically I noted that she had been shot from the rear at close range. There were powder marks on the back of her lavender robe, and the profuse bleeding in front seemed to indicate that the bullet had torn straight through. So Higgins had been right! We were still in danger!

Clumsily Mike deposited a basin of water beside me. He seemed hypnotized, incapable of speech. And I was glad of it.

"Find the Skipper!" I said hoarsely, starting to bathe the wound with my handkerchief. "Hurry, Mike! Her heart's bad and—"

The Skipper was there beside me before he could seem to move. Her face was grim and set.

"Give me that, Jim," she said sternly, kneeling beside me. "There's a first-aid kit in the bathroom. Get it, please."

I got up with difficulty. I couldn't seem to get my mind away from the fact that I would be suspected of this shooting. It took me at least three minutes to find the first-aid kit in the cabinet over the basin. While I was fumbling around in the process, I could hear Gay's high excited voice. The thing must have been heard all over the house. In another minute the servants would be tumbling in on us. Vaguely I wondered, as I crossed the few steps to the Skipper's side, what had kept them off so long.

Mike and I were of about as much use as an oil burner in the Sahara. But the Skipper worked quickly and carefully. Between us, we lifted M. Farrington to the bed and stood waiting while the Skipper applied restoratives. Slowly, in a series of unpleasant groans, the old lady came out of it and was immediately acutely ill. I made for the door as fast as I could go, only to bump smack into Higgins, straightening himself from an obvious keyhole attitude in the hall.

"What has happened, sir?" he said without a trace of embarrassment.

I closed the door behind me with a jerk. "What are you doing, Higgins?" I countered.

"Miss Barbara was giving me some instructions in the lower hall. We heard what sounded like a shot and hurried up here. I stayed in the hall at her request to keep the servants out of the way, sir."

"Very pat, Higgins." Glaring at him, I noticed suddenly that he was holding something in his hand—something wrapped up in a handkerchief. And he saw my look.

"I found this on the stand here just now. I thought perhaps you had better take care of it until the police arrive."

Deliberately he unwrapped from the handkerchief his own revolver, to my knowledge the only one on the Bluff. I reached for it involuntarily, and to this day I don't know what stopped me. Perhaps it was the sudden realization that even as he offered it to me, Higgins was carefully avoiding direct contact with the gun. I managed to take it, handkerchief and all, without touching the metal. Furiously I hurled questions at him. No results that meant anything.

Cook was in the kitchen. He was sure of it because she had been there when he answered Miss Barbara's ring and both William and Annie were certain that she had not come up the back stairs. They had just left him. They claimed to have been in their rooms when they heard the shot, and he believed that they were because they had not been in the kitchen when the Skipper rang. They appeared immediately after the shot was heard. It was all very upsetting, just when we had been sure that the trouble was all over. He would very much like to know what had happened.

"Someone shot and painfully wounded Miss Farrington," I said bluntly.

He staggered back against the wall. "Painfully wounded," he repeated in a thin whisper. "Painfully—"

A thought was dawning in my head. "Merely a flesh wound," I said deliberately, with my eyes on his face. "She's quite conscious and there's no danger."

It didn't work. His eyes were on the floor, his face expressionless. When he finally spoke, his voice was cool and collected. "This is horrible, Mr. Jimmie."

"Yes." My plan crystallized. "Wait here, Higgins."

I went into the Skipper's room and, after considerable rummaging, located a box of bath powder. Holding the gun by the tip of the barrel with my fingers carefully wrapped in the handkerchief, I dusted the thing liberally with powder and then blew. A faint white film remained on the shiny metal, but it was an even film. There were no fingerprints on the revolver. And Higgins, who had possessed the presence of mind to wrap his own hand in a handkerchief before touching it, had just attempted to thrust the thing into my outstretched bare hand.

"Until the police arrive," he had said.

13

That second shooting was one of the most sinister episodes of those days and nights of terror. In broad daylight with everyone up and about, we had hitherto considered ourselves safe. It was puzzling, too, for it seemed to represent an inexcusable slip in the killer's otherwise workable plans. He had managed to convince the entire household of the guilt of Norman Farrington, who would never be able to disprove the charge. Why had he ruined all his work and why, of all people, would he shoot M. Farrington?

Martha herself had little evidence to offer. She had just gotten out of bed, she explained, with the intention of dressing for lunch. As she sat down at the dressing table, someone knocked at the door. Thinking that it was the Skipper, she called out, "Come in," without looking up. And that was all she remembered. She thought she caught a glimpse of a man's coat sleeve reflected in her mirror, but she wasn't sure.

We could get nothing more out of her. She was panic-stricken and hysterical. There was no sidestepping the fact that my presence in the room was singular, to put it mildly. The gun which Higgins had found was undoubtedly the weapon used. One bullet had been fired from it. And anyone could see that it would have been a simple thing for me to have fired from the door, deposit the revolver on the stand in the hall, and be the first person on the scene of the accident.

We sat in the living-room, waiting for the Skipper's report on the effect of the sleeping powder which she had just administered to her sister. Higgins had been ordered to tell the other servants that the revolver had gone off while I was cleaning it, and that no one had been hurt. As Gay pointed out, we might at least have some decent meals for the next few hours. We were apt to need them.

Gay and Michael sat close together. I think she was telling him the Skipper's story. In any case, he was listening intently, although his eyes strayed to me from time to time, clouded with something that puzzled me.

I had plenty of time to review the facts and to appreciate the overwhelming extent of my danger. In the first place, I had once been in love with Jude Blinshop. In the second place, no one had seen me on Friday night from the time the Skipper left me until Michael roused me at something after eleven o'clock. True, I had been in full sight of everybody when Cook had screamed from the kitchen, but it seemed fairly evident that Mike's father had been responsible for that mêlée in the kitchen. Certainly it would explain his reentry into the house.

I had been in the living-room alone when Gay and Mike heard prowling footsteps in the hall. William had clearly suspected me of hitting him over the head and dumping him down the back stairs. My own experience at that time could be explained all too easily by a clever prosecutor. There would always be Norman Farrington for him to fall back upon whenever his logic ran amuck.

I had been the first upon the scene of the latest crime, found there by several witnesses. No one but myself could account for my actions after I left Higgins downstairs. Good Lord! That conversation with Higgins! A first-year student of law could make considerable out of that!

Murderer, warned that suspicion still exists, becomes desperate, etc. My head was buzzing with it. Over and over again I reviewed that ghastly moment with Higgins in the upper hall, when by the fraction of a second I had escaped putting the final, damning link in the chain of evidence—my own fingerprints on the fatal weapon.

Higgins announced lunch rather early, explaining that Miss Farrington was not yet asleep and that Miss Barbara had ordered him to serve at once. But the Skipper's plan failed utterly. Far from creating diversion, lunch was an even more depressing experience than doing nothing in the living-room. Without either the Skipper or M. Farrington to keep us going, we picked at food in uncomfortable silence. I could not bear to look at Higgins. Had he offered me that gun deliberately, knowing that it had already been wiped clean of the murderer's fingerprints? Would he have denied the entire episode in court?

I thought that he would. In my imagination the frail old man was beginning to take on the proportions of a Faustian Mephisto. What had he started to tell me before he changed his mind? Anything? He might have been building up that chain of circumstantial evidence deliberately.

Higgins was the owner of the gun which had in all probability killed Jude Blinshop and wounded M. Farrington. Our searches had disclosed no other weapon in the house. Whoever used that gun on Jude must have cleaned and reloaded it before it was handed to Michael on Friday night. And who had as good an opportunity for doing that as Higgins? True, he had been with the rest of us when the episode in the kitchen transpired, and in the room with all the others when William and I met our fate. But in both those cases the active presence of the lunatic was not only possible, but distinctly probable. The noiseless tread that had always seemed pleasant to me before suddenly became threatening and sinister. I jumped every time the man came near me with food.

There was no longer any sense in dodging the fact that the murderer must be a recognized inmate of the house. The possibility of a second unknown wandering the Bluff in darkness was absurd. It was obvious that the person who shot M. Farrington had known just where to find her, just where to dispose of his or her gun, just where to conceal himself or herself after the shot had been fired.

And the murderer was a person of nerve. The murderer must have stood calmly in the hall, wiping off that gun, knowing that the report of it must have been heard all over the house. There was my one stumbling block. I could not conceive of Higgins as a person of that type. Staid and pompous, yes. But nerve? The man had been shaking practically continually since our arrival on Friday. In the light of the Skipper's story, it seemed quite probable that he had been shaking for some time before that, too.

Gay ended my speculations momentarily by rising from the table.

"I'm going to beg one of those powders from the Skipper and lie down," she said.

Michael and I rose, too, I with sudden misgivings.

"Don't do it!" I said sharply.

Her eyebrows rose. "For Heaven's sake, why not?"

Feeling more foolish by the minute, I stuck to my guns.

"It isn't safe in this house. Take some more aspirin or something."

She stared at me blankly, and her voice took on an acid tinge. "Why, Jimmie, you haven't poisoned the sleeping powders, have you?"

Her words startled more than they annoyed me. My mind had been dwelling on the foolhardiness of heavy slumber in that devil-ridden house. The possibility of poison had not occurred to me. Like the dull fool I was, I allowed my face to register my consternation.

"So you have?" said Michael softly.

I whirled on him. "Do you believe that?"

"My dear Jimmie," he was actually chuckling, "I'm beginning to think I could believe anything."

It was really happening. Mike was standing there, cold sober and without a trace of rage, calmly hinting that I was the murderer!

"I see!" I said heavily. To save myself I couldn't think of a thing to say to either one of them. I faced them for a brief second, turned on my heel, and strode into the library. If they already half believed the case against me, what would be the attitude of a disinterested jury? I went through a pretty bad five minutes before Mike joined me. He was loading a pipe and he strolled to the window without even glancing at me. I was tempted to do two things. I was tempted to knock his block off, and I was tempted to stalk out of the room without speaking to him. I did neither. I stayed right there, waiting for him to speak.

"We were only kidding, Jim!"

I took plenty of time before I answered him. "Sorry, I can't pretend to be amused."

He worked at the pipe a while. Then, "I'm on an impossible spot! Counting out the servants, I'm obliged to suspect my family, my girl, or my best friend. It's not so easy."

I could see that, but I still didn't care about being considered the worst bet in the crowd. I was silent.

Finally he turned around. "A couple of hours ago I was suspecting myself."

I couldn't restrain a sulky grin. Applying a match to his pipe, Mike grinned back at me.

"No hard feelings?"

"No hard feelings."

That was too much for me. We were suspecting each other of murder as we might have been suspecting each other of salting the rice pudding. The sound of my own laughter fascinated me. I experimented with it. Michael didn't join in.

"Don't do that, for God's sake!"

He was regarding me with a puzzled frown.

"Sorry," I wheezed. "It's so damn silly."

"Yes." His face was very grave. "Jim—have you had anything to do with this?"

I would have laughed again, but I hadn't the energy.

"No," I said. "Word of honor, Mike. Not a damned thing!"

He looked me straight in the eye. "Neither have I—unless I'm out of my mind."

Until that week-end I would have accepted his word against a Supreme Court decision. I half believed him even then. But I had believed Gay and the Skipper and M. Farrington also. And they had all lied. The thought was disconcerting. Mike, reading it in my face, grinned.

"You see?" he said. I did see—all too clearly.

"Mike," I said after a slight pause, "did Gay tell you what the Skipper asked her to?"

His eyes turned toward the fire. "About my father?"

"Yes."

He nodded. "I saw him last night, Jim. When the Skipper fainted. He was standing in front of Jude's door. There was so much fuss that no one noticed, and I didn't sing out because—because I knew him. Funny, isn't it? Twenty-odd years I've thought that he was dead, but I knew him on the spot—even knew what was wrong with him."

So that explained Michael's sudden notion that he was insane. It also explained how the maniac had gained admission to Jude's locked room. He had been there, under the sheet, when I first locked the door. And Jude's body— It wasn't a pretty picture.

Well, at least we had a fairly good idea of Norman Farrington's activities. Escaping from Higgins' room, he had somehow managed to get out of the house on Friday night. The chances were that he had spent most of the night in the garage, except for the short time when the Skipper had scared him away. It was even probable that he had tried to escape from the Bluff in a car, only to find that the bridge was down. He must have gained access to the house by the back door, mowing down Cook and Annie as he came. Then he had prowled the house, upsetting M. Farrington's room and killing the cat in just such a fit of insane frenzy as the Skipper had been fearing. He had probably scuttled for the nearest door when he heard us on the stairs, and his manner of concealment within that room was gruesomely evident. During our excitement over the Skipper he had crept down the hall to William's room where—

My thoughts came to an abrupt halt. I had locked the door of Jude's room *before* William and I met our accident. It was still locked when we examined it later, and the lock had not been tampered with. Yet the madman must have entered that room at least once in the meantime. When the Skipper and I had discovered Jude's body, we had also discovered a lock that *had* been tampered with. Why? If Norman Farrington could go through that door once without forcing its lock, why should he have forced it later? Had someone else lured the poor bedeviled old chap to his death? I glanced at Mike. He was staring into the fire, his eyes heavy and brooding, his teeth clamped tightly on his pipe stem.

"Mike," I said, "are you sure he was standing in front of Jude's door?"

He looked up in surprise. "Positive. Why?"

"Just wondering. Did you see him go in there—Jude's room, I mean?"

"Why, no. He was still standing there when I helped you pick the Skipper up."

Well, it didn't matter. Whether Norman Farrington had been seen entering that room or not, there was nothing to indicate that he had stayed there—nothing but our inability to find him in the rest of the house to indicate that his hand had placed Jude Blinshop where we found her. The wading was getting deeper and deeper. I had a growing conviction that the death of Michael's father had been no accident. Unpleasant as it would be for all of us, I began to wish that the police would arrive.

My mind reverted suddenly to M. Farrington's assertion that she had seen a man's sleeve reflected in her mirror. It was possible that the old lady had been mistaken. It was also possible that she had been attempting either to shield or to incriminate someone. The last idea wasn't exactly cheering. The only person who had been in any way incriminated was myself. And the idea of M. Farrington's intending such a state of affairs was preposterous.

I began to consider M. Farrington carefully. It occurred to me that I should like to examine her room again. I should like to know a thing or two about the angle of her mirror and the distance from the hall door to her dressing table. The would-be murderer had stood in that doorway, of that much I was sure. It would be the only logical place to stand in order to allow for a quick disposal of the weapon. And there were powder burns on the back of M. Farrington's robe. Yes, I very much wanted to see that room.

There were only two people in the house that M. Farrington would attempt to shield in such an instance—Mike and the Skipper. Gay, I felt sure, she would have betrayed without a second's hesitation. Since I knew that I had not been in that doorway, there was little point in trying to decide whether or not she would have shielded me. Would she protect Higgins? The question seemed very important.

Higgins was as much a fixture on Farrington Bluff as the old house itself. With every breath she drew, Martha Farrington defended anything that pertained to the old order of things. But would she defend her butler at the risk of involving the nephew whom she regarded almost as a son? I thought not. In short, I came to the conclusion that if the angle of the mirror would allow a glimpse of anyone standing in the doorway, M. Farrington had seen a woman's arm. If not, she had merely imagined that she saw something. The person who had killed Jude Blinshop was the same person who had tried to kill Martha and the same person who had lured Norman Farrington over the cliff to his death. And that person must be in the house, known to every one of us.

If that individual had pried open the locked door of Jude Blinshop's room, he was a person of considerable strength. Michael had only one hand. Higgins was too feeble. Annie and M. Farrington were not conceivably strong enough. William, Cook, Gay, and myself were left—possibilities, but not probabilities. I was getting too involved in the subject.

"Mike," I said, "there'll be a boat from shore by morning at the latest. Have you decided what we'll say to people?"

His clouded eyes had a somber look. "We ought to consult everyone before we decide. For Aunt Martha's sake, I think we should hush it up as much as we can. Old George Foster's the coroner. He can tell us what to do, and we can let him handle the police."

"What about the Blinshops?"

Michael's face was growing darker and darker. "As soon as we can get across, I'll go down there. I think— I should."

I knew what he was thinking. Everything would depend upon Jude's family. We could tell them that she had been shot by accident while one of us had been playing with a gun. If they would accept that statement and the coroner in action was no different from the coroner on a fishing trip, the name of the body in the billiard room might be left out of the case altogether. We could—

Right there I stopped, struck by an unhappy thought. If we were to smooth this thing over—hush it up—we would be running a terrible risk. Either at Farrington Bluff or among us in town there would remain a dangerous homicidal maniac, unknown and therefore infinitely dangerous. On the face of the thing, I wondered that Mike could consider it.

"Do you think we have a right to risk it?"

He glanced up at me swiftly, and then back to the fire. "Yes," noncommittally.

"But suppose something else happens?"

It was a squeamish way to put it, but he understood me. Leaning forward, he surveyed me with weary, patient eyes.

"You'll have to trust me a little, Jim. I don't think anything else will happen."

I stared at him. M. Farrington shot down like a rabbit! And nothing else would happen!

"Have you any reason for thinking so?"

"No, of course not." Michael roused himself, knocked the ashes out of his pipe, and slipped the thing into his pocket. "Don't be so jittery."

"You wouldn't be so calm yourself if the police were scheduled to arrive within a few hours and everyone from the kitchen maid up suspected you of three murders."

"Three?" He shot the word at me, suddenly on the alert. "How do you figure three?"

"Well," I said cautiously, "one certainty, one possibility, and one attempt."

"So you think my father was murdered, do you?"

"I think it's damned likely that someone coaxed him out to that bluff."

"You're crazy!" said Michael roughly. "Why the devil would anyone—"

Gay's voice jumped at us from the door. "Have you seen the Skipper? I've looked all over the house. I— I can't find her!"

14

"She's in Aunt Martha's room," said Michael. "What are you talking about?"

Gay leaned against the door. "But she isn't! I've looked three times. And I've been all over the house—upstairs and down."

Michael went to her. "The Skipper is all right. You probably missed her on the stairs or in the kitchen."

She shook her head doggedly. "I've been to the kitchen."

Michael and I looked at each other.

"Is Aunt Martha asleep?"

"Yes. At least, I think so. She looked—all right. I didn't notice much."

If Mike was alarmed, his face didn't show it.

"You just stay here a minute with Jim and I'll find her."

It was quite plain from Gay's face that she didn't in the least relish the idea of staying anywhere with me again—ever. But Mike was out of the door before she had time to object. Eyes big as saucers and her red hair rumpled about her chubby face, she looked exactly like a terrified twelve-year-old. I felt sorry for her.

"Don't be afraid, Gay. You've been alone with me before without being murdered."

It was the right line. She hesitated imperceptibly and then managed a wavering smile.

"Come along," I continued briskly, steering her into a chair and thrusting cigarettes at her. "If you see me beginning to look ferocious, just hum *Auld Lang Syne* and I'll control myself for auld sake's sake!"

This time the smile was steadier. With my ears straining for the sound of Mike's returning footsteps, I rattled on.

"Tell you what. You be the Ancient Mariner and reform me. I'll bet that within twenty minutes I'll be loving both man and bird and beast. You might even get a confession out of me, and then you could—"

"Jimmie," she said, "you're an ass and only another ass could think you guilty of anything. I'm all right really. It was just—sort of a shock."

I could believe that. Not ten minutes ago Mike had been confidently assuring me that nothing more would happen, and I had half believed him. Why didn't he come? Was he building a house instead of searching one?

"Well," I rambled, "how did you enjoy your sojourn in the donkey world?"

She was listening, too. I could see the cords of her neck tight with the effort. But her voice was light.

"Meaning that I did suspect you? Well, I suppose I did a little. It's impossible to talk to you and think so, but you must admit that the evidence looks pretty bad."

Was that Michael on the stairs? Gay had heard it, too, for she was half out of her chair. He was going down the hall in the direction of the servants' quarters. I continued the cream-puff chatter feverishly.

"Don't mention that evidence. I'll dream of it for months. I'm sure of it."

She didn't answer. Our pretense of lightness was very flat. We were sitting there, gripping the arms of our chairs, waiting—waiting for an eternity of dragging time. Then at last came Mike's steps in the dining-room. Gay fairly bounded to meet him.

"Well?" she demanded before he was in the room.

He was worried. There were sharp lines around his mouth, and his scowl was bewildered.

"Aunt Martha's awfully quiet. Do you know anything about these damned drugs, either of you?"

I shook my head, but Gay was clutching his arm.

"Did you find the Skipper?"

Michael averted his face. "She's probably out feeding the dogs. Poor mutts must be nearly starved. I'll just run out and find her. I'm sure she's there."

Gay looked on the point of screaming. I shoved in my oar.

"Wait a minute, Mike. I don't mind looking. I'll take William along to guarantee my conduct. You stay here with Gay."

I knew that he wanted to do the searching himself, but one look at the chalky face at his elbow changed his mind.

"Thanks, Jim," he said. "William's getting his things on—I've already called him. You'll find us up with Aunt Martha."

I hurried into the hall, where I found a conglomerate assortment of boots and oilskins in the closet. Kicking off my shoes, I dragged on the likeliest looking pair of boots and headed for the kitchen, struggling into an oilskin as I went. At the game-room door, a disturbing thought halted me.

Snapping on a light, I stepped to the billiard table and lifted the white cloth. This time there was no mistake. The table held what it was supposed to hold. I started to replace the cover, when I had another idea. One by one I went through the soggy pockets of Norman Farrington. And sure enough, in the breast pocket of his coat, I found what I was seeking—a key.

Replacing the cover, I stepped to the door and tried the key in its lock. It worked immediately. I turned out the lights and moved through the hall to the dining-room door. It worked in that lock too. A skeleton key! Then someone had certainly enticed Norman Farrington to his death. Only a person without a key would have broken the lock to get into or out of Jude's room. And mad as he was, Norman Farrington had left that locked room at least once.

With the weight of evidence already against me, I dared not be found with that key. I polished it hurriedly with my handkerchief and returned it to its original resting place. There was only one consolation. The murderer either did not know of or had overlooked the key's existence. I switched off the game-room lights a second time. There was no help for it. I must take the risk of his remembering and finding that key.

The servants' hall was empty and rapidly darkening in the gloom of the February twilight. I passed through it quickly into the kitchen, where I found all the servants. Higgins, Cook, and Annie were at the table drinking coffee. William in his boots and oilskins was coming down the stairs, a sou'wester in his hand. It didn't take a Sherlock Holmes to deduce what they had been talking about. There was a dead silence. Annie began to blush furiously. So either William or Higgins had talked, after all.

"I'm going with you instead of Mr. Michael, William," I said. "His arm is bothering him. I don't think he should go outside."

To say that this information was not well received would be to put it mildly. William favored me with a sullen stare. Annie started to say something and was heavily shushed by Cook. Higgins' face held a positively malignant leer.

"I think that's a good idea, sir," his voice was silky. "While you're in charge, it's only right that you should do *all* the searching."

I tried to ignore him. "Have you a good flashlight, William? It may be dark in the stable."

William's answer might best be described as a sort of grunt. But he dragged a flashlight from his pocket and handed it to me. At the door I paused with one more question.

"Have any of you seen Miss Barbara at all this afternoon—or heard anyone leaving the house?"

"No," said Cook and Annie in the same breath.

"Not that I recall, sir," from Higgins.

William followed me out into the late afternoon. It had cleared miraculously. The wind, if not altogether dead, was rapidly dying, and there was a crisp snap in the air, infinitely refreshing after the caged atmosphere indoors. Gratefully I filled my lungs with the salty tang, forgetting for an instant the urgency of my errand. A single star glowed in the red-rimmed west and beyond it to the south, the gray-and-white tumble of the Sound stretched before us. William allowed scant time for observing it.

"Are you in a hurry, Mr. Wells?"

I was in a hurry. I turned on my heel and led the way down the rapidly freezing drive toward the stable, William stalking sullenly behind me. Halfway down the drive, I stopped short.

"We shall have to go back, William."

The man was watching me like a hawk. "Why?" curtly.

"I'm pretty sure the stable's locked, and I forgot to get a key."

"I've got a key here."

His laugh grated on my nerves. We went on in silence. I reflected that if the stable were locked, the chances of the Skipper's being inside were very slight. I could, however, check up very easily on whether or not the dogs had been fed. If they had, it would be a simple matter to check back and find out whether someone other than the Skipper had fed them.

"Who usually feeds the dogs, William?" I inquired.

"Miss Barbara. Always."

"Always? Even the last few days?"

"Once or twice I've fed them for her—but not lately."

Of course not. I might have known that William would say just that.

"Then who did feed them these last few days?" I demanded bluntly.

"I don't know," and William plodded on.

The stable and garage doors were both securely padlocked. William opened the former without a word, and we stepped inside.

"Skipper!" I shouted at the top of my lungs.

There was no answer, except for the yowling of the dogs. I looked into every one of those stalls. Some of them had a little water, but there was no food in any of them. The animals were ravenous. The collie bitch sprang at me viciously, subsiding with a whimper when I spoke to her. The others were tugging wildly at their chains and yelping mournfully. So the Skipper had forgotten to feed her dogs—from the looks of them had forgotten it two days in a row.

"William," I said, "the minute we get back to the house, see that these dogs are fed."

"Yes, sir." The Skipper's forgetting her dogs was equivalent to Napoleon's forgetting his army. "It's—funny, sir."

I agreed that it certainly was. With poor old Farrington stretched out on the game-room table, these dogs were the only earthly reason for the Skipper's leaving the house. And she had not been near them. Where the blazes was she then? I mounted the ladders and peered into one loft after the other, shining the light all around them. One disclosed the few dusty footprints that I myself had left there yesterday. On the other, the undisturbed film of a decade still rested. I came down slowly.

"We may as well look in the garage," I said.

William's grunt might have meant almost anything. We locked the stable door behind us, and entered the garage. The cars stood as I had seen them the day before. The dry smears of clay hopelessly blurred under our impatient feet. The place smelled stuffy and dead. I called again and again, but there was no answer.

"Upstairs?" suggested William.

For the second time in as many days, I mounted those steps. The first time I had feared to find something up there. Now I was praying that I would—praying against a heavy weight in my chest that told me it was useless. It needed no flashlight to tell me that the room was empty—empty and exactly as we had left it. Walking to the wardrobe door, William flung it open. The hat and trousers still hung where we had found them. Picking up the former, William turned toward me, a puzzled expression on his face.

"What's this?" he said heavily, pointing to the bullet hole in its crown.

Like a flash of lightning another brainstorm struck me. I had fired Higgins' gun in the garage yesterday morning. The Skipper had fired it in the library yesterday afternoon. But only one bullet had been fired from the revolver which Higgins claimed to have found in the hall. Unless someone had cleaned the butler's gun at least twice, there must be another revolver on Farrington Bluff, and that revolver must be in the possession of the murderer!

My stare was making William uneasy. "That's a bullet hole," he said.

"I'm sorry, William. I did that yesterday morning. Miss Barbara and I thought we heard someone in that closet and we weren't taking any chances. I'll get you another hat."

He didn't believe it. I wondered what sort of evidence he could be piecing together in his stubborn mind around a bullet hole in a discarded old cap.

"Come along," I said briskly. "It's still light enough to take a quick look around outside, if we hurry."

We hurried. Clumping down the stairs, we raced into the open air. This time it in no way revived me. I felt as if a tremendous weight suspended over my head was being lowered by a slow, inevitable pulley. It was much darker than it had been for our search the day before, but the clearness of the air made it possible to see farther with less difficulty. It took but a fraction of a minute to ascertain that the rocks on which the buildings stood and the beach below them were deserted. I was already sure that there was nothing between the bluff and the house, for I had stood staring in that direction when I first stepped outdoors. I figured that by following the driveway we could get a pretty good view of the entire northern lawn.

Accordingly, down the drive we went, William watching to the right and I to the left. There was nothing unusual. Only numerous sticks and limbs blown down by the storm. In one place half of a huge elm had been snapped off and hung suspended on a few retentive fibers, waiting for a breath of wind to send it hurtling to the ground. At the foot of the drive, water still seethed through the narrow gut separating us from the mainland.

From this point, where the bridge usually stood, the driveway of the Bluff sweeps off in a rough circle—one section going toward the garage, the other toward the house. We followed the latter, and at the house we branched off to the path which runs from the west terrace to the tennis courts and beyond them to the boathouse. Even less of the pier was standing now. A few piles still held their ground, but they were shaking prophetically in the boiling water. The boathouse was still completely inundated. Slowly, with difficulty we climbed the rocks, scene of Michael's downfall. No one and no trace of anyone.

"Well, William," I said, "we may as well go back to the house."

He made no reply. I puffed down the rocks, nursing my stiff fingers and treading gingerly on numb feet. The weather was getting colder by the minute and our raincoats were not exactly adequate. The storm, decidedly, was over.

William had nothing to say throughout the walk back to the house. I fancied him busy with his own thoughts, in which he was no doubt hanging me with the last bit of evidence. My own thoughts were dismal. I was thinking that the things happening during the Skipper's first disappearance weren't exactly calculated to cheer us up about this second one. Where the devil could she be? She had been left taking care of M. Farrington before lunch, and no one had seen her since but Higgins, when he received his orders for an early lunch. That was three or four hours ago.

Avoiding the game-room door, we swerved along the rear terrace in the direction of the kitchen. As we did so, I was struck by an appalling thought. My eyes swept toward the bluff.

"We forgot one place, William."

He got what I meant—and showed it plainly.

We crossed that strip of lawn like two old men who have indulged in a skating spree and have difficulty with their underpinnings. I forced myself to look over the edge of the bluff. There was nothing but sand, water, and dead scrub grass. The tide was well out. If there had been anything there a few hours ago, it had long since washed away, and the chances of its ever being found again on Farrington Bluff were slight. The sight of Norman Farrington's body there that morning had been pretty bad, but the mental picture of the Skipper floating for days in that churning, half-frozen water was worse. We turned dumbly back toward the house.

We let ourselves in at the main door. An unearthly silence seemed to settle down upon you in that house, enveloping you like a blanket. It was dark—much darker than it had been outside and more terrifying. I didn't want to face Michael just then, and the idea of my own company was insupportable. I followed William into the kitchen.

They were waiting for us at the kitchen table, Higgins with a dilapidated old pipe in his hand and Annie trying furtively to extinguish her cigarette. Cook's face was red, her eyes bleary, and her breath strongly alcoholic.

"Did you find her?" burst out Annie. Under drawn brows, Cook was regarding us oddly.

"No," I said. "Which one of you fed the dogs last?"

There was dead silence. Then Cook rumbled, "They ain't been fed. I forgot 'em, and so did Miss Barbara. The meat's there in the ice box like always."

"Who fed them Friday?" I demanded.

Cook's voice, if anything, was a little thicker. "Miss Barbara fed 'em of course. They ain't been fed since."

"Are you sure?" I snapped.

"Sure I'm sure. I handle that ice box!"

"Feed them now, will you, William?" I said. Since Higgins had obviously told some of the story, there seemed little use in keeping them in the dark. The results might be disastrous when the police arrived.

"We can't find Miss Barbara," I told them. "There seems to be some danger of her having fallen over the cliff. Did any of you see her this afternoon?"

There was no answer. They were all staring at me. I turned to Higgins.

"When did she give you the order for an early lunch?"

His reply was prompt. "At eleven-thirty. When I heard the bell, I glanced at the clock to be sure I had not failed to start things at the usual hour."

"Where did she ring from?"

"She rang me on the house phone and gave me her orders then."

"You mean that you didn't actually see her at eleven-thirty?"

"No, sir."

More complications. "How many rooms are connected on the house phone?"

"All of them, Mr. James. You may overhear a conversation from any room in the house, but the buzzers are independent for each room. You push the one you want."

Then the Skipper might have called from any room in the house—or someone else might have called for her. Had the early lunch been part of the plan? For the life of me I couldn't see why. I turned wearily to the door.

I paused for a second outside of M. Farrington's door to get my breath before I went in.

Gay and Michael were both leaning over the bed, and the faces they raised to mine were drawn. I shook my head.

"Not a trace of her."

Gay's breath came sharply, and Mike turned away from us. My eyes fell to M. Farrington's pillow. Her face was colorless. Even in that silent room her breathing was imperceptible.

"Look at her, Jim." There was a catch in Michael's voice. "She looks—queer."

15

Queer was hardly the word for it. Her mouth was drawn and tight, her throat working spasmodically. Groping for her pulse, I found her hand to be like ice. If her pulse was stirring at all, it was stirring very feebly. I stared up into Michael's smouldering eyes.

"Find those damned powders!" I ordered. "Gay, see if any of the servants know anything about this stuff. Hurry!"

I was trying to remember what I had ever heard about poisoning, and I couldn't remember a single thing. One used a stomach pump, I supposed, but where the devil were we to get a stomach pump? White of egg? They had given me that dose once when as a kid I had amused myself by eating toadstools. But was that of any use a long time after the poison had been taken? The memory of a very poor collegiate practical joke flashed across my mind. Ipecac! There might be ipecac in the house.

Michael came rushing out of the bathroom, a plain gray box in his hand. It was half full of powders; but on the top was written merely, "Sleeping powder. Dr. Foster," and the date. No help there.

"Get hot-water bottles," I said. The chances were that it was the wrong thing to do, but the chances were better that if left in that condition much longer M. Farrington would be finished. I raced into the bathroom and ransacked the medicine chest. Everything from sodium bicarbonate and iodine to a nerve tonic. But no ipecac.

"Get those hot-water bottles as fast as you can, Mike," I said and tore into the hall.

One by one I went through every medicine chest on that floor. There was enough stuff there to cause a druggist to turn cartwheels. But no ipecac. Coming out of Mike's room, I caught sight of Gay coming up the stairs with William at her heels. One glance at her face told me that there would be no help from downstairs.

I shouted, "Is there any ipecac in the house? Ask Higgins! Ask—"

He nodded. "Miss Barbara had it for a dog that got some bad meat. It's in the kitchen. I'll get it."

Mike had hot-water bottles in place and was working for all he was worth. We hastened to help him. My arms were already aching by the time William appeared with several bottles and a whole trayful of glasses. Without waiting to read instructions, I poured out a dose. I knew that amount hadn't killed Hog Fowler at school, but that was all I did know. We had difficulty in making her swallow it, and when we finally got it down, there was no effect. We rubbed and rubbed. William was obliged to take Michael's place. We rubbed some more. And then things began to happen—with startling suddenness and considerable force.

But what little vitality she had left seemed to go after that. Gay tried to pour some whiskey down her throat, with no success. We all tried. Useless. Finally Mike straightened up and met my eyes.

"She's dead," he said in a still voice.

Sweat was running down my face into my eyes. My throat was hard and dry. "She can't be! She—"

William's hand coming down heavily on my back froze the words in my mouth. He pushed me to one side.

I'm not quite clear on what followed. William had taken charge. We were all moving mechanically, obeying his orders. As I remember it, I was holding the old lady's uninjured arm up over her head, flaying it back and forth from her sides in a sort of windmill motion. What the others were doing I have no idea. Finally, beneath the wheezing noises of her rescuers, M. Farrington began to breathe—faintly, spasmodically at first, and then with more strength and steadiness. Mike and I stopped simultaneously, but William made us keep going.

Weariness was floating over me, but through it droned words, "The Skipper! The Skipper!" We must hurry. But where? Where? Just as M. Farrington's eyes flew open, I had the answer.

"Stay here, Gay," I whispered and unceremoniously yanked Michael into the hall.

"The cellar," I told him.

For once Mike didn't wait to argue. He followed me down the hall into the servants' quarters as fast as he could go. I could feel his breath on my neck all the way. We sprinted through the narrow corridor and took the back stairs three at a time.

I was fumbling at the door of the entry and the confounded thing wouldn't seem to work. Behind me there was a banging of drawers, the crash of a chair going over, an awful uproar.

The clatter on the back stairs was probably William, but I didn't turn to see. Frantically, I tried key after key on that cellar door. It was an age before one of them turned, and the door flew open. Inky black, the cellar gaped below us.

"Where the devil are the lights?" I rasped.

Mike's hand found a switch and the cellar stairs, narrow, crooked, and dusty lay ahead of us. Farrington Bluff was built in the days when cellars were designed for foundations of a house in which food and drink might be incidentally stored. We went down those stairs at top speed. As my feet left the bottom step, I heard the door above closing loudly.

"Where's William?" I snapped at Michael.

"Went back upstairs. The women are having a fit about being left alone."

On the spot, I dismissed William from my mind. By the light of the dim bulb over the stairs, we could see a good part of the vast old cellar. We were standing at the end of a long passageway, flanked on the left by the wall of the house and on the right by a room of some description, the door of which was practically at my elbow. Under what must have been about the main hall upstairs, the passageway seemed to open out into a larger room. The beam of my flashlight picked out a wooden structure rising almost to the rafters and blocking off all but a small entrance into the center room.

"Stand here and keep your eyes open," I ordered, and pushed open the door at my right.

I was looking into what must have been the Farrington wine cellar, a large, low-ceilinged room, almost square in shape. My light disclosed tiers of bottle racks, mostly empty, completely surrounding the room. Here and there a barrel or a keg. Over the whole a perfect curtain of dust and cobwebs. Cobwebs hung in long, lacy festoons from the ceiling beams, from the racks, from the barrels. Dust lay in a thick, undisturbed carpet on the floor. Of any human being, there was not a trace.

I let the door swing softly to.

"Where does this passage take us?"

"Furnace-room and fuel bins. Storage-room after that."

Silently I led the way along it. Our footsteps echoed through the ghostly, empty place. After we had taken a dozen paces, the dim light over the stairs was of little use.

"Aren't there any more lights?" I whispered. There was no reason for whispering, but the atmosphere of the place already had its grip on me.

"No. Aunt Martha's stubborn about improvements." Unconsciously Mike was whispering, too. "Skipper was always telling her that Cook would break her leg down here and sue us for plenty."

I flashed my light around the furnace-room. Oblong in shape, running across the entire center of the house, its left and right walls consisted of enormous coal and wood bins, respectively, piled right to the ceiling. A huge, old-fashioned furnace stood in the exact center of the room, its pipes running overhead in all directions. Some orderly hand had been at work, for there was no dust, and there were no cobwebs. And no sign of the Skipper. Apparently the wall nearest the passage was also the wall of the wine cellar which we had just left. In the center of the wall opposite it, was a door for which I made without further ado. But it was locked.

If I had fumbled with the keys upstairs, I nearly tore them apart now in my excitement.

"What's stored here?" I grunted.

"Vegetables—preserves—junk!" Michael's words were coming in spasmodic jerks. He may have been thinking the same thing that I was thinking—that with the wine cellar left unlocked, it was odd to find the preserve closet fastened.

The door opened at last.

A room about the same size and shape as the furnace-room and neat as a pin, lay ahead of us. From floor to ceiling it was lined with high closets—wainscoted. In the center of the room stood a large kitchen table with an antiquated tea wagon beside it. Otherwise, the room was empty.

"Skipper!" I shouted, flinging myself against the nearest door.

"Are you there? Skipper! *Skipper!*"

The impact of my shoulder on the solid wood of the closet sent a steadying stab of pain through me. I turned to look for a poker.

The furnace-room offered better than a poker, however. Mike made straight for the wood bin. There, propped against the wall, was an ax. I snatched it from him and rushed back at the closets.

The pen may be mightier than the ax, but my blows on that hard wood would have been equally effective with either. The ax glanced and twisted, and twisted and glanced.

"Use the butt of the damn thing," grunted Michael. The light was wavering in his hand.

I did. Wood splintered and crashed. There was a tinkle as of broken glass. Something wet and sticky was in my eyes. I was still trying to clear them when Mike yelled, "Try the next one!" I blinked at a closet full of broken jars. The mess drooling down my face seemed to be strawberry preserve.

I tried the next closet and the next and the next. Splintered wood, broken glass, and a mess of fruits and vegetables. Mike took the ax from me and I stood hanging on to the light while he bashed in two more doors. Then I took another turn and he took another. Before the last closet we paused, looking at each other.

I went at it quietly. Perhaps we were lucky that it was to be in the last one. I shuddered to think of the effect our wild smashing would have had on a person inside any of the others. It took more time this way. The wood gave way slowly with a dull, tearing sound. I seized a loose board and ripped it away—then another and another. Mike's face was turned away, his shoulders hunched. Snatching the light from his hand, I flashed it upon—six orderly rows of canned lima beans.

"I suppose," poor Mike's voice was hollow, "we'd better get back to the others. They'll be—wondering."

I couldn't look at him. "I'm sorry, Mike," I said. "I—I'm damned sorry."

"Forget it!" His laugh was a pretty weak attempt. "Boy! Will Aunt Martha be wild when she sees this!"

It struck me that M. Farrington might never see it.

"Let's get back upstairs."

We left the ax where we had found it, and started down the passage, our light flashing ahead of us. Mike's hand closed on my arm suddenly.

"Jim," he whispered, "wasn't there a light over the stairs?"

I stared into the blackness ahead, and my heart did a flip-flop.

"It was an old bulb," I said. "Probably burned out." But the echo of my own voice wasn't reassuring. I breathed a sigh of relief as we gained the top of those rickety steps and my hand found the door knob.

"What the devil's the matter?" demanded Michael.

I had to swallow before I could answer.

"The door's locked on the outside—bolted." The reflected light from the kitchen shown clearly through the keyhole when I extinguished our torch.

I handed Mike the flashlight and without a word he went back for the ax. I put my shoulder to the door. It was useless. On that narrow top step there was barely room for steady footing, let alone for bracing yourself for a push. The steepness of the stairs made a running leap out of the question. I was obliged to stand there waiting for Mike, my ears cocked for sounds from the kitchen beyond—sounds that never came. By the time an advancing ray of light appeared down the passage, my imagination had me on the run. I imagined that the killer had come down into the blackness of the cellar to finish his work. I imagined that I had sent Mike down to his death while I stood at a door. I saw the glint of light on the steel ax, and swallowed hard.

"Here you are. Hurry!" Mike's voice was urgent.

It didn't take me ten seconds to crash in that door. With a screech of tearing wood, we tumbled pell-mell into the entry and threw open the kitchen door upon an empty room.

The picture in my mind sent me tearing up the back stairs. On the landing, Mike nearly knocked me down, attempting to pass me. I flung open M. Farrington's door, but Mike was into the room ahead of me.

16

M. Farrington was sleeping. Gay was sitting beside her, and in a far corner of the room William and Annie were whispering together. They all turned sharply toward us.

"All right, I think." Gay answered our unspoken question. "Mike, what under the sun—"

I interrupted her. It seemed to me that this was no place for telling the story.

"My fault, kid," I said. "I thought I'd had a revelation or something."

"But—"

"Not here. Mike will tell you about it. You two go on down and start Higgins rustling up some food. I'll stay with Aunt Martha."

I shoved them both into the hall, still protesting. Why had William bolted that cellar door? I was almost positive that he had, and I was equally positive that there would be no use in asking him. He had certainly saved M. Farrington's life, but— At any rate, I sent both him and Annie down to help Cook. Alone, I sat down beside M. Farrington.

She looked better, but not enough better for much rejoicing. The Skipper's words, "Her heart is bad," were drumming in my head. Well, as long as she was sleeping there was nothing more we could do. Sitting there with anxious eyes glued to the old lady's face, I went through a bad half hour.

One terrible conviction was gnawing at me persistently—the conviction that the Skipper alone was responsible for our week-end of horrors. Her peculiar actions had been the direct cause of our presence at the Bluff. We had only her unsubstantiated story to explain her invitation, and that story was bizarre, to put it mildly. It was possible, of course, but it was difficult to believe that Norman Farrington had lived all these years unknown to his own son. Was it plausible that Martha Farrington, who possessed above all things a generous amount of common sense, would have insisted upon harboring a dangerous lunatic in that deserted spot?

Another stumbling block was the presence of Jude Blinshop. Surely a person of the Skipper's determination could have found a dozen pretexts for revoking a commonplace invitation when she realized the very real danger involved. And why the unusual attitude of both sisters toward poor Jude? With Michael flaunting Gay under M. Farrington's nose, the old lady had almost ignored Jude. And the Skipper's "Keep Michael away from Jude!" still rang in my ears—unexplained.

Step by step I once more reconstructed the events of the case. We had come there because of the Skipper. Her attitude had been strange, particularly in regard to Jude. She had been out of doors for an indefinite space of time on the night of the girl's death, and her actions were none too satisfactorily accounted for. She would have known more about the whereabouts of firearms at the Bluff than anyone else in the house. And Jude would have followed the Skipper into the storm without a moment's hesitation. She had been in my own sight during the episodes of Cook, Annie, and Christopher, and she had been in the sight of all the others when William and I met our assailant. But again, we had Norman Farrington to reckon with.

The Skipper had run from Jude's room straight to the exact spot of her brother's fall, just as if she had known what she was looking for and where to find it. She had particularly requested that her doubtful story about the old man not be repeated to her sister, the only person aside from Higgins who could in any way substantiate or refute it.

Her alibi with respect to the shooting of M. Farrington rested exclusively on Higgins, who would have died for her with pleasure. Higgins had been in a bad state of nerves since our arrival. I could not forget that he, intentionally or otherwise, had almost succeeded in causing my fingerprints to be planted on a weapon that he certainly believed to be the one used on M. Farrington.

It all boiled down to the fact that the Skipper was the center of the horror that engulfed us. She could use a gun quickly and well—we had seen her do so in the case of the cat. Her story could be substantiated only by Martha Farrington, and Martha Farrington's life had twice been threatened since we had heard it. The Skipper had been left alone with her sister, who, but for our chance arrival, would be dead. And the Skipper was missing.

My mind began to consider the unsuspecting rescue party that would probably put in an appearance by morning. I wondered what they would say—what we should say to them. I speculated upon who would be in that boat. I pictured to myself old Andie Darrel, with the salt water running down his wrinkled face and his enormous mouth gaping at us. Andie would be in that boat. And after Andie—I couldn't seem to decide on anyone else. Well, we should say that two people had been killed, a third both wounded and poisoned, and a fourth disappeared. Andie would gape at us, and then—blankness. I went over the same ground a dozen times before William came in.

"Mr. Michael says to come down to dinner, sir. I'm to stay with Miss Farrington."

William was to stay— Well, suppose he had locked that cellar door? He had saved the old lady's life first, and he would hardly have gone through all that if he were planning another attempt. After all, it was Michael's aunt and Michael's decision. I went down to dinner.

I have eaten some bad meals in my day, but I have never been confronted by anything equal to that one. Hash-browned potatoes, cold and reeking of grease, underdone pork chops, limp and slimy, burnt peas fresh from a tin can. Mike threw down his fork in disgust.

"Higgins," he exploded, "what the devil is the meaning of this?"

Higgins had been quite well aware of what he was giving us. He had served the appalling meal as quietly and carefully as he might have served a banquet for the Duke of York, and yet I had the impression that he had been enjoying an excellent joke. His face never moved a muscle.

"The meaning of what, sir?"

Michael nearly strangled. "Don't mimic me! What do you mean by serving this disgusting mess? Has Cook lost her mind?"

"No, sir. Cook is a bit upset, sir. I'm very sorry."

"Sorry!" Michael's face turned purple. "Do you mean to—"

But Gay interposed quickly. "Shut up, Mike. Is there anything in the ice box, Higgins?"

"There might be, miss. I will look."

Gay pushed back her chair. "Never mind," she said. "We'll look ourselves."

Unexpectedly Higgins planted his back against the door. His face was expressionless, but it stopped all three of us.

"If you'll excuse me, miss, I wouldn't advise your going into the kitchen just now." His words were civil enough, but his tone was commanding. It took Michael several seconds to be able to speak at all.

"Why not?"

"Cook is not quite herself. Nerves and a little too much stimulant, sir."

I glanced back at the untouched meal. "Do you mean she's drunk, Higgins?"

"No; not exactly."

Brushing past the butler, Mike strode into the kitchen with Gay at his heels. I took a good look at Higgins. With a slight shrug, he stepped to the table and began to clear it. I wanted to knock some answers out of the man, but his back told me plainly that I might just as well save my breath. Reluctantly I followed the others.

An arresting scene presented itself in the kitchen. Cook sat at the head of the table, a huge spoon in her hand with which she from time to time dipped into an enormous bowl in front of her. The woman was not drunk. She was doped. Her eyes and skin betrayed that. Mike was staring at her, dumbfounded. But sheer terror was written all over the face of Annie, who crouched on a stool at the other end of the table, apparently under orders not to move. Through the open door into the entry, I could see Gay rummaging in the refrigerator.

"What's the matter with you?" said Michael sternly. Cook waved a roguish, dripping spoon in his direction and began to curse fluently. We couldn't quiet her for a long time.

Finally, she turned the full benefit of her glassy, muddled eyes on my face. Then, grunting like a ponderous animal, she wobbled to her feet and wove an unsteady course up the stairs, still clutching the repulsive bowl in her arms. Four of us gaped after her. Mike flung himself into a chair.

"Oh, hell!" he muttered wearily. "What next? Damn it all, what next?"

I didn't answer him. My attention for the moment was fixed upon Annie, still shivering at the end of the table.

"Annie," I said, "have you ever seen Cook like this before?"

The girl nodded dumbly.

"Often?"

"No—no—only once."

"When?"

"Last winter. It was only once, Mr. Wells. She ain't done it in years except then. It was—was an awful storm, sir. And she had a toothache."

I chewed that rapidly. "Did either of the Miss Farringtons know of it?"

Annie was on the verge of tears. "No, sir. We—we said she was sick—me and William. There wasn't no use in letting on to Higgins. He'd have gone straight to the missus, and—it's hard to live things down, sir. I used to know Cook when I was little. She'd given it up, sir. And anyway, it wasn't like this. She was just quiet. Mr. Wells, you're not going to—"

"I don't know," I said. "Go help Miss Palmer scare up something to eat out there."

She went, but I had to help her to her feet. As soon as she was out of earshot I whirled on Michael.

"She's doped to the gills now. That means—" I was just beginning to realize what it did mean. The second attempt on M. Farrington's life had been made by dope. And either Cook had once been an addict or Annie was a liar. No help was forthcoming from Michael. He sat staring at the floor, not even listening to me.

"What do you think, Mike?" No answer. Impatiently I shook his shoulder. But the entrance of Gay and Annie stopped me. They had found food all right—plenty of it.

But for once a successful raid afforded me no satisfaction. We all ate because we needed food, not because we wanted it. Higgins made quiet entrances and exits to and from the dining-room, assured us that he had already eaten, begged permission to retire, and took himself off upstairs with evident relief.

Over and over in my mind, I mulled the possibilities that this new angle lent to the situation. If Cook was now doped—and there seemed very little doubt on that score—there was a possibility that she had been in the same condition on the night when Norman Farrington made his dramatic entrance into the house. In that case, all of our previous calculations of time were worthless. There was no telling how long Annie had lain bound and gagged in the entry. And the unquestionable fact of William's lathered and partially shaven face dwindled in importance. He might have taken all the time in the world to prepare that evidence.

The whole question of M. Farrington's accident was thrown into a hopeless jumble. Higgins' extraordinary behavior with regard to the fingerprints on the revolver might be explained as nervousness. Cook might have used that gun from M. Farrington's doorway, left it in the hall, walked a few paces toward the servants' corridor, and turned, giving the appearance of having rushed out at the sound of the shot. The fact that both the Skipper and Higgins offered the same alibi rather tended to substantiate this theory. Could the Skipper, later on, have left M. Farrington alone with Cook, and might Cook have augmented the sleeping powder with a preparation of her own? Had Cook in some mysterious way lured the Skipper to whatever fate she had encountered? It seemed rather senseless. Cook had been at the Bluff for several years without any such outbreak. What possible motive could she have for embarking on a career of wholesale slaughter?

It was doubtful that she had even heard of Jude Blinshop before that week-end. She had certainly not recognized her assailant in the kitchen. To the best of our knowledge, she did not even know of the poor lunatic's presence in the house. How, then, would she have known that there was anyone concealed in Jude's room? And why would she bother to annihilate him, even if she had?

"Has William had any dinner, Annie?" said Michael suddenly.

"No, sir."

"Go tell him to get some now. Would you mind staying with Miss Farrington for a little while until one of us comes up?"

The alacrity with which Annie leapt at the suggestion was amazing. Whatever terror the house held for her was seemingly not increased by being left alone on the upper floor with the sick woman. She rushed up the stairs eagerly.

"It stands to reason," said Mike heavily, "that the house can't be full of homicidal maniacs."

Gay giggled. "If it comes to that, it stands to reason that all this can't have happened in your own house. Try again, Mike."

Michael sat up. "We have enough evidence to hang almost anyone in this house. That shows pretty good planning on someone's part. And offhand, I'd say on the part of the person against whom there's been no evidence."

"But there's been no evidence against *me*—" began Gay indignantly.

Michael eyed her coolly. "Precisely. And you have been the person who's so hot to have almost anybody confess. Does that suggest anything to anyone's mind?"

"Why—" Gay stared at him in blank amazement. "Why— Are you suggesting that I—"

The upward swing in her voice brought me to my feet.

"Of course he isn't!" I said loudly. "Now, *I'm* suggesting that we get down to business. William will be down in a minute. Why don't the three of us start now and go inch by inch over every bedroom in this house? We might find something—helpful."

I think we would have been in for a spirited debate, but the sound of William's footsteps on the back stairs brought them to a quick decision.

"Let's," said Gay, simultaneously with Mike's grunted assent.

Silently we herded into the hall, taking care that the kitchen door was not left swinging after us. One thing that none of us relished was the idea of William prowling through the deserted house on our trail—William, Higgins, or anyone else. At the foot of the main stairs Michael, finger to lips, beckoned us into the living-room. We followed him on tiptoe and he closed the door softly after us.

"The radio," he whispered. "Turn it on for a blind."

I had forgotten that there was a radio at the Bluff. Why the dickens hadn't he thought of it during those unspeakable hours of waiting? Mike is not usually a person for details. I watched him in startled silence as he turned on the radio and most of the lights in the room with it.

"Wait," Gay whispered. "Help me move this davenport, Jim. Now the chair. That's it." Working rapidly, she completed the setting of our little stage. The davenport was turned before the fire and a heavy chair drawn up beside it, so that both were turned from the hall and game-room doors. With the aid of a couple of steamer rugs and many pillows, Gay swiftly constructed an amazing semblance of three people dozing before the fire. I suppose we had all done that very thing a dozen times, but we watched it now with no anticipatory glee. We were in deadly earnest. I for one was thinking, "She's clever. She keeps her head and thinks of details. And she's the only one above suspicion. The only one!"

"There!" said Gay with finality. "Mike, throw some logs on the fire. I think that will do."

Michael moved to obey her. "The only trouble is," he said, "that this will be a pretty obvious gag if anyone happens to look through the windows. And it would sound damned fishy in front of a jury."

I reflected that practically anything we could do in the way of fooling the murderer would be twisted against us later, if his cunning succeeded in involving us.

"We'll have to take some risks," said Gay; but she went back over her handiwork, creating a fair illusion of three people given to sleeping with their heads under blankets.

"Let's get going," said Michael.

At the door an unexpected problem presented itself. We no sooner stepped into the hall than a loud blast of swing music echoed through the entire house. William or anyone else would have to be deaf not to know that a door had been opened. I took a wild shot.

I said very loudly. "All the hall lights are on. Shall I douse them?"

Mike stepped back into the room. "No," he shouted, "leave them on!"

I closed the door after him with a careful bang. There was of course a very good chance that William had been watching us through the keyhole of either the library or the dining-room door—or even through the crack of the door to the servants' hall. He could command a good two-thirds of the first floor from the kitchen without once coming into the hall. But there was no help for it, and none of the doors had moved.

At the foot of the stairs, we were confronted with another danger. Higgins and Annie, both supposedly upstairs, might have been watching the entire performance from the landing, and even if they had not, we were now apt to be detected. If they were both where they should have been, they were both very near the head of that staircase, Annie in M. Farrington's room, its door not six feet from us—Higgins in his own room, its wall right beside us. If he were sitting in a chair, separated from us by a few inches of mere plaster, the slightest sound would ruin the whole show. There were a few things in our favor—such as the sturdiness of the old stairs, with never a creak in them, and the thickness of the carpet.

Facing the west end of the house, we were confronted by M. Farrington's room on the left with the Skipper's beyond it. On the right were Gay's room and Jude's. To the east my room and Mike's both faced the door to the servants' corridor. We didn't dare whisper. By some tacit agreement, we seemed to have decided that the person we sought was one of the four servants, and that observation by any one of them must be avoided above all things.

Michael pointed to Gay's door, and without hesitation I unlocked it. We crept in. Gay switched on the small light on the bed-stand. Her face was rather flushed, but for once she went through an ordeal without fireworks. She even waved us toward the suitcase, lying open on a stand.

Aside from clothes and the usual odds and ends, it contained three letters which, at a nod from Gay, I opened. They were from friends and in no way startling. We went through the dressing table, desk, and bed-stand, removing drawers and turning them upside down. Nothing. We tore the bed apart and even felt under the mattress. Nothing. We went through her closet, Mike even looking through her shoes. I investigated coat linings and pockets. We lifted the rug. We leafed through all the books in the room. To save me, I couldn't think of anything else.

"Jude's room," I suggested reluctantly, the very thought of my latest experience in there turning me a little sick.

That business of rifling the possessions of a dead friend in sight of her lifeless body still remains one of the most unpleasant jobs of my life. I couldn't seem to shake off the idea that the person who had killed her might be one of the persons now rattling among her things. I couldn't drown the memory of that ghastly sight on the closet shelf and the still, sheeted figure that had not been Jude Blinshop. I would have given anything to have thrown Gay and Mike bodily out of that room—and myself after them. But I went through with it.

At last only one thing remained to be investigated—the bed and its silent occupant. Great beads of perspiration stood on Michael's face. But we had failed to look at that bed once before, and our failure had been disastrous. I took a deep breath and stepped toward it. Moving so lightly in my clenched hand as almost to throw me off my balance, the sheet came back. Jude Blinshop lay where I had placed her. I replaced the cover quickly.

The stillness of that room seemed to follow us down the hall to my quarters. No one spoke during the entire performance of dumping all my things on the floor. I couldn't get Jude's disfigured, staring face out of my mind. It seemed to be reproaching me for something. I'm afraid I wasn't of much help at that stage of the game. Michael's voice was hushed as he asked me if I was all right.

I said that I was. I stumbled after them into his room and helped paw through his belongings. There was a devil of a mess there, but nothing more. And that brought us to a halt. Aside from the servants' quarters, there remained only the rooms of the two Aunts. Annie and M. Farrington were in one of them, and the bathroom door into the other probably still stood open. Cook and Higgins were in their rooms—or should have been. That left William's room and Annie's. Annie, it seemed to us, would be more apt to remain where she was than William. We decided on his room first.

Breathlessly we tiptoed across the main hall to the servants' quarters. Not a sound. One dim light was burning just above the stairs in the narrow hallway. We listened at Higgins' door. A light was burning inside, but there was not a sound. We crept down the corridor to Cook's door where the sound of heavy breathing was clearly audible. Pushing open William's door, I groped for a light.

The tumbled bed still bore testimony of my struggles there. The trunk straps that had held me lay on the floor as Michael had flung them. Inch by inch we went over that room—through the dresser, the wardrobe, his uniform pockets, under the rug, all over the bed and its mattress.

I finally shrugged helplessly and turned to the door.

"Wait a minute." It was Michael at the window against which reposed a small leather cushion of the sort used in the driver's seat of a car. Mike picked it up. We all crowded around him and as we did so a section of the cushion unsnapped. Two letters fell to the floor. I stooped and picked them up.

They were both in plain white envelopes, one typed and one addressed in a vertical, firm handwriting. In the corner of the typewritten one, I read *Office of the Warden, Wethersfield Prison, Wethersfield, Connecticut.* It was addressed to Mr. William Miller, 137 Nassau Street, New York City. My hand shook so that I could hardly get the letter out of the envelope. The date was in July of the previous year. I read:

> *"I am sorry to learn from our mutual friend that you have encountered difficulty in securing employment. It is my suggestion that you get in touch with Mr. Blinshop who, in spite of the fact that he was obliged to take the stand against you, bears you no malice, and is most eager to help you now.*

> *"He is a generous and sympathetic man. In spite of the trouble you have caused him, you need not hesitate to accept his assistance. 1 heartily endorse the plan of a fresh name and a fresh start.*
>
> *"Do not lose your nerve. Please keep in touch with me."*

It was signed by the Warden of the prison.

17

"Dear Bill," read the other letter, *"I was glad to hear from you. You've been on my mind for a long time. I'd hate you to think that I had any grudge against you because of your tough luck. I felt then and I still feel that you were a good chap in a tight spot.*

"Fortunately, I think we can manage to get you a job where you will be just as well off as you were here. Then you can forget the whole business. With your permission, I'll drop in on you Wednesday at 11:00 a.m. and we can go around and see about it.

"It bucks me up to have you write to me after all. Let me know if Wednesday isn't all right.

Yours sincerely,
John Blinshop."

So William had known Jude Blinshop! Worse than that, he had apparently gotten into trouble while working for her father and been prosecuted for it. For the first time, we had discovered a clear and plausible motive.

Michael spoke first. "The rat!" he said. "After a guy went to all that trouble to give him a lift!"

There were several things about the situation that puzzled me. Why should William have kept those two letters? He was not a sentimental soul, nor yet an imaginative one. Assuming that he had been responsible for Jude's death, he was a treacherous, cold-blooded devil. I couldn't seem to imagine such a man keeping incriminating evidence to gloat over when the nights were long and lonely. The evidence was right under my nose, but I wasn't satisfied with it. Could this be what Jude had told Michael? Perhaps she had not been aware that the aunts knew William's identity and wanted to warn them. Perhaps—

I asked Michael—for the sixth or seventh time—what Jude had told him in the game-room.

I don't know what I expected him to do, but he certainly didn't do it. His eyes jerked from the letters in his hand to my face. They held a startled, panicky look that turned rapidly to one of rage.

"I told you that she warned me about the chimneys." His voice was thin and tight. "Perhaps you could understand it better if I repeated that it was none of your business."

Gay's face turned a dull red and her eyes began to glitter.

"You listen to me—" She had Mike by the arm, and another scrap was close enough for me to see the whites of its eyes.

"Cut it out!" I snapped. "Gay, shut up. I thought that it might have been about William, Mike. That's all. Was it?"

"No."

I believed him. Well, at least I knew of one thing that Jude had *not* talked about.

"If William is our man, we're on a bad spot," I said. "If he's the murderer, I'm pretty sure he has another revolver. And furthermore, he knows how to use it."

Michael gave a violent start. "He was alone with Aunt Martha for—"

He didn't finish it. He didn't need to. We were all thinking the same thing. We started down that hall in a body. All in a heap, we burst into M. Farrington's room.

Annie had been sitting beside the bed, reading. On the bed M. Farrington, wide awake, was surveying us with a chilly eye.

"Are you running away from something?" her dry voice demanded.

Michael found his tongue first. "Sorry, Aunt Martha. We—got worried about you."

"Quite sudden, wasn't it?"

Despite everything, I couldn't control my laugh. Good old M. Farrington. Queen Victoria perched on a cyclone! I roared, and the others along with me.

Queen Victoria continued to sit sedately waiting until we gradually subsided. Gay was still giggling when the old lady spoke.

"Now, if you have all had your little joke, perhaps one of you would tell me what this is all about?"

Michael sank down on the bed beside her. "Aunt Martha," he said, "you're marvelous, only in our present weakened condition we aren't up to you."

"Hmmph!" observed M. Farrington.

For want of something better, I asked her how she felt.

"Amazed." The dry voice was getting drier. "Well?"

Mike took a deep breath and plunged in. "Well, you see none of us had been in to see you because we didn't want to disturb you, and we—the idea struck us all at once that you might not be all right. We—er—we got worried."

I opened my mouth to elaborate upon the subject, when Michael's foot dealt me a savage kick in the shin. He glanced significantly at Annie, and I realized that I had been about to narrate our whole case against William in front of the girl. And it would not be safe to send her out of the room. She would head straight for William, and the door of his room was probably standing wide open, exposing a perfect record of our activities.

"We're getting a little jumpy," I put in lamely. "Do you mind a bit of company for a while?"

We had not bluffed the old lady, I was glad to see. M. Farrington's advice was something I could do with right then, if only I could get the coast clear to ask for it.

"Annie," said M. Farrington, "I wish you would find my glasses. I think I left them on the table in the library."

I nearly swallowed my tongue. Annie was going to get a sight of either William's room or the living-room only over my dead body.

I said, "I've forgotten my cigarettes. I'll be right back."

It was an obvious ruse—too damned obvious. But Gay didn't understand. "I have some here, Jimmie."

"Wrong brand," I said, glaring at her and edging myself toward the door. I followed Annie into the hall.

I stepped into the living-room and watched her until she disappeared in the direction of the library. Our little tableau was just as we had left it. Whether or not it had been discovered by anyone, I couldn't tell. I switched off the radio, shoved the furniture back into position, and yanked the dummy sleepers apart. A good alibi was on the tip of my tongue for anyone who might interrupt me. I was looking for my cigarette case. But no one interrupted me.

Galloping up the stairs, I cut down the hall and into the servants' quarters. William's door was closed. The shock of that sent me crashing through it. The light had been extinguished by someone—someone who was no longer in the room. Drawers had been returned to their places. Everything had been tidied. In the faint light from the hall I could see that even the cushion had been returned to its place at the window. I strode over to the thing. Its snaps had been refastened. Someone—possibly William himself—had been covering our tracks. Why?

I closed the door and crept to the head of the narrow staircase. From below I could hear the faint rumble of voices—William's and Annie's. Not William then. Not unless he had been standing just outside his door as we rushed out of it, worked with remarkable speed, and rushed down to the kitchen when he heard my steps in the hall. I had lost all conception of time. Whether or not such action would have been possible, I couldn't say. Had we been gone from that room more than five minutes?

If William were eliminated, only Cook and Higgins were left. Cook's room was straight across the hall from the scene of activity and Higgins' was right next door to it. They were both in their rooms. It was possible. But why should they cover our tracks? Why should anyone do that, unless—the thought struck me like a thunderbolt—unless the Skipper was still in the house?

If the Skipper was in the house, her disappearance must have been of her own choosing. Why? In my excitement I bumped smartly against the wall. Higgins' door flew open and Higgins, an apparition of nightshirt and spindly legs, confronted me.

"Who's there?" His voice was nervous. "What do you want?"

I had no intention of frightening him. I didn't answer him at once because I expected him to step into the hall where he would have seen me standing against the wall next to his door.

"I heard you," he quavered. "And I know where you're hiding."

"It's only me, Higgins," I said, stepping into his range of sight. "Don't be alarmed."

Whatever he had been afraid of, I apparently had not been involved in it. With a gusty sigh of relief, he leaned heavily against the door.

"Oh, it's you, sir. I—I wasn't sure. My nerves aren't so good any more."

Was he acting or wasn't he?

I said, "Have you been in William's room at all to-night?"

He stared at me blankly. "No, sir. Why?"

"Have you heard anyone in there since you've been in your room?"

Sleepy or not, his eyes were on the alert. "No, sir."

"That's odd. Mr. Michael, Miss Palmer, and myself were searching that room just a few minutes ago."

I was giving him his chance. If the confidence he had almost given me concerned William, there would be little point in his withholding the information now. He was no fool. He would normally conclude that if we had searched William's room, we must in some degree suspect William.

"That's strange, sir," he said. "I've been asleep, and I didn't hear a sound."

Whether he was lying or speaking the truth, something was troubling him. It suddenly flashed across my mind that he might be speaking the truth for an excellent reason. Perhaps Higgins had not been in his room at all. Perhaps—

"Higgins," I said point-blank, "is Miss Barbara in this house?"

He blinked at me like a great sleepy owl, but the eyes behind the drooping lids were not sleepy. "I'm sure I don't know, sir."

I gave it up. "All right. Go back to bed. Everything is fine. I was just looking around."

The instant his door closed upon me, I stepped quickly to Cook's door and listened. Not a sound. I knocked softly at first and then louder and louder. No answer. I tried the knob and the door swung open easily to my hand. Dim light permeating the room from behind me showed me at one glance all I wanted to know. The bed was tumbled and untidy, but the room was empty. I made my way quickly and as quietly as I could to the head of the back stairs and listened. The words were indistinct, but there were two voices—neither of them the strident tones of Cook.

Why I did what I did next is a question. For once I had an opportunity for a little investigation before the entire household joined in the sport. The immediate thing was to find Cook. And one room on the upper floor had not been searched recently—the Skipper's. I made tracks in that direction. The proximity of M. Farrington's room made me doubly cautious. I sidled through the Skipper's door and closed it behind me.

My extreme caution was creating certain difficulties. I couldn't find the light, and there was considerable danger of my clattering over some of the furniture in the dark. Frantically I searched my pockets for a match, found one, after three attempts managed to strike a light, and took one step forward. That one step did the trick. My foot caught on something on the floor, and in another moment I was crashing head over heels in an uproar fit to rouse the militia.

In the darkness I struggled to my knees, listening to rapid feet coming through the bathroom from Mr. Farrington's room. I was discovered, but I didn't care. Rocking back and forth on my knees, I waited for the light to come through that door and disclose the body of Cook. I almost thought that I could see it in front of me without the light.

The door came open with a bang. Michael stood on the threshold, a heavy silver box raised in his hand as a weapon. At the sight of me, his mouth dropped open. Slowly, fascinated, I swung my eyes down in the path of light streaming through the bathroom door. They encountered an ordinary rag rug, one end of which had been kicked up in the air—in all probability by my own foot. The other end was held firmly to the floor by a leg of the Skipper's bed. Of bodies—or traces of them—there was not a sign.

"What are you doing now?" said Michael blankly.

I was becoming aware of a banged elbow and a barked shin, and I was also conscious of the picture I cut there on my hands and knees.

"Playing potsy!" I said. "Any suggestions?"

He stepped over to a stand and switched on a light.

"Are you hurt?" he inquired without too much interest.

I got clumsily to my feet. "I'll barely live."

Michael surveyed me thoughtfully. "Suppose we go into the other room?" he said.

I went. The indignity of my position momentarily seemed more important to me than the mysterious disappearance of Cook. M. Farrington was sitting in a chair, clad in one of her eternal lavender wrappers, sharp eyes on my face. Gay sprawled on the bed, cocked up on one elbow, her attitude thoroughly alert.

I addressed myself to Gay, the least disconcerting of my audience. "Where's Annie?" I said.

But M. Farrington was not to be ignored. "Annie," she declaimed, "is still looking for the glasses which are over there on the dressing table. Would you mind telling us what *you* were doing?"

"Someone got to William's room before I did," I said, not pausing to ask whether or not they had told her the whole story. But M. Farrington had been missing no tricks.

"How do you know? Were the letters gone?"

The letters! "No," I said quickly, "Mike has them, haven't you, Mike?"

Michael's hands flew to his coat pockets and on through his vest and trouser pockets.

"Gay has them," he said.

Three pairs of eyes swung to Gay's face. It was blank.

"But I haven't. You have them yourself, Mike. You took them from Jimmie."

There was silence.

"Michael," said M. Farrington crisply, "search the hall. You may have dropped them in your excitement."

It was a forlorn hope, but it was the only one. Mike went on the gallop. M. Farrington took command of the situation.

"Now, James, you have not explained what you were doing in Barbara's room. Don't look so vague."

I tried to do as I was told. As calmly as I could, I told her what I had discovered. Gay gasped once and, when I came to the episode of the rug, giggled nervously. But M. Farrington's gimlet eyes never left my face.

"Why didn't you go down to the kitchen?" she snapped before I had drawn a breath on my last period.

"I couldn't hear her. You can always hear Cook, and—"

"Hmmph!" said M. Farrington cryptically just as Mike came through the door.

His face told the story long before his tongue could.

"Didn't find a thing."

"I guess it's time we looked at that kitchen," I said.

M. Farrington's smile was sardonic. "Are you quite sure, James?"

I was.

The smaller corridor was still in semi-darkness. I listened outside of Higgins' door for the faint sound of his breathing. Cook's door was still closed, but I was taking no chances. I pushed it open and satisfied myself that she had not returned to her room. Then, feeling my way carefully, I started down the back stairs.

The mumble of voices was lower and more indistinct. I could no longer distinguish one from the other, let alone any of the words. Slowly I crept down until the turn of the landing brought me within full view of the kitchen, where I halted, open-mouthed.

William stood at the end of the kitchen table, leaning over talking excitedly to Annie, who was sitting beside him. Beyond them in a capacious rocking chair, her eyes glittering and her large hands clenched tightly in her lap, sat Cook. She was not talking, but she was listening spellbound to the other two.

"Is it proof enough?" I was obliged to exert every ounce of balance I could command to avoid falling over the banisters in my eagerness to hear Annie's whisper. "If we was to fall through with this, he could make it awful hot for us. There ain't many jobs, Bill. You'd oughta know that."

William brought his fist down on the table expressively but without sound. "The guys like us is the ones that'll get blamed. It took me three years to learn that. And here's another thing. We got enough evidence on Higgins to send him to the chair tomorrow!"

18

At this moment I leaned too heavily upon the railing. It wasn't a very loud squeak, but William spun around. I tried to flatten myself against the wall, but I had been discovered.

I stuck my hands into my pockets and ambled down the stairs.

"What I'd like to know, William," I said, "is what you just said. Something about evidence against Higgins, wasn't it?"

With a ridiculous pretense of calm I seated myself on the table, my back to the massive figure of Cook. "If you'll take my tip, William, you'll get the whole story off your chest. What do you know about Higgins?"

He was gripping the table as if he meant to smash it to pieces.

"What makes you think I know anything?"

"You do." I strove to keep my voice level. "You're full of surprises. What, for example, do you know about Higgins that would send him to the chair?"

I pitied the fellow. His eyes were bloodshot and his face was drawn. "You can't prove I said nothing. You can't prove nothing. I ain't going to talk."

I took a long shot in the dark. "As a matter of fact, William," I said, "I can prove several interesting things about you. And it so happens that my evidence is very fine evidence indeed. And it won't do you any good to dispose of me in order to get hold of it."

Cook, I really believe, would have throttled me at that point, if William's arm had not sent her hurtling back into her chair. He drew a long breath.

"All right," he said faintly. "What are you going to do?"

I shoved a chair at him with my foot. "Sit down," I said, "and tell me about it. It's all bound to come out anyway."

He sat heavily. Annie was beginning to cry.

"I been three years in the pen." His voice was slow and dazed. "I was driving for the Blinshops and a ring was pinched. They pinned it on me. The old man felt sorry for me and got me a job here with Miss Barbara. I ain't done a thing—but it's gonna look bad." He was mumbling as if in his sleep, and his voice was weary, hopeless, and sick.

"Did anyone but Miss Barbara know about this—anyone in the house, I mean?"

He shook his head drearily. "Miss Judith knew."

Jude! It was going to look bad! And yet, if the Skipper had known all about his record, he would have had no reason for— I leaned toward him.

"You know better than I do that you're in a tight spot. Your only way out is to find the guilty man."

Cook's roar this time brought me to my feet.

"Damn you!" she bellowed. "Damn you for a lying devil! Leave him alone!"

"Suppose you finish the story, William," I said.

His blazing eyes snapped from Cook's face to mine. For an instant I thought I would be obliged to fight my way out, but only for an instant. William's eyes fell and he sank back into his chair.

"All right, then," his words were barely audible. "Cook knew it—and my wife."

An entirely new train of thought was popping into my head.

"By that you mean Annie?"

"Yes."

The silence in the kitchen was unbroken. Annie had ceased to sniffle. I was doing some rapid thinking.

"You'd better answer questions, all of you," I said at last. "How did you manage to get here, William? Did Cook arrange it?"

"No. I told you once, Mr. Blinshop did. Cook's been here a long time. She got Annie this job when they sent me up. And then—I just happened to get here. I might have known there'd be some hitch to a break like that!"

"Did anyone here know that you were related?"

William shook his head. "I didn't want to take no chances."

Every word he uttered dovetailed with a wild idea forming in the back of my mind. Right then, it seemed too bizarre to be true, but I was to think better of it.

"What did you do with those letters?" I said.

"What letters?" His face was bewildered.

"Don't be a fool," I snapped. "We searched your room just now and found the letters from your Warden and from Mr. Blinshop. A few minutes later, when we came back, the letters were gone. What did you do with them?"

William's face was twisted in terror.

"As God's my judge, Mr. Wells," he said, "I didn't have no such letters."

I lost my temper. "You had them or someone in your family did. I saw them. This won't get you anywhere. The first policeman who comes into this house can have you identified. Where are they?"

"Do you know what he's talking about?" William turned dazedly from Cook to Annie. They both shook frightened heads. "What—what was in them, sir? Where was they?"

"They were in your driving cushion," I said. Slowly, as accurately as I could, I repeated their contents. Before I was halfway through, my bewilderment redoubled. As surely as I was sitting there, not one of the three had ever heard my words before. It was insane and pointless. They had absolutely nothing to gain by denials. William voiced the conclusion that was formulating in my own mind.

"Somebody put 'em there! Put 'em there and then swiped 'em."

"Did you ever have such letters?" I demanded.

His eyes clouded. "I don't know. I had references from the Warden and Blinshop once, but I forget what I done with them. I—think—I showed 'em to Miss Barbara when I got this job and then chucked 'em. It's—crazy."

It was all of that. I turned to Cook.

"How long have you been down here?" I inquired.

"Huh?" Cook's heavy jaw dropped and then snapped together. "In this kitchen? I come down with Willie to git him some supper."

"Has she been here ever since?" I directed the question at William.

His face darkened. "Sure, she's been here. What do you think? You needn't try to pin anything on her, too."

"I'm not trying to pin anything on anybody," I said patiently. "I'm trying to find out what happened. Two people are dead, and if we don't want to be in their shoes, we've got to find out what happened. We won't find out anything until everybody tells all he or she knows."

I paused to gauge the effect of my words. It was considerable.

"Now," I said quietly, "did either of you straighten up William's room after we searched it a few minutes ago? No one can hold it against you if you did. It will just keep us from running up any more blind alleys."

"No," said William earnestly, "I swear I didn't!"

Annie's negative was thin and wavery but Cook's came forth torrentially.

"Very well, Cook," I said curtly. "Annie, did you leave Miss Farrington alone—even for a second—after William came downstairs?"

Annie answered without the slightest hesitation. "No, sir. Not for a second even!"

One point was settled then. Almost anyone in the house might have placed those letters in William's room, but there was only one person who could have removed them—Higgins. Everyone else was carefully checked. Unless the Skipper was in the house! Or either Gay or Michael was withholding them for a purpose. The only purpose that I could imagine for such an act was to conceal the fact that either had put them there.

I picked my words slowly. It was important that William should tell me all he knew about Higgins without being frightened into withholding any information. I wanted to know what he had been on the verge of telling the others when my blundering entrance into the kitchen cut him short. I had constantly in mind the fact that either William was a felon or William had served three years in jail rather than give information about someone else.

"We're all in the same boat," I said. "Either we catch the culprit red-handed or one of us is apt to become his third victim. And another one of us is pretty certain to be tried for these killings." I didn't point out which one of us. I left that to William's imagination and he got the point. His hands clenched convulsively. "What have you people noticed about Higgins?" I inquired as casually as I could. "To my mind he is the only person who has had access to William's room recently."

In the heavy silence it seemed as if my attempt had failed. Just as I was about to try again, William spoke.

"He's been funny," he said. "Long before you and Mr. Michael came he was funny—jumpy. Used to go roaming around the house at night and nearly went crazy if you caught him at it or asked him a question." William paused uncertainly.

"That wouldn't hang a man very high."

"Maybe not. That first night—the night you folks got here—he acted almost nuts. Had Cook in such a fuss about the dinner, it's a wonder you got anything to eat at all. Laid me out in fine style for not bringing him some stuff from the drug store, when I'd already told him I couldn't get it unless Miss Judith's train was late. Made me go all the way back to town after it.

"And then, when Annie and Cook was both downstairs, I heard him talking in his room. Thinks I, 'The old boy's gone screwy.' So I knock at his door. And was he wild! Told me he was reading poetry out loud and I'd better mind my own business if I didn't want to start looking for a job. Threatened to knock me down. Can you tie that?"

I couldn't decide whether William was rambling in an attempt to gain time or because he really considered the details of his story important. There was nothing to be gained from the faces of the others. They were both seemingly engrossed in the story.

"Is that all?"

William plunged on eagerly. "All? Christ, no! After we'd went to bed, we couldn't get to sleep, like I told you. The noise was awful and Annie was pretty scared. We was in my room. Along about eleven o'clock or a little after Annie got so excited I went out to see if I could get something to make her sleep. Cook didn't have nothing, so I knocked at Higgins' door.

"There was a light inside, but nobody answered. I figured he couldn't hear me on account of the wind, so I open the door and walks in. Higgins wasn't in that room and neither was anybody else. I didn't think nothing of it then. I figured he was out fastening up blinds and things, and thought he was a stubborn fool not to ask me to help him. But next day I done considerable thinking when he tells you he went to bed at eleven o'clock."

I restrained a snort of impatience. "But that doesn't mean a thing, William. Higgins only made a rough guess at the time. It would really be suspicious if he'd hit it right on the dot."

William shook his head stubbornly. "Not for Higgins. That bird wouldn't think of rolling over in bed without looking at the clock to see if it was the right time for it."

There was an idea in that. "Just how does it happen that you are so sure of what the time was when you went into his room?"

"That's why I went out at all. I'd been kidding Annie to make her think there wasn't nothing wrong in her not being asleep yet. She made me turn on the light and look at the clock. And then I went out."

William was no slouch himself as an alibi artist. "And you think you can turn Higgins over to the police," I said, "because he happened to be a few minutes off in his calculation of the time he went to bed? Use your head."

"I am using it!" doggedly. "Annie finally got to sleep, but by that time I was jumpy myself. I thought, 'Maybe I'd oughta go out and help the old cuss. This is a hell of a night and no mistake.' So I got into my pants and shirt and started after him.

"There'd been a light on in the hall before, mind you, but it was out now. You couldn't see your hand in front of your face. I was looking for the light and I hear a door downstairs bang hard. I turn toward the stairs, thinking that something had been blown open and better be fastened, and all of a sudden I hear someone coming down the main hall like a house afire.

"I thought someone was sick or something, but before I could more than turn around, the door into our hall swings open and Higgins comes tearing through. There was a light in the big hall and I could see him plain as day. He had all his clothes on and he looked like all hell was after him. Before I could open my mouth, he'd tore into his room and I could hear him locking the door."

William paused for breath.

"Go on!" said Annie and I simultaneously.

William frowned. "I didn't know what to do. If he'd needed help he could of woke me easy as not. And he hadn't. He'd locked his door. I think, 'He's cracked for fair, that's what, and I'd better tell Miss Farrington first thing in the morning.' So I start to go into my own room, but before I could close the door I hears someone else tearing down the main hall. I opens my door just a crack and sees Mr. Michael come rushing in and begin to pound on Higgins' door. He was soaking wet and pretty excited. I open my mouth to sing out and ask what's up and just then Higgins opens his door. Damned if he ain't in his night-clothes, blinking like he'd been asleep since noon!

"I wasn't going to get caught listening, not with Higgins the way he'd been lately. I closed my door, but I stood there listening, and the first thing I hear is Mr. Michael saying, 'Wake up everybody in the house! I can't find Miss Barbara and Miss Blinshop!'

"I knew right off that the first thing the old boy would do would be to come through the bathroom after me, and there was Annie sound asleep. I routed her out quick and got her over by the door. The minute she hears Higgins' door close, she skins across the hall into Cook's room. With Mr. Michael only halfway down the hall, it was a tight squeak, but it worked!"

"William," I said roughly, "if you'd told this story in the first place, you might have saved at least one life. Do you realize that?"

The man's face was troubled. "Jobs is scarce."

"Lives are scarcer!" I snapped. "Is there any more?"

It was a stupid attitude to take, and I realized it the minute the words were out of my mouth. William's lips set in a grim and stubborn line. He was silent.

"He ain't been withholding no facts!" rumbled Cook indignantly.

"He *has* been withholding facts—important ones," I said. "Now look here, William, I'm not blaming you. You've had a rough time. But your negligence has caused plenty of trouble. The best thing you can do now is to be sure that you haven't overlooked anything."

William's voice was sullen. "I don't know nothing more."

I took a wild chance. "It will be interesting," I said, "to find out what a fingerprint expert thinks about who locked Mr. Michael and myself in the cellar."

There was dead silence. William's eyes were fixed on the floor.

"All right," he said at last. "I ain't denying it. I went off my nut. It—it seemed like you was the guy that konked me, and I thought you'd just tried to bump off the old lady. When we was looking for Miss Barbara you acted like you was stalling, and— Well, you didn't say nothing about where you was going."

I stared at him. "You're not very consistent," I said. "I thought you were just now accusing Higgins?"

"I was!" His expression was mulish. "I was wrong about you maybe. I got to thinking while I was sitting with the old lady, and I admit I was wrong. But there's too much fishy business about Higgins."

"Such as—?" I knew he was ready to continue.

"Well, yesterday, when he was supposed to stay in the kitchen till you sent for him—when you were in the living-room and the rest was in their rooms—he went upstairs. I saw him."

So Higgins slaughtered that cat! My throat tightened and there was ice at my back.

"Why didn't you say so?"

His eyes were still on the floor. "Where I've been, sir, if you don't learn nothing else, you learn to keep your mouth shut."

"Not when it may cost you your life!" I said savagely.

I was certain that Higgins had removed those letters from William's room. All the years that I had known the old man, all the years that I had considered him as much a part of Farrington Bluff as Long Island Sound itself, fell away from me. Higgins owned the only revolver known to be on the Bluff. He had lied about his whereabouts on the night of Jude's death, and certainly he had been out of his room when it occurred. He had had opportunity for mutilating the cat and dismantling that bedroom. The Skipper was missing, and she would have followed him anywhere. Poor Norman Farrington would have trusted him implicitly. He had been among the first on the scene of the shooting of M. Farrington. I had found him with the gun in his hand, and he had almost tricked me into planting my own fingerprints on it. My head was spinning with the mass of evidence.

I again asked William if there was anything else.

Getting slowly to his feet, he plunged a hand into his back pocket and drew forth a leather case which he flung upon the table.

"That!"

I picked the thing up gingerly. It contained about two dozen keys of all sizes and descriptions. They conveyed nothing to me.

"That fell out of his pocket when he was getting the dinner and I nailed it. Higgins always carries a key to every room in the house," said William slowly.

19

A sound from the stair railing grated on our ears, spinning us all about simultaneously. Higgins, fully dressed, stood on the landing, staring down at us. How long he had been there, we had no way of knowing. It is one thing to confront murderous fiends in tabloid headlines, but it is quite another to stand face to face with one in the form of an old family servant whom you have known for a good part of your life. My lips were dry as I slipped the key-case into my pocket.

"Hello, Higgins," I said. "Come on down. We were just talking about you."

The silence got under my skin. I waited for the man to answer, for Cook to explode, for Annie to scream. Nothing happened. For a space of fully fifteen seconds we stood there while the old man studied our faces.

"Were you, sir? I can't seem to sleep and I thought I would make myself a pot of coffee."

He came down the stairs slowly, as deliberately as he had ever descended them in his life. Habit is certainly a powerful factor. If ever I had wanted to collar a man, Higgins was that man. And yet—I couldn't.

I said casually, "Sure. Make enough for the rest of us. I guess we can stand it."

No one spoke. We sat there and watched him measure out coffee, pour in water, and set the pot on the stove. He turned from the operation, smiling.

"I'm glad it's nearly over, Mr. Jimmie. There will be a boat here by morning, see if there isn't."

I could do nothing but murmur, "Yes."

He was guilty. I was sure of it. But sitting there looking at him I couldn't see myself telling him so. I cleared my throat.

"Higgins," I said, "you've lied to me on every single question I've asked you—haven't you?"

For one fraction of a second the eyes turned toward me were the sick, tired eyes of a very old man. In the next instant they were veiled and calculating.

"What gives you that impression, sir?"

I stood up. "You were seen out of your room on the night when Miss Blinshop was killed. You were seen going into your room fully dressed just before Mr. Michael called you and reappearing as if you had been asleep a moment later. You own the only gun in the house. You were seen coming down the stairs immediately before we discovered the injured cat, when you swore that you had been in the next room. You were on hand when Miss Farrington was wounded. You even tried to get my fingerprints on the revolver. William and I are going to lock you in your room. You will be kept there until the police arrive."

Those strange eyes never once left my face, not even after I had completed my distasteful task.

"Mr. Jimmie," he said very quietly, "you've known me for a long time. Do you believe what you are saying?"

"I'm sorry, Higgins. Yes."

A ghost of a smile crossed his face.

"I see," he said. "Do you object to my having my coffee before you lock me up?"

"Don't take no chances with him," cautioned William.

And so we sat there waiting for that coffee, waiting to be served by a man whom we intended to deliver into the hands of the law to lose his life. I was too busy with my own feelings to notice particularly what went on in that room. Once or twice the clumsy shuffling of Cook's feet penetrated my consciousness, but that was all. I doubt if any coffee on the face of the earth ever took as long to boil as that did.

At last Higgins moved to the closet and set out five cups and saucers. Cook stood grimly over him while he poured, her mind running, I imagine, to all the varieties of poison that could be dropped into those cups. My own mind was too full of all the other cups Higgins had handed me—of all the decent little favors he had done me. I choked trying to drink the stuff. Higgins drank his calmly and set the cup down.

"I'm quite ready, Mr. Wells," he said.

But I wasn't. Suddenly, strangely, I felt that I was making a great mistake. Where and how, I could not see, but I was sure that I was making one. I had a strong conviction that if Higgins were guilty, he would never have taken the accusation as he had. If Higgins had done all the things we had imagined his doing, Higgins was insane, for he was without a conceivable motive. And an insane man, confronted with captivity, is not usually as placid as he was. At least, I didn't think so. It was a straw, but I gasped at it frantically.

"Higgins," I said, "haven't you anything to say to defend yourself?"

"Not a thing, sir."

William and I took him upstairs. It was consistent with my general stupidity that, although I had many qualms about his guilt, I no sooner slipped the key of his locked door into my pocket than I regarded the entire episode as closed. It was all over. And now—what?

William stirred uneasily at my elbow. "I feel like a rat, sir. He's an awful *old* man."

I wanted to get away from William.

Without replying I made off down the corridor to the main hall. Lights still glared there, and I could hear the intermittent murmur of voices in M. Farrington's room. I knew that I should go in there and tell them what had happened. I knew that they were in all probability working themselves into a fine frenzy waiting for me. But I was in no mood to face M. Farrington—or even Michael.

I went downstairs into the cold, deserted library, where I made a fire, helped myself to a stiff drink, and sat down to think. For the most part I was concerned with the whereabouts of the Skipper. That Higgins in his right mind would in any way injure the Skipper seemed to me out of the question. And I could not convince myself that Higgins was not in his right mind. I went over and over the question. I took another drink and then another. I threw myself down at the desk and tried to write. The feel of a pen in my hand was comfortingly familiar. More to quiet my nerves than in hopes of proving anything, I set to work.

HIGGINS

> *Knew of the presence of Norman Farrington. Whereabouts at the time of the death of Jude suspicious. Easy to imagine him in the confidence of every single person molested to date—Jude, Norman Farrington, M. Farrington, and the Skipper. Seen upstairs when the cat was killed and the room torn up. Lied about it afterward. Only person who might have removed letters from William's room. Witness for his alibi on the shooting of M. Farrington (Skipper) missing. Obtained something from drug store.*

> *Poison? Started to tell me something. A confession? Tried to get my fingerprints on the gun used on M. Farrington. Carried keys to every room in the house. Note: Standing at my own elbow when Cook was attacked. Locked in room with others when William and I were attacked. Has seemed afraid of something from the beginning. Seems relieved to be locked up. Motive inconceivable.*

Pausing for a cigarette, I surveyed my results. A pretty disorderly mess. Well, it could be straightened out later. At least my nerves were steadying down.

WILLIAM

> *Convicted of felony. Served full term in spite of interest of Mr. Blinshop. Seems to indicate that no vindicating evidence has yet been found. Knew the Blinshops. Only person with conceivable motive—revenge. Only person to give evidence against Higgins. Substantiation of all his evidence comes from his wife and Cook, who are clever enough to have fooled the household over a long period of time. Knew of Higgins' gun and admits to being a good shot. Alibi covering killing of cat and braining of wife and Cook questionable. Proof of whereabouts during death of Jude again rests on those two. Found Jude's body. Might have dealt with me in his room. Might have planted and removed letters to cast suspicion elsewhere. Suggested the locking of upstairs rooms. May have had Higgins' keys at the time. May have seen Norman Farrington when Michael saw him. Servants' gossip from the Blinshops' might have told him who Norman was.*

Might have had Higgins suspecting him. Strong enough to have overpowered both the Skipper and her brother. Seems well versed in drugs. Admits going to drug store. Note: Was injured when I was. (Might have thrown himself down the stairs.) Did revive M. Farrington. Admits locking us in cellar.

I placed the two lists side by side and considered them with unabashed delight. It seemed to me that the case against William overshadowed the case against Higgins. I fumbled for more paper and hurried on.

MICHAEL

Has refused point blank to answer questions. Received some mysterious communication from Jude—perhaps the last she ever made. Was outdoors at some time near that at which Jude met her death. Furiously opposed to any investigation. Suggestion of hushing up whole thing uncharacteristic. No proof that he did not kill the cat and wreck his aunt's room. First one on the spot after the shooting of M. Farrington. Would have been trusted by all the victims even more than Higgins. Might have pocketed William's letter. Seems to have had some inside knowledge since the first night.

Note: Could not have beaned either Cook, Annie, William or myself. Ignorance of his father's existence singular. Bare possibility that his dive over the rocks was an attempt at suicide. Motive incomprehensible.

I brooded over that sheet for several minutes. Not much evidence, aside from his queer actions that first night. Nothing definite. Just a vague, insistent undercurrent of duplicity totally unlike Michael. His rows with Gay were encouraging in that they might have been expected. Mike was set up rather like an August day—warm and sunny with occasional thunder-storms. For the dozenth time I cursed him for not taking me into his confounded secret, whatever it was. That close-mouthed attitude was not like him.

Gay, I wrote next and stopped at a complete loss. As far I could remember at that moment we had not one shred of evidence against Gay Palmer. True, no one had actually seen her in her room on the night of Jude's death, but no one had seen her out of it. The same applied to the episode of the cat and the dismantled room. She had been in the library when Cook and Annie were attacked, in her own room with all the others when William and I were brained. She had not been at the scene of a crime in one single instance. Her actions, as far as I could see, had been perfectly natural and absolutely predictable. There was no trace of a motive, unless we were to go back to that little flare of jealousy so characteristically exhibited on that first evening. Her slate was so clean that for a moment my mystery writing habits sent a thrill of suspicion buzzing through my head. But I was obliged to laugh at my own suspicions. I wrote, *Evidence—none. Motive—none.*

My temples were beginning to pound like steam pipes. I knew that the time which I might decently allow myself for sulking in a corner had long since elapsed. I knew that the others upstairs must be getting impatient. But something in the back of my head told me to go on. I must think quickly, and my thoughts on paper were worth a dozen of my thoughts left to themselves. I needed another drink, and I took one.

COOK

A dope fiend at some time in her life. Very hot-headed. Strong as a bull. Capable of cleverly managed deceit over a long period of time. Possible motive—same as William's plus the slightly unbalanced mind of the addict.

I wrote my next idea down with fingers that trembled with excitement.

Episode in the kitchen might have been an act designed by her to throw the authorities off the scent. Same applies to mysterious appearance and disappearance of William's letters. No evidence of her whereabouts at any time given by anyone but William and Annie. During the episode in William's room, William might have acted for Cook, whom he was fond of. The mess in M. Farrington's room was the sort of thing that might be expected of a drug-crazed person. Both of the Farrington sisters trusted Cook. She is as strong as a man. Might have bodily removed either the Skipper or Mr. Farrington. Note: All hypothetical. No real evidence.

Nevertheless, I experienced a thrill over that possibility. In its light, I could explain the entire performance. Cook, aiding William and Annie to execute revenge for his imprisonment, might have been obliged to go to appalling extremes in order to cover their own tracks. It was highly possible that the poor old lunatic, wandering around in the dead of night, had observed something he was not meant to see and had, accordingly, been done away with. The only substantiating witness to Higgins' alibi had thus been removed. Perhaps M. Farrington had seen something, too. That would explain the several attempts on her life. What could she have seen? Apparently she was unaware of its importance. The coat-sleeve that she thought she saw in her mirror might have been William's.

Time was passing. A very few hours remained before the probable arrival of a rescue party from shore. Unless we were to go through a worse ordeal than any we had yet encountered, it was vital that we have our culprit bagged and ready for delivery when that first boat touched shore. Gritting my teeth, I pushed on with my notations.

Annie

Also capable of good bluff. Least so of the three. Was certainly tied up by someone else. Hysterics might have been due to strain instead of fright. Has seemed unafraid of empty house since first night. No definite evidence. Incapable of any of it alone. Might do anything for or with William. Motive plausible.

M. Farrington

Invited Jude here. Heard last conversation between Skipper and Jude. With Skipper when person was heard, in upper hall. With others during attack on Cook and Annie and attack on William and me. Brother would have trusted her implicitly. Not strong enough to remove anyone bodily. Last person to see the Skipper. Nearly killed twice. Apparently withholding evidence, consciously or otherwise. With Annie when letters were removed from William's room. Has acted characteristically throughout. Motive—none.

There was only one person left, and for a moment I hesitated. There was something repulsive about sitting there sorting evidence against the Skipper when the chances were that her body was floating somewhere in the churning waters of the Sound. And yet, having gone so far, I wanted to finish it. I wrote her name at the head of a fresh piece of paper and rattled on.

> Skipper
>
> *Upset from the very beginning. Motive obscure. By nature would stop at nothing to gain an end that she believed in. Before the cyclone, asked me to keep Michael away from Jude. No real evidence as to her whereabouts when Jude was killed. Apparently the last person to see Jude alive. Knew of Higgins' gun. Had been seen to use it when she considered it necessary. Unusual for her to forget the dogs. With M. Farrington when prowler was heard in upper hall. With whole party when both attacks were made. Would have been trusted by anyone. Seemed to know just where to look for brother's body. Alibi about second shooting substantiated by Higgins. Last person with M. Farrington before her second accident. Both disappearances coincide with disaster. (First—Jude's death. Second—M. Farrington's near death.) First person to notice forced lock on Jude's door. Capable of any sort of bluff at any time.*

In all probability, Michael was searching the house for me by that time. Nevertheless, the odds were against my getting another chance to think things out alone. Time was pressing. The dial of my watch registered 2:45. I imagined that the boat from shore would be at the Bluff by eight o'clock at the very latest. That left us a little over five hours. I forgot old Higgins locked in his room waiting for the police. I forgot everything. Feverishly I pored over those scribbled sheets.

I thought that the evidence pointed to one of two things—to an elaborate plan of revenge on the part of William Miller and his wife, aided by an old friend in Cook, or to an obscure and inexplicable misunderstanding between Michael and the Skipper. It was clear that, in the latter case, the two culprits were not in each other's confidence. Michael had searched the Bluff for his aunt like a madman. Far-fetched as it might seem, I really believed that he had been ignorant of the existence of his father. All of his actions seemed to indicate that he had stumbled upon some evidence against the Skipper. He was neither a fool nor a coward, and I could explain his anxiety to have the investigation dropped in no other way. It was an impenetrable mess. But the Skipper's guilt tallied with the evidence against Higgins.

There were few people in the world whom I could imagine Higgins trying to shield. Barbara Farrington was one of them. In her behalf the old boy would go to trial without a murmur. He might have taken those letters in an attempt to shield the Skipper. He might have substantiated her alibi and tried to get someone else's fingerprints on the revolver. He might have been with the Skipper when William found him out of his room on the night of Jude's death. It was possible that he had been about to confide the whole story to me that day in the living-room when he saw someone outside the window. Could that person have been the Skipper? But what motive—what earthly motive—could the Skipper have for killing the daughter of an old family friend, for killing her only brother, for twice attempting to kill her only sister? It was preposterous! I turned hopefully to the other view of the case.

The Millers had motive and opportunity for everything that had happened. One of them could have shot Jude in premeditated or sudden revenge. William might have cut me down as I was about to stumble over some evidence. Any of them could have enticed Michael's father from his hiding place. Either William or Cook could have killed the cat and upset M. Farrington's room after guessing old Norman's identity, in an attempt to throw the house into a panic. It was highly possible that M. Farrington unconsciously held some evidence against them. Any of them could have both shot and drugged her and subsequently done away with the Skipper, who might have witnessed the latter crime. But if the Millers were guilty, how could I explain the behavior of Michael and his aunt?

I sat there for a long time, frowning at that paper. Even if the Skipper had been telling the truth, what of Michael? What had he and Jude talked about? Why had the Skipper been so anxious to keep that pair apart? I couldn't seem to get anywhere.

Michael, in the doorway, put an end to my speculations.

20

I recited the case against Higgins to M. Farrington myself. Michael raged, stormed, and threatened to tear me limb from limb. He would, he shouted, believe Higgins in opposition to Saint Peter. But M. Farrington took it silently, almost coldly, as if she had been expecting it and was in a measure relieved.

"You were quite right, James," she said, cutting short Michael's tirade. "It seems unfortunate, but we must take no more chances."

My sympathies, I am afraid, were entirely with Michael. The logical thing for me to do was to present my case against William, but I hesitated to tell that story to M. Farrington. An opinion once lodged in her head had a tendency to stay there, and if I were wrong two innocent people would be jobless when the whole business was over. Higgins was safe and quiet. Since Gay was taking M. Farrington's view of the case, I let it go at that.

At her own request, we left M. Farrington to sleep. She seemed really much better and announced her intention of joining us downstairs a little later. Gay wanted to stay with her, but she wouldn't hear of it. Pretty much involved in our own thoughts, we made a weary trek down the stairs. In the lower hall, I grabbed an old jacket of Michael's and slipped out onto the terrace.

It was a beautiful night, starry, crisp, and clear. The salt air felt good. Leaning against a pillar, I closed my eyes and listened to the steady roar of the surf. I stayed there until the uproar in my head had cleared a bit.

Then, lighting a cigarette, I strolled aimlessly in the direction of the bluff with some vague idea of watching the effect of the spray on the rocks below. As luck would have it, I roamed unconsciously over the exact ground that I had traversed so frantically that morning. I found myself pulling up with a jerk at the scene of Norman Farrington's death. The ground was packed and trampled from the impress of many feet. The marks of our skidding as we tugged on the rope glistened icily in the starlight.

Wordsworthian reflections on Nature deserted me. I leaned over and looked down. Somewhat marred by the imprint of Higgins' feet, but still clearly defined in the sand below was the shape of poor old Farrington's body. Apparently it had landed hard without sliding or rolling. At almost any other point on the whole bluff, a heavy weight going over the edge would have rolled and slid to the beach below. Slid!

If the Skipper had gone over the edge, the extent of the bluff's outward slope would make it necessary for her to have struck sand. And if she had struck sand, the mark would still be there. The rain had stopped long before she disappeared, and the sand was too wet to be much disturbed by the wind. It would be impossible for anyone to jump clear of the bluff into the water, even at high tide. There was no moon and I was without a light, but my eyes, already accustomed to the darkness, had seen the mark of Norman Farrington's body without any trouble. I raced along the top of that bluff, my eyes glued to the sand far below me.

When I finally halted on the rocks beside the stable, I knew beyond the shadow of a doubt that the Skipper had not gone over that bluff into the water. She might, of course, have fallen from the rocks either where I stood or where Michael had fallen across by the boat-house. We had already examined that possibility, with no result.

I turned moodily back toward the house. That night couldn't end too soon for me. I tried to look at my watch, but my matches were gone. Striding rapidly along, I wondered what Gay and Mike were doing. It would be pretty terrible if the Higgins issue precipitated another row.

The hall was still vacant, and the sound of voices rumbled in the living-room. Peeling off the jacket, I made hastily in that direction, and just as my hand touched the knob, Gay's voice came through the closed door.

"Then would you mind telling me why you were searching your father's pockets a while ago, and what you wanted with the key you took out of them?"

I flung open the living-room door in the silence.

"Well, Mike?" I said.

Closing the door behind me, I leaned against it. The person who had forced the door of Jude's room to lure or to force Norman Farrington out toward the bluff must have known that the old man was there and that he had used a key to get there. No one else should have known of the existence of that key. And Norman Farrington's son had gone in search of it and found it! He was standing there gazing at me as a man might gaze at a snake which had sprung at him in the middle of Fifth Avenue.

"You heard that, I suppose?" Michael's voice was bleak.

"Yes." Suddenly, unreasonably I thought, "We are three characters in a play. Nothing has happened. Nothing will happen until we remember the lines."

Michael's hand shot into his coat pocket and dragged out something which dropped into my own hand. I found myself staring down at the skeleton key from Norman Farrington's pocket, staring at it and wishing violently that I had never seen the damned thing.

"How did you know it was there?"

"Guilt!" Michael's voice was hurt, not bitter. And Mike was no actor—or was he? The radio stunt—

Gay rushed to his rescue. "This is ridiculous! I was being a sap. That's all."

"So you think!" This time Michael's voice was harsh. "But Jimmie doesn't. Look at his face."

"Hold on, Mike," I said. "I haven't said a word. Answer me decently, can't you?"

He looked at me and suddenly his face creased into a grin. "All right," he said. "I went snooping around. Saw the broken lock on Jude's door and just happened to think that if my father had a key in his pocket, we could be pretty sure that you were right about his fall not being an accident. You see, if he was the guy who crowned William, he must have gotten through that door after it was locked. I saw you examine it afterward, and it was all right the second time you locked it."

I didn't believe him. He was following my own train of thought—but I didn't believe him. Would anyone ever be able to trust anybody after this ghastly mess was over?

"Good." The friendliness of my voice was a little lesson in hypocrisy all in itself. "That was what I was thinking. We're letting ourselves get too jumpy."

Gay sprawled on a sofa. "I'm cured!" she sighed gustily. "If I ask another question, wring my neck! Who has a cigarette?"

Watching Michael's lighter flare, I observed, "A few more questions and we'll all go gaga. It's time this outfit did a little relaxing."

But we didn't do any too well at it. There we sat, three people who forty-eight hours before would have sworn on a stack of Bibles that we would have trusted each other till the end of time. And we hadn't—and didn't. I was distrustful of Mike. Gay had precipitated the whole scene because she shared the feeling. And Mike, if he were innocent, could have taken that key for only one reason—to prevent the murderer's finding it. If he had been sure that neither of us was the murderer, he would certainly have told us of his discovery. If he were innocent—if he had been sure. If! If! If! The word beat a weary rhythmical refrain in my head the while we chatted aimlessly about little Tessie Blake and her meandering husband, about the inadvisability of looking for a new apartment until our plans for the summer were more definite.

The conversation dragged, dwindled, and finally expired. Coherent thought, it would seem, expired with it. If I tried to think about the Skipper's whereabouts, the probable guilt of the Millers obtruded itself into the picture. If I tried to come to any conclusion about the Millers, I immediately thought of Higgins. And so it went. Out of the long silence came Michael's voice.

"They had trouble with Cook after you went out. Hysterics with all the trimmings."

I jumped at a loophole for escape. "Cook?" I said. "Hysterics? I'll just have a look at her. Be right back."

"Meaning that we'll see you at breakfast?" demanded Gay testily.

William, his face decidedly strained, opened Cook's door.

He didn't seem to have any intention of letting me into the room. "She's better, sir. I guess she'll be all right. Has Miss Barbara been—" He left the question dangling.

"No," I said shortly. "Do you mind?" And I elbowed past him.

Cook's hysterics had been genuine enough. Her face was ghastly. There were great sagging circles under her eyes and her chin was quivering painfully.

"How are you now?" I tried to sound kind.

All of her remarkable volubility was gone. She played restlessly with the covers without looking up.

"I ain't so good, sir." It was the weak, exhausted voice of a sick woman. "I ain't so good."

Well, considering the state she had been in when she had prepared dinner, that was not at all surprising.

"It's nearly morning now. It will soon be over."

"Yes," closing her eyes, "yes—nearly morning."

I waited for William to close the door after me. Then I stepped across to Higgins' room, found my key, knocked softly, and went in. The old man had been sitting on the bed, head in hands and fully dressed. His face was haggard.

"It's only I, Higgins," I said, sitting down beside him. "Don't be frightened. I came to see how you were."

"I'm doing very well, sir." With a start I realized that he had been crying.

"Higgins," I said. "I don't for a minute believe that you are guilty and I'm trying my best to prove that you're not. Do you believe that?"

For a fleeting second his eyes rested on my face, but they immediately looked away.

"Yes—Mr. Jimmie," he said shakily.

I put a hand on his shoulder. "You almost told me something once," I said. "Tell me now. No one can hear us, and it may be important."

"I can't, sir. It ain't that I don't trust you. I'd trust you like I would Mr. Michael himself. It ain't that at all, sir."

"Then what is it, Higgins?"

"I was wrong, sir. And you might not believe that I was, and—and that would be awful. Awful! I found out how wrong I was. I can't tell you nothing, sir!"

"Can't you tell me what you found out? It might be just as important."

"No!" The fierceness of his answer made me jump.

Lighting a cigarette, I got to my feet and began to pace the small room. His head in his hands, the old man seemed to forget my existence. He was not guilty. But he knew who was—or thought he did. He was withholding evidence—evidence that I had to have right then. I looked at my watch. It was four-thirty.

I made one last desperate try. "Miss Barbara is alive." All the conviction I could muster rang in my voice. "We know that for a fact, Higgins. But unless she is found within the next hour, she may not be."

He got to his feet like a man staggering into a warm house out of a blizzard.

"Are you sure of that?" he whispered hoarsely.

The pressure of my clenched fists was driving my fingernails into flesh. "Positive!"

"Then—then—" For one awful moment I thought he was going to strangle before he got the words out. "Don't—don't tell no one I said so. I ain't sure it's right. Look for the old loft."

I stared at him blankly. "Loft?" I echoed.

"Yes. Take Mr. Michael. He should be able to find it."

21

"James!" It was M. Farrington on the davenport. "Stop it this instant! What is it? Where are you going?"

I had scant time for entangling my wits with Queen Victoria!

"The loft!" I shouted. "The loft! The Skipper may be there." I had Michael by the arm and was tugging him in the direction of the door, but he held back.

"The loft?" he echoed. "You're crazy! There isn't any."

Higgins' last words were ringing in my ears. *Take Mr. Michael. He should be able to find it.*

"Another of your sudden inspirations, Jim?" came Gay's voice sweetly.

I seized Michael. "Don't lie to me!" I howled. "You're taking me there or I'll break your lousy neck!"

Michael threw me off easily.

"Don't be a fool," he said quietly. "You're not going to tell me whether or not there's a loft in my own—" His voice trailed off and his eyes suddenly widened.

"Good Lord!" he said hoarsely. "There is a— Come on!"

I didn't stop to find out what he was talking about. There was a rush of voices behind us, but we tore for the front stairs. At the head of them Michael swerved to the right and sprinted once more toward the servants' corridor.

He swung into the other hall before I was halfway from the stairs. By the time I reached the swinging door, he had a ladder-like set of steps pulled straight down from the ceiling directly in front of the head of the back stairs.

"Not in use," he panted. "Forgot it completely." He disappeared into blackness.

I followed him, barking my shins again as I went over the edge.

"Skipper!" he was calling. "Skipper! Skipper!"

In the darkness, there was no sound but our own heavy breathing. The air was dusty and heavy. Squatting on the edge of that trap door, I felt a sneeze coming, tried to muffle it, failed.

"Damn it!" said Michael. "Shut up, can't you?"

He was listening. I could feel the tension of his body where he crouched against me. But there wasn't a sound.

"Are there any lights, Mike?" I whispered.

"No."

It was like us to be without a light at that moment. I didn't have heart enough to swear. Michael was edging himself away from the trap into the darkness. He bumped into me as he went and I felt a bulge in his coat pocket—the bulge of William's flashlight.

"Mike!" I said. "You have the flashlight. In your coat!"

His hand flipped into the pocket. There was a grunt of relief and the next moment a beam of light gradually disclosed a section of the room we were in. It was low and directly under the rafters. The eaves sloped down to the floor and at its highest point it was not over five feet high. If the old carriage loft had brought to my mind the dust of other decades, this gave me a feeling of the dust of other centuries. It was full of Farrington relics. Furniture, clothes, mattresses, trunks, suitcases, chests, bedding. Apparently it ran over the outer section of the servants' quarters and had not been used in years. The atmosphere was musty and stifling.

Michael's light came slowly down to the floor at our feet. At the head of the trap door the floor was polished clean as a whistle by the clothes of persons coming up from below. The glancing of the light on my own knees showed me a gray film of dust coating my trousers. But beyond that polished space and beyond the hodgepodge of our footmarks, a clear trail of footprints led off in the direction of the other end of the loft. There were two sets of them, blurred as if made by people walking either in stockinged feet or slippers. Michael's light flashed around in a circle. Not five feet away from that double trail was a single set—returning.

We painfully skirted trunks, old bureaus, and wash-stands. Once we narrowly escaped disaster when Michael, banging into a cedar chest, dropped the light. The air got thinner and mustier as we proceeded. It was dawning on me that we should have to work rapidly. There were no windows in that loft. If the Skipper was there, she had been there for hours.

"Mike! Mike! Where are you?" It was Gay from the direction of the trap door.

Michael shouted, "Go back! Stay with Aunt Martha. We'll be there in a minute."

A thick row of old draperies hung from the rafters. A pile of bolsters. I nearly yelled when I banged into an old bustled dress. As we went along the chances of the Skipper's still being alive seemed to grow slimmer and slimmer. I tried to think what one did for a case of suffocation, but the only word that came to my mind was, "Dead—dead—dead!"

"Could a person live six hours in this?" I whispered to Michael.

His only answer was a grunt. Leading the way around a tall old mirror, he pulled up with a bang, his breath whistling into the silence. Over his shoulder I peered into the circle of our light. The footprints had stopped. There was a blur of stirred up dust and a long trail of smooth, clean boards leading directly up to a heavy cedar chest. Right at our feet, scattering out as far as our light would reach, were the broken pieces of some horrible china contraption—probably a vase.

Before I had half taken in the situation Michael leapt forward. His head rapped smartly against a sloping rafter, and he staggered back, grunting. In another instant he was crouched and in under that eave. The chest was crashing out of the way, nearly upsetting me.

The Skipper was lying on her side, her hands bound behind her with strips of white cloth and her ankles securely tied with similar pieces. A crusty, dark streak ran across her entire face.

Between us we managed to get her out into the open. Michael thrust a penknife in my hand.

"Cut the damn things. Cut them! Cut them!" He was weaving around me in circles, his voice clamorous.

I wasn't much more use. The knife twisted and turned in my hand and the cloth seemed to be made of iron. Dropping the useless blade I tore madly at the knots. It went on and on. And Michael continued to bellow. Flinging down the final strip at last, I felt for the Skipper's heart. I couldn't hear a thing—only the mad pounding of my own pulse.

"Get out of the way!" I lifted the Skipper in my arms. "Hold the light, can't you? We've got to get her out of here."

He held it, after a fashion—unsteadily, wobbling back and forth in and out of my range of vision. We made but slow progress through that maze of relics. The Skipper was an unresisting dead weight in my arms, and it was necessary to bend almost double to avoid the rafters. I could hear Michael's breath now at my side, now in back of me. I nearly tripped a dozen times. My arms ached and I couldn't seem to breathe by the time the light of the trap door finally appeared.

"Get William," I wheezed. "Yell for him."

Michael yelled, his voice ringing wildly through that empty loft. An answering roar came immediately from below, and the next instant William's head appeared through the trap.

"Get down a few rungs!" I panted. "I'll—hand—her—down."

William was quick and efficient. Slowly we lowered our limp bundle into his waiting arms. I followed him with Michael clattering behind me. I could hear M. Farrington's excited voice in William's room, interrupted by Gay's soothing one. I saw Annie, white and trembling, in Cook's doorway. But William was halfway down the corridor. I caught up with him as he strode into my room and laid his burden on my bed. His large hand went immediately to the Skipper's heart and stayed there for at least ten seconds.

"Get a mirror," he said at length in a hushed voice.

I leapt to obey him. Without a word he held the thing over the Skipper's nose and mouth. I was obliged to hold on to Michael to prevent interference. And then William turned the mirror up. It was covered with a fine mist.

His voice barked at us, "Open the windows! Quick!"

I did—and a great many other things in the next half hour, until I became violently ill myself—and had to be taken out.

William was just lowering the Skipper's head to the pillow as I reentered the room shakily a long time later. The glass he had handed Gay was empty, but the patient's face was still ghastly, her eyes closed, and her breathing now painfully audible from across the room. I caught sight of Michael. Beads of perspiration were standing out on his forehead. His hands were clenched, his eyes shut.

I went out into the hall, groping for a cigarette and trying to deafen my ears to the sounds from the other room. I had had enough. Even the thought of the approaching hour of reckoning failed to move me. The Skipper would tell her story. The police would come. And for my part at that moment, I didn't care what she might tell them or what they might do about it. I was through. Or so I thought.

It must have been a good ten minutes before I realized that Michael had joined me.

"Got a cigarette?" he said.

The gloomy vigil had just begun. After a long time

I became conscious of the scene outside the window.

The trees along the drive were standing out in sharp relief. I could even see the outline of the drive itself in the misty gray light. My watch said five minutes of six. We were within a few hours of the end.

"It's getting light, Mike," I said pointlessly.

Michael, staring fixedly out of the window, didn't stir. I put an impulsive hand on his shoulder, half expecting it to be shaken off. It wasn't. And so we stood there. A hollow feeling in my middle and a lightness in my head spelled breakfast, but I had a feeling that once confronted with food I would not be able to eat it. Suddenly I wanted to get back into that sick-room to find out—whatever there was to find out. But I didn't like to propose that to Michael and I didn't like to leave him alone.

A hand falling on my arm made me jump. Gay was standing there.

"She's going to be all right. She's asleep finally."

Michael spun around. "Are you sure? It may be hours before we can get a doctor."

"Of course I'm sure. Her breathing is all right now and her pulse is good. I took it myself. Mickie—" Her voice was doing things that could mean only a sentimental interlude. I interrupted peevishly.

"Did she say anything?"

Gay glanced at me briefly. "She said she was sorry to be such a damned nuisance. If anyone should happen to ask me, I'd say we got out of this pretty darned lucky."

I tiptoed into the Skipper's room. She did look better. There was a slight tinge of color in her face. But God! How haggard she was! Her cheek bones stood out sharply; her eyes were great black hollows; and her hair in the dim light of the bed lamp showed almost entirely iron-gray. And only a few months before— It was unthinkable!

I found myself reverting to one all-important question. Jude's family. Who was to tell them? It would be sheer cruelty to leave the job to any one of the three Farringtons. Gay had never met the Blinshops. And that left me.

Right then and there I began to lay plans. We would say absolutely nothing to the natives who arrived from the village. I would go back with them and straight to George Foster, the coroner. I knew Foster, a fat old boy who loved above all thing to troll for bass. I would tell him the whole story and leave it up to him. He had spent a lifetime in such messes, and he had been a lifetime friend of the Farringtons. If anyone knew what to do, he would. Then I would either hire a car in the village or borrow Foster's, and head straight for Blinshop—

Screaming through that silent house came the unmistakable sound of a pistol shot, fired at no great distance from where I sat.

22

My eyes darted to the Skipper's face. She hadn't stirred. Reaching over, I found her pulse to be strong and steady. Without hesitating I dashed into the hall in the direction from which the sound had come—the other side of the house, near my room. It must be in the servants' quarters. As I crashed through the swinging door I saw the door of Higgins' room standing open, and two more steps brought me within range of all I wanted to see.

Higgins lay sprawled grotesquely over the bed. In one hand was the much discussed revolver. A small, blue hole showed in one of his temples. There was a great deal of blood on the coverlet. The house was ringing with pounding feet.

"He's done it!" shouted William. "He's done himself in!"

I tried to answer, but I couldn't get out a single word. So it was Higgins after all. Higgins, the dignified, pompous old codger, to die like this! There were screams in the hall, screams and babbling voices. M. Farrington was resisting Michael's attempts to turn her away from the ghastly sight, and Gay on the other side of the old lady was doing her best to help. Beyond them in the hall, Annie was standing in her nightdress, wide-eyed and shaking. I took Gay's arm roughly.

"Go back to the Skipper," I said. "Don't leave her for any reason." Gay seemed to be the only person there with even a mild trace of sanity. She went without a word.

"Please, Aunt Martha!" Michael was saying. "Come away. Please—"

M. Farrington's voice went zooming up the scale wildly. "I will look! I must! I don't believe it! He was here before I was born! He—"

I tried my hand. "Aunt Martha," I said, shaking her none too gently, "Mike can't stand any more of this. He's all in. Take him out of here."

For an instant it was touch and go, whether the ruse would work or whether she would go off in hysterics. I could see them rising in her spasmodically working throat. And then, "Of course. Of course!"

The look of relief on Michael's face was enough for me. I turned back into the room, hearing William's voice in the distance ordering Annie to go back and watch Cook. Once more William and I faced each other over the body.

"I suppose," I said through stiff lips, "we could do something to stop this bleeding. It's—messy."

William's voice wasn't steady. "I wouldn't touch nothing, sir. The police will want to see it just like it is."

"It seems beastly to—leave it—alone like this."

"Well, wait a minute, sir."

Before I could stop him, William was out of the room. It was all I could do to keep from shouting after him. I turned away from the sickening sight and leaned heavily upon the dresser. Something bulky under the scarf attracted my attention and I lifted the thing automatically. Lying face upward on the dark oak surface were the two letters that had so mysteriously disappeared from William's room. I was still glaring at the things when William reappeared with a dark blanket which he drew carefully over the bed.

"Look here, William."

There was more curiosity than surprise on his face as he took the things. "So that's it. He wasn't a bad sort until something got under his skin—whatever it was."

I blinked dazedly. That was the question. What earthly reason could there be for Higgins' amazing actions? A contented, gentle old man with the rest of his life mapped out for him as pleasantly as anyone could wish, suddenly goes hay-wire and kills a girl he has known since her babyhood, a man whom he has spent a good part of his life caring for, and finally attempts to kill the two people who represent all the family and security that he has. It didn't make sense. There could be no question of money as a motive. I happened to know that the entire Farrington fortune had been left in trust for Michael by his grandfather with a request that Higgins be provided for as long as he lived. The only solution seemed to be insanity.

"It's a hopeless mess, William. Can you think what could have ailed him?"

William shook his head. "Must have been plumb nutty, I guess. Didn't seem like that, but he must have been. Funny. You know, when I was working for the Blinshops I always thought Higgins was crazy about Miss Judith."

I looked around that bare little room and shivered. Then I walked out—very softly.

My watch said twenty minutes past six. There was little point in trying to hustle people off to bed. We were bound to be routed out again within a very few hours, and I knew from experience that a little sleep is worse that none at all. It was highly doubtful that anyone would be able to sleep anyway. Snapping on the low lamp on the dresser, I turned out the glaring overhead lights. Gently I closed the door on Higgins' room and made off in the direction of the main house. Cold showers, breakfast, and a plan of action were in order.

Michael's room was empty, but in mine the Skipper was still sleeping soundly. Gay was standing at the window.

"Where are the others?" I whispered.

"I'm not sure. They went down the hall somewhere—Miss Farrington's room, I guess. Jim—are—are you sure it's over?"

"Absolutely sure, Gay. Was the Skipper disturbed at all?"

"No." Her hands were restless. "Whatever possessed him? Does anyone know?"

I drew her into the next room. "I doubt it," I said, "and I doubt if anyone ever will. Now listen, kid. Go take a cold shower and freshen up. William will stir up some breakfast. See that Aunt Martha does the same thing and send Mike along to me. All the majesty of the law is going to be loose around here in a little while and it isn't going to be much fun."

"O.K." There was something about the jaunty tilt of the kid's chin that I liked. I stopped her.

"Gay," I said, "there'll be a pretty big fuss over this in the papers. If Mike suddenly gets noble ideas about not soiling the hem of your gown, don't let him get away with it."

She flashed me a grin that sent my spirits soaring.

"Sonny," she said, "if he thinks he can get away from me now, he'll need the militia to help him."

Her feet clattered cheerfully down the hall. Hauling out clean clothes, I felt a little better. It was over at last. I was jumping around in the shower when I heard Michael come in. Grabbing a towel, I strode dripping after him.

But if my spirits were up, his were hitting a new, all-time low. He flopped down on the bed.

"Don't be such a damned Pollyanna!" he growled.

My spirits began to slide. "How's M. Farrington?"

"How do you think? Jim, what the devil do you suppose ailed him? Why did he do it? It's—it's—"

"Cut it out, Mike," I said. "We don't know and probably we never will. What difference does it make now? Get into that shower. You're all in."

Michael kicked at the rug. "It makes a lot of difference. Higgins never had a thing wrong with him in his life. And he never did a thing in his life but look after my damned family."

Michael has an Irish streak which calls for the noble and highly dramatic. Right then I had no answer for him. I felt rather like a person lost in the woods who knows there is an animal of some sort behind him, but doesn't dare turn around to look. Higgins must have had a motive. But just then I didn't care to turn around and look at it.

"The police," I said, "will have no reason for thinking anything but that the poor old chap lost his mind. You haven't either. Stop trying to dig yourself up a family skeleton. Go take—"

"The hell with your shower!" Michael exploded. "Who gives a damn what the police think? I've got to know why he did it. I've got—"

"—to take a shower," I finished grimly. Picking him up clothes and all, I carted him, struggling, into the bathroom. It was something of a job to hold him, but he was thoroughly doused before he managed to send me crashing on my ear and stalk out. I threw him a towel.

"Take a rubdown," I said.

"You go to Hell!" But he caught the towel with his bad hand. I grinned and set to work on my own dressing, leaving him to his fuming. The atmosphere was so natural that I could have whooped for joy. I was busy with my tie before he got to the point where he could directly address me.

"Do you suppose there is any way that they could leave the Aunts out of all this? If the story about my father hits the headlines, Aunt Martha will never get over it. Foster ought to be able to keep them away from the Skipper for a while anyway."

I said, "I think the best thing to do, Mike, is for me to go into the village on the first boat that gets here. I'll go straight to Foster and leave it all up to him. Then, if he'll let me, I'll push on to the Blinshops'. Ought to be back by seven tomorrow night, easily."

Michael was silent for a moment. "That's decent of you, Jim."

I climbed into my coat. "Forget it," I said. "Keep your ear cocked for the Skipper. I'll see how the breakfast is coming."

In broad daylight, the effect of the electricity in the hall was rather ghostly. The sooner we got all the lights out and the house nearly normal, the better for everyone concerned. Switching them off as I went, I headed down the hall and into the servants' quarters. At the head of the back stairs I remembered the lights in Higgins' room and in Jude's. I turned back. With my eyes averted from the bed, I made for Higgins' dresser. And then something leapt into my throat.

Directly in front of me at the level of my eyes, was a splotch in the wall plaster, and within that splotch the bullet which had ended Higgins' life. Passing a bewildered hand over my eyes, I looked again. There was no mistake. The bullet was there. Was my memory of the situation blurred? I rushed to the bed and flung back the blanket.

Higgins lay on his back with his arms flung out at his sides, the revolver tightly clenched in the right hand. In his right temple was the bullet hole, and in the left, the nasty gash made by the bullet tearing through. But the mark in the plaster was in the wall on his right!

Ideas began bouncing through my head. A man falling in a faint or for any reason other than a blow, falls on his face. Unless Higgins had been sitting on the bed, he could never have landed in that position. Could he have been sitting? I crouched until my head was approximately at the level of a person sitting on the bed. For a bullet to have passed through both sides of the man's head and landed where it had, it must have passed right through the top of his skull. And Higgins' wounds were in his temples.

Much as the idea of the old man's guilt hurt, I wanted the whole thing to be over with. Perhaps, I reasoned frantically, the impact of the bullet spun him around. Perhaps— My next realization sent me staggering against the wall. The revolver was in his right hand, and Higgins had been left-handed! Murder number three!

Right then and there my state of mind clarified. All along I had been nearly as much afraid that we would catch the murderer as I was that we wouldn't. But I thought of that tortured old face as I had last seen it alive. I took one more look at it as it was then. And I wanted that murderer. If it was Michael himself, I was going to see him die before my own eyes. My mind began to work as coldly as if it were dealing with a problem in bridge. Not the Skipper. I had been sitting beside her when the shot was fired. Furthermore, the murderer had put her behind that chest. Higgins must have seen them, to his undoing.

I checked them off on my fingers. Gay, Michael, M. Farrington, William, Annie, and—yes, and Cook. Ill as she was, Cook could have crossed that hall, fired, wanted a trap—a trap that no alibi could spring. And I wanted it before they all collected for breakfast and the murderer had a chance to suspect that his plan had not worked.

There was only one question on which any trap could hinge—the reason for the presence of the revolver in Higgins' right hand. It could have been put there because the murderer was ignorant of the fact that it should have been in the left hand, because the murderer forgot in his excitement, or because the murderer desired to throw suspicion on someone else. They all seemed good possibilities. The choice depended entirely upon the identity of the culprit.

Of all the people in the house, Gay was the only person who could have done it out of ignorance. She was also the one person in the house against who there had been not one shred of evidence at any time. She was impulsive and hotheaded. The murderer might or might not be either. The murderer certainly was cold, logical, and capable of swift action. In a crisis Gay was all of those things. It was possible that her rows with Michael had been a safety valve for more nerve strain than we had realized. Yes, Gay was capable of those murders, but I could not even remotely guess at a reason behind them.

Michael, on the other hand, certainly knew all of Higgins' characteristics. If Michael had placed that gun in the butler's right hand, he had done it because he lost his head. And Michael in such a situation would be quite apt to lose his head. His aunt, on the contrary, would be very cool. And M. Farrington did not like Gay. I could not help feeling that if M. Farrington were ever aroused to the point of committing a murder, she would not hesitate to cast suspicion on any luckless soul who had incurred her dislike. It seemed as if both Cook and Annie would have lost their heads in such a situation. But William would be cool as ice. But, without exception, every one of them knew that Higgins was left-handed.

I sought a trap that would hinge around those characteristics as I saw them and around the peculiar circumstances in which the body was found. The sight of the body was not much help. I covered it.

Then I started methodically and worked my way from the bed around the room, under the rug, under the bed, through the pitifully few possessions in the dresser and wardrobe. Not many spoils to show for seventy-odd years of hard work. For my purpose, nothing to show at all.

It was quarter of seven. At any time now the round-up for breakfast was apt to start and something told me that I must question the suspects individually or give up the whole attempt. Hopelessly I stared at that room, trying to wring its secret from it. A trap! I must spring a trap—now. And my mind was a blank. I stared down at the figure on the bed and the idea came. Three strides took me into the hall. Conclusive proof or otherwise, I knew what I was going to do.

23

All the way to Gay's door I was thinking of only one possibility. What if she wasn't there? But she must be!

"Come in!" called a cheerful voice. "Oh—hello, Jim, I was just going to start down. Why—what's the matter?"

I put a finger to my lips. "Shhhh!" I said hoarsely. "Don't let the others hear you. Come quickly."

She gave me one awful look and the brush in her hand fell clattering to the floor. "Jimmie, what is it? Oh—"

But I clapped a hand over her mouth before the scream was fairly started.

"Quiet!". I hissed. "I've just discovered something they'll all have to see. You'll have to—show me how to break it to them."

I had not underestimated Gay Palmer. She was suddenly as calm as if I had merely come to escort her to breakfast. When the panic was completely gone from her eyes I removed my hand.

"Is it Mike?" she demanded levelly. "Don't fool with me, Jim. Is he all right?"

"He's all right," I said, leading her into the hall. That short silent walk to Higgins' room was ghastly. I was obliged to concentrate on all the worst features of the crimes before I could force myself to push open his door. Gay walked in without a sign of alarm, and I followed her, closing the door and putting my back against it. Swiftly her eyes swept the room from the bed to the far wall and back to my face.

"Why—what is it?" she said blankly.

There was a dead, heavy weight in my chest. Whatever she had done, this was the girl that Michael wanted to marry. Violently I wished that my slow wits had been able to devise something quick and conclusive in place of my slow, questionable scheme. I was banking desperately on the Skipper's evidence. Briefly, I had reasoned that if one of the servants was the culprit, the Skipper's evidence added to the circumstantial chain which I had built up against them, would be all that was necessary. However, if a member of the Skipper's family or a person who might shortly become a member of it was guilty, the Skipper would lie, and it would be necessary for someone else to prove their guilt.

Going back over the scene of the finding of Higgins' body, I had realized that neither Michael, Gay, nor M. Farrington could possibly have seen the body as it lay on the bed. Annie and William had been standing in the doorway, completely blocking off their view. Consequently, if any one of them knew in what position both the body and the gun had been found, that person was the murderer.

I intended to ask each one in turn to help me prove that Higgins was a suicide. The murderer had had plenty of time to ponder over his or her blunders. Therefore, if any one of the three could reconstruct the scene of the crime, satisfying in full all of its peculiar circumstances, that person was the person I wanted. If not, we had simply to wait until the Skipper was well enough to tell her story.

"Jimmie! What ails you? Are you sick?"

I shook my head to clear it. "No," I said, "just tired. Listen. We'll have to send for the police as soon as someone gets here from shore. And there's something wrong with this. If Higgins killed himself in here, the bullet ought to be here. It's the first thing the police will look for. And I can't find it anywhere."

"Hmmm," said Gay slowly. "That's so." She paused a moment and then her face brightened. "Well, look! He must have been either standing by the bed or sitting on it. If he was standing, the bullet ought to be in the door. If he was sitting, it must be in the wall above or behind the bed. The darned thing could have gone right between those iron bars."

She was assuming that Higgins had used his right hand, and that there was nothing peculiar about the wounds in his head. Hedging for time, I examined the door carefully, felt along the wall above the bed, and even moved the bed to look at the dusty surface behind it.

"That's funny," said Gay.

I had some thinking to do. "Wait," I grunted, moving the bed back into place. "Let me think. Yes, of course! The door was open!"

If there was anything in her face but an unflattering opinion of my intelligence, I couldn't see it.

"Then the thing must be in the hall, you sap!" she said scornfully. I followed her into the hall and examined the wall solemnly. My head wouldn't seem to clear. I had the impression that my bright little scheme was flopping.

Gay's face was worried. "This is ridiculous, Jim. It must be here!"

Was she acting? I played my last card. "Good Lord! Am I a lunkhead! The old boy was left-handed."

Sincere or feigned, there was plenty of disgust in the look she leveled at me. Perhaps I was gullible, but at that moment I was sure that my information meant nothing to Gay Palmer.

"Not a lunkhead," she said in a withering voice. "Just a moron!" Walking back into Higgins' room she swept the far wall with eager eyes and moved straight to the hole in the plaster. "Here you are, sleuth. Sometime when you're short of cash, why don't you sell that head of yours for a curiosity? You wouldn't miss it."

I tried to look crushed and I managed to beam like an idiot. "I must be getting old," I murmured.

"Or feeble-minded," said Gay. "Come on to breakfast."

"Go ahead down. I'll collect Michael and the Aunt. I think the Skipper will be all right for half an hour."

There was one danger that I had overlooked—the likelihood of our being intercepted in the hall. But Gay solved my problem before I could begin to tussle with it.

"I'll go through the kitchen and see if they need help," she said. "Do you think you can get two whole people down the stairs before another brainstorm strikes you?"

I turned my back on her, but I didn't move until I heard her reach the kitchen. Then I turned and galloped down the hall at full speed. Outside Michael's room I paused long enough to screw my face into a glum expression and thrust my hands dejectedly into my pockets.

Michael turned a red face from his one-handed struggle with a tie.

"It's about time," he said. "Fix this damn thing, will you, before I go completely nuts?"

I fixed it, sank gloomily upon the bed, and took to a studious contemplation of the floor. Michael grunted into a vest, swore himself into a coat, selected a handkerchief to his taste, and finally became conscious of me.

"Well," he said irritably, "now what's the matter? Aren't things bad enough without any high tragedy from you?"

"Mike," I said, "I don't like it."

"You don't say. Now look at me. I just love it! Another minute and I'll be turning handsprings."

That mood always annoyed me. I let my irritation go with a vengeance.

"Don't be any more of an imbecile than you have to!" I snapped. "And keep your voice down. There's no crying necessity for waking the Skipper that I can see."

"Who's waking the Skipper?" He flipped open his cigarette case, found it empty and flung it violently on the bed. "Damn it, Jimmie, I simply request that you do something besides run around looking like Banquo's ghost. For God's sake get over the idea that you're the only person with a headache! I'm the host of this damned murder fest, if you happen to remember."

I was ashamed of myself. It was bad enough to plan cold-bloodedly the proof that your best friend was a murderer, but to bait him was inexcusable. Stealing a glance at him, I nearly abandoned the whole idea. He looked terrible. Something about his face reminded me of the Skipper in the next room.

"I'm sorry," I said. "I'm—I'm sorry."

He stared at me a moment. "Don't look like that!" he growled. "It's my fault. I'm jumpy. Forget it."

"All right." I shoved my cigarettes at him. "Any sound from the Skipper?"

"No. I wish we could get a doctor here now. Jim—" The flare of the match lighted up his drawn face. "You don't suppose this will have any after effects—heart or anything—do you?"

"I don't see why it should," I said.

"If it does," said Michael bitterly, "I'll never forgive myself."

"You?" Great God! Was the crazy fool going to confide his guilt to me just as I was busily trying to prove it for myself? "Don't be absurd, man! What have you got to do with it?"

"If I'd insisted on her going south, she would have been forced to tell me what was on her mind, and my father would have been sent back where he belonged."

It took me fully ten seconds to get my breath. "You think your father's presence caused all this?"

"It must have. It was the only unusual thing that I can think of."

Michael crushed his barely lighted cigarette. I studied his face.

"Do you think that also explains Higgins' extraordinary behavior?"

"No." The face was cloudy. "Damn it, it doesn't explain anything. Jim, what could have ailed him?"

"You've got me, Mike," I said truthfully. "Has it occurred to you that there's something mighty peculiar about the way Higgins died?"

He whirled on me. "What do you mean?"

"Well," I was picking my words with care, "when a bullet goes through a man's head, it lands somewhere. Of course, the police will be better than I was, but I'll be damned if I can find it—anywhere."

His eyes were boring into my face. "Are you sure it went through?"

"Positive. There's a mark where it went in and a gash where it came out."

I delivered the end of that sentence to an empty room. Michael had started for Higgins' door, and if he got a glimpse of the face under that blanket before I had staged my act, it was all over. Everything I had went into the sprint that brought me up to him just as he halted at the side of the bed. Two seconds later and I would not have been in time to grab the hand he reached toward the blanket.

"Don't, Mike," I said. "It's—pretty bad."

Ordinarily wild horses couldn't have stopped him. Was it exhaustion or was it guilt in his face and trembling hands?

"Perhaps—you're right." His voice was muffled. There was a silence and then he straightened up. "All we have to do is reconstruct the scene. He must have been either on the bed or beside it—unless someone moved him. Did anyone touch him?"

"Not so far as I know," I said in the steadiest voice I could muster.

"Then he must have been doing one of the two. That means that the bullet—" His eyes turned to the far wall and picked out the splotch in the plaster immediately. His voice stopped. The next instant his grasp on my arm made me wince. "What the devil is the big idea?"

I was fighting to keep my voice down. "What do you mean?"

"That bullet is right where it should be. What kind of damned stunt is this?"

I shook him off. "I don't know what you're talking about," I grated. "There isn't any bullet. I've been over this door a dozen times—even moved the bed and looked in the hall. If you find anything, you're better than I am!"

There was an awful moment of silence, and then Michael began to chuckle—a chuckle that sent the blood back into my singing head.

"Jimmie—" he said. "Jimmie—you're a dud! Higgins was—oh, Lord!—left-handed! Look." He pointed to the far wall. "Here's your bullet, right where it ought to be."

Either I was witnessing some masterly acting or Michael had no conception of the state in which the body had been found. I stared at that tiny section of cracked plaster as if I had never seen it before in my life.

"Come along," he said at last. "You need food!"

If my little attempt did nothing else, it had at least restored Michael to a good humor. He was still chuckling when we reached the head of the stairs.

"Go look after your love-life," I said. "I'll get the Aunt. I'll cough when—"

"It won't be necessary," said Michael, clattering down the stairs.

M. Farrington alone remained, and I rather relished the idea of an encounter with the irascible old lady. I knocked on her door and called, "It's Jimmie, Aunt Martha."

There was a slight pause and then a truculent voice said, "Come in."

M. Farrington was dressed and waiting. I could see at a glance that she had been crying, but her mood was far from mellow.

"It's about time you put in an appearance, young man," she said curtly. "Where under the sun is Michael—or that Palmer girl? Am I to sit here all morning waiting for my breakfast?" No, *mellow* was not the word.

"I'm sorry, Aunt Martha. Mike's been having a bad time trying to dress himself. I sent him down to Gay to see if she couldn't calm him."

It was the wrong approach. "Calm him!" snorted M. Farrington. "That little red-headed thing has had him on pins and needles ever since she got here. How is Barbara?"

"Sleeping." I tried to make my voice soothing. "She'll be O.K. when she wakes up."

"Hmmph! Under the circumstances you might find a better word for it. I suppose that if I am very good my chauffeur will allow me to see her for a few moments just before dinner. Come along, James! Now what is the matter?" I was hesitating with my hand on the door.

"Aunt Martha, there's something I wanted to talk to you about before the police arrive."

Her eyes blazed indignantly. "Police? Is that quite necessary? You may tell George Foster that I won't allow it!"

"I'm afraid it will be out of his hands," I said. "He can help with the papers, of course, but—Aunt Martha, we ought to establish the fact that Higgins was a suicide, before the police get here—and—and—"

"Don't stutter. I shan't scream. And *what?*"

"And in order to prove that, we must prove that the bullet which killed him came from the gun in his hand."

Her eyes widened. "Then find the bullet, James!" she said sharply.

"I've been trying to. It—it just isn't there."

"Nonsense! It must be. Did you look in his head?"

"It passed right through his head."

Her chin went, if anything, a little higher. "James, you couldn't find anything if it were tied to the end of your nose. Never could. Open that door."

She was something to look at, I can tell you, with the tears still wet on her face, striding down that hall like a major-general. The rest of us might be ready for sanatoriums before we were through, but not Martha Farrington.

"Children should be brought up with a little self-reliance," she stated. "If a man is shot, he is shot by a bullet. Obvious."

"Yes, ma'am," I said meekly, and we paraded forthwith into Higgins' room.

Her face grew grim as she caught sight of that bed. But her voice was ragged.

"Poor Higgins," she said. "Poor, loyal fellow. James!"

The last word came with such unexpected force as to make me jump. "Yes, ma'am?" I said in the involuntary tone of my youth.

"Were you the first person to find him?"

"Yes. He was lying just as he is now."

"I see." Her face screwed in thought. "He was about your height. Stand over there by the wall."

Without a word I obeyed her.

"Now then, a man about to kill himself is in no state of mind to sit down. He must have been standing here," she suited the acted to the word, "with his gun in his hand like this." She stood facing the bed dramatically. "He pulls the trigger, is spun completely around by the force of the explosion, and lands on his back on the bed. The bullet must be over your head there, James."

The blanket over the dead man's face had not been moved. From the moment that I realized that M. Farrington, who had known Higgins all her life, was depicting that death scene with the imaginary revolver held in her *right* hand, my limbs had gone suddenly stiff. Even after she had finished speaking, I could not move. Her voice rang out sharply.

"Don't move, James! As the expression is, *I have you covered!*"

She had reached under the blanket and removed the revolver from Higgins' hand. It was trained straight at my heart.

I muttered something that didn't make sense.

"Quite so, James." Her smile was unpleasant. "You see it happens that my brother Norman was not insane. Barbara did not believe that. I would have showed her quite convincingly if that fool Higgins had held his tongue. Norman could not see that he might better be dead than back in that place. Therefore, I showed him. As for Judith, she was in the way. So was Higgins, much as I regret that fact. So are you, James. Therefore—"

But she never finished. I made the most perfect football charge of my career. We went down in a heap together, simultaneously with the deafening report of the revolver. Long before I managed to get to my feet I knew that Martha Farrington was dead.

24

I stood at the living-room window, gazing out across the cluttered sweep of lawn and drive toward the gut where a boat from the mainland should be appearing. Breakfast, such as we could manage to choke down, was over. William and Annie were clearing it away. Between Michael and Gay on the davenport, sat the Skipper. She should have been in bed, but we could do nothing with her. A very short time would bring relief, and with it a doctor. There was a weird sense of unreality in the room, a sense of awakening from a bad nightmare, an illusion intensified by the Skipper's quiet voice.

"Your grandfather, Mike, was a pretty unlucky person. He was only a kid when he married Martha Waterman. Pretty little thing, I've been told—good family. They had about five years of happiness and then—with two kids on their hands—it developed that the wife was insane.

"They didn't put people in asylums in those days if they could possibly help it. He kept her here for three years. And then in one of these winter storms, she got away from her nurse and went over the bluff. She was killed.

"He got over it in time. There were the two kids, both seeming—er—normal and healthy. Eventually he married my mother, whom he had known all his life. I was born about a year later, and the three of us grew up together.

For a long time the other kids didn't even know that my mother wasn't theirs. But servants talk and there was gossip in the village. They found out and they brooded about it. When Norman was about eighteen and Martha about twenty, he began to show unmistakable signs of insanity. Whether he had actually inherited it or brought it on by brooding and fear, we never knew. Anyway, it was there.

"I was about thirteen at the time and I didn't understand much about it, but I did know that Father was in a terrible state. Remembering what happened to the mother, he clapped the youngster into a private nursing home. I think that when Father died, he was still expecting Norm to be cured. He never was. He came home once for a short time, but we couldn't manage him. We sent him back and he never came out again until a few months ago.

"Martha had always been crazy about the boy. When they sent him away, they had a time with her, I can tell you. She accused Father of trying to kill him, among other things. Insisted that he had also murdered her mother. But the doctors assured Father that she was merely neurotic—not in the least insane. Father always felt that Martha's attitude had a great deal to do with my mother's death. But that was absurd. My mother died of pneumonia shortly after Norm was taken ill, and that finished Father. He drew into his shell and left us to our own devices.

"I'm not trying to excuse myself now. I just want Mike in particular to understand how things were. You see, the servants had adored my mother. Consequently, they took great delight in pampering me. And Martha, for such a proper soul, got a big kick out of my escapades.

"And then—" The Skipper's voice faltered but immediately picked up again. "Then something happened. There was a youngster I used to play with—Jack Blinshop. I used to golf with him, gun with him, boat with him. We'd always been cronies—"

Again the Skipper paused. There was an awful wait before the level, expressionless voice went on.

"I was about nineteen and Jack must have been twenty-three. He'd been away at school, and he'd come home to his father's law office, which he hated, and married a girl his family liked, only to find out that he hated her, too. He was wretched, and I felt sorry for him. I wouldn't listen to Martha's warnings. Neither would Father. He told her to mind her own business.

"The upshot of the whole thing was that I suddenly found myself violently in love. He was a handsome kid.

"In those days you couldn't divorce a person just because you hated the sight of her. Jack had no grounds and his wife refused to divorce him. Sounds silly now, but it didn't then. People had a habit of being pretty consistently horrible to anyone who even mentioned such a word. And she was the sort of person who cared a great deal about what people have to say. I didn't blame her much, but I wasn't that type.

"So Jack and I were gloriously happy for a short time, and then—our kid was born. Make no mistake about it, Mike. You were born because I wanted you. I knew what I was doing. You were a cute little devil, if I do say so myself. I wanted to name you after your father, but no one would hear of it.

"It was in February." There was a smile in the quiet voice. "You have no idea what an uproar you caused. In her way I don't think Martha blamed me, but she had been tearing her hair for months. She had thinned the servants down to the few old faithfuls— among them Higgins. The entire household knew, and the stage was set for a nice, private, Victorian scandal—the one thing above all others that I wanted to avoid.

"We had some lovely scenes. I intended to flaunt my child in the face of all society, and Martha's ravings on the side of convention meant nothing to me. But my father's did. He blamed himself for ruining my life and went on in awful fashion. Jack's wife nearly died of shame. She entered the final count that licked me. She pointed out that I would be playing a filthy trick on the child. That got me. So they all took up the refrain and rubbed it in.

"As a result, old boy, you'll never find another person who will admit that you were born here on Farrington Bluff one February day. Six months later an infant named Michael Farrington II supposedly arrived from the far south where young Norman Farrington and his hypothetical wife had met with a fatal and hypothetical boating accident.

"That ended the chapter—or should have ended it. It ended a lot of things for me, at any rate. They did a good job on me when they set about showing me what I had done to you. Your father and I have never been alone together since you were two weeks old. The risk was too great. I made a little nightmare of my sins to brood over when the nights were long and lonely. Perhaps if I hadn't, this horrible thing would never have happened. But it's too late now."

She smiled wanly. "On the whole it's been worth it—or I thought it had until recently. You're not a bad brat, Mike. I used to flatter myself that you hadn't suffered because of my pigheadedness. You had everything a kid could need. You and your father were good friends. I was a pretty happy old fool. And then—poor Norman escaped.

"I've told you about that, but I didn't tell you all of it. He turned up here at night in the middle of a snowstorm. He was—pitiful. Half-frozen, half-starved, and entirely lucid. He wanted protection from the entire world—and above all from 'that place'.

"Martha was frantic. If you've been my fetish, Mike, Norman was hers. I knew from recent alienists' reports that for all his seeming sanity, his condition was in reality worse than ever. But Martha wouldn't believe it. Norman pleaded and wept; Martha begged and stormed. You see, Father had left the money and everything else in my hands and it was up to me. I finally agreed to let him stay for a while, but I intended to send him back and Martha knew it.

"It was then that I realized my mistake. Martha was not merely upset. She was insane—as insane as ever her poor mother and brother were, but in a craftier, deadlier way. Suddenly she began urging me to send for you kids, and when I flatly refused, she threatened to write and tell you the whole story. I was an ass. I see that now, but I didn't then. I would have walked off the bluff to keep you from knowing the truth. I was dumb enough for that. I sent for you.

"On the night you arrived, she sprang her whole amazing trap on me. She told me that she had also invited Jude, whose name I had mentioned in my invitation, more to make it sound natural than for any other reason. She said that Jude was arriving within the hour. Her proposition in a nutshell was that either I promise not to send Norman back or she would arrange a marriage between Blinshop's daughter and Blinshop's son.

"I didn't know about you, Gay. Mike is a close-mouthed infant when he wants to be. I did know that Jude was a stunning kid—and that Mike used to be fond of her.

"I was on the verge of doing almost anything when Jude's arrival diverted me. I left her with Martha and went out for a tramp in the rain to try and collect my wits. That was another fatal mistake. It seems that Jack had just told his daughter what I didn't have the courage to tell my son. And Jude, poor kid, proceeded to confide her knowledge to my sister, blowing the whole plan sky-high unless Martha could prevent both Michael and me from talking to Jude. If Michael had heard that story, Martha's last hold over me would have been gone. To make matters worse, Higgins, in the dining-room, heard it all. If only he could have told me so before he did!

"Well, anyway, you three walked into a pretty mess when you came here Friday night. Martha knew that her game was up, but I didn't, and her one aim was to keep me from knowing it. She made one bad slip. She didn't know that you talked alone with your sister in the game-room. She didn't know that Jude had told you the whole thing. And I knew nothing. I lived centuries Friday night when I realized that you were together. I threw out one desperate line to you, Jimmie, and you must have thought I was crazy.

"Upstairs we had an awful session, but the storm cut it short. You see, I consented to let you come on one condition—that Norman was not to be allowed in the house until after you had left. Late Friday afternoon we fixed him up in the boathouse where there was heat, and he seemed quite comfortable. But in the middle of our row we realized that the storm was whipping up a flood tide and that the boathouse wasn't safe. He had an old skeleton key of Father's, but he might have fallen asleep and would be trapped there.

"I thought of William's summer quarters over the garage. I got into my oilskins and went down the back stairs and out along the porch. You were still in the game-room, Mike, and I suppose you saw me through the window. I saw you."

Michael nodded.

"Yes. Well, Norman had left the boathouse and I couldn't find him. I thought that sooner or later he would head for either the house or the garage. I got to the garage just as you were coming out of it. Norman had already tried to escape in one of the cars. I doubted that he would go to the house. As a matter of fact, I mostly told the truth about where I was that night. The poor collie was in a bad way when I got to the stable. I stayed there a long time, and when Norman failed to arrive I started back.

"As luck would have it, I didn't get a chance for a private word with Higgins. He told me his story just before lunch yesterday. It seems that he had kept his eye on Martha's door. As I went down the back stairs, Jude came up the front ones, looking for me. Martha met her in the hall, crying and wringing her hands. She told Jude that I had just rushed out the front door shouting that I was going to throw myself off the bluff. Jude rushed out after me. Martha stood behind her on the porch and shot her with Higgins' revolver before the old man could stop her.

"I suppose she thought she had done away with all possibilities of Mike's hearing about his father. She handed Higgins the gun and went quietly back to bed. Poor Higgins made sure that he could do nothing for Jude. He cleaned and reloaded the gun and resolved to talk to me before he said anything to anybody else.

"As for me, my situation got increasingly worse from the moment I walked into the kitchen. I felt sure that either Martha or Norman had done it, but I had not one shred of proof—and didn't have until Higgins spoke to me yesterday. Martha staged a frightened, elderly woman act. I could get nowhere with her. I did nothing because we were as much on our guard as we could be and I wanted to avert panic.

"How the dickens Norman managed to elude us when we searched the grounds in broad daylight, I don't know. He may have let himself into the house more than once with that key. I don't think there's any doubt that he was the intruder who dealt with Cook and Annie. That handkerchief he used on Annie was yours, as a matter of fact, Mike. He'd been using some of your clothes. Higgins was the prowler in the hall. He told me so. But poor Norman must have ransacked Martha's room and mutilated the cat in just the sort of frenzy the doctors had predicted.

"I'm sure that you and William suffered at his hands, Jim. Then, I imagine, he let himself into Jude's room with his key and concealed himself in that horrible fashion. Martha must have known that he was there. I suppose she really thought that he was better dead than confined. At any rate, the minute I realized that he was gone, I could think of only one thing—the spot on the bluff where his mother died and where Martha used to brood for hours as a girl. In her mind she had made a martyr of her mother. Something told me that she intended to do the same with her brother. I knew what we would find at the foot of that cliff before I had taken a single step.

"You see, I still hadn't talked to Higgins. I knew that we were at the mercies of a homicidal maniac, but I had not one shred of proof and my chances of being believed were pretty slender. I put her to bed and I thought she was sleeping when I left her. Apparently she wasn't. Higgins was on the verge of telling you the whole story, Jim, when he saw her standing outside the window in my oilskins—listening. She frightened him half out of his wits. What she was doing out there I don't know. Looking at the scene of Norman's death possibly. At any rate from then on she began to distrust Higgins. After you went looking for Mike, Jim, he let her in. And she threatened him, poor old boy! He was terrified. He got her to her room and went in search of me.

"Meanwhile you got the wacky notion that you were insane, Mike, and I did the hardest thing I've ever done in my life. I went to Higgins' room, got his revolver, and walked straight down the hall to Martha's door. In view of Higgins' story she must have just left the oilskins in my room and started to undress. She was at the dressing-table and as she turned toward me, I shot her. Unfortunately, my aim was rotten. Higgins had caught sight of me in the servants' hall. As I turned around he was right at my elbow. He never said a word. Took the gun out of my hand, wiped it clean with his handkerchief, and shoved me to the head of the stairs. To all intents and purposes we were coming up them as you rushed down the hall, Mike. Higgins had the alibi right on the tip of his tongue.

"When I heard that I had failed, I knew that I had endangered your lives more than ever. Martha knew who had shot her, although I don't think she actually saw me. She knew and she laid her plans accordingly.

"I was with her for some time, you may remember. She pretended to be asleep, but I knew that she wasn't. She was my sister—practically my mother—and—and a grand girl. God! How I pitied her! But we sat there within two feet of each other and planned each other's death. I waited until she asked for another sleeping powder. I went into the bathroom to fix it, where she could not possibly see me, and I put a half a box of the damned powders into her glass.

"But she was ahead of me. I came back to find her crying. It wasn't as if her state of mind had been her fault. Seeing her that way—got me. I tried to comfort her, but she wouldn't listen for a long time. Then something appeared to snap in her and she poured out a story. She said that she had lured you into the old loft, Mike, and shot you. Then, frightened, she had put you inside one of the cedar chests and left you there—alive.

"If I had stopped to think, I would have known that she was lying. She hadn't been out of my sight since you had left the room. But she knew me well enough to know that I wouldn't stop. That loft was used as a sort of strongroom in Grandfather's time. I had forgotten its existence.

I tore up to it, dragging her with me. And when I got to the place where she wanted me, she simply crowned me with something. The rest of that—let's not talk about."

The Skipper's pauses were becoming longer and more difficult, but she went on.

"I think Higgins suspected her, but the place had never been used in his time. He didn't know how to get into it, and he knew that Martha was watching him. I heard someone tapping around down here trying to find the opening, and I imagine it was Higgins. Also, he probably wasn't sure of himself. Martha's nearly dying after she finally took the powders probably made him wonder whether I hadn't simply attempted to murder her a second time and then beat it to escape being caught. I heard him calling to me several times through the floor in his room. He apparently knew I was there, but thought I could answer him or come down if I wanted to. When Martha knew that I had been found—dead or alive—she knew that Higgins would talk. Poor old Higgins had been protecting her with his life. He even removed those letters that she planted in William's room. She begged the originals from me long ago and kept them all this time. Those letters were forgeries, of course. Higgins had saved her life, but now he was dangerous. And so—she killed him."

The Skipper stopped abruptly and the sudden silence was painful. Michael sat with his head in his hands, motionless. Gay's subdued face was turned toward him, and her eyes were anxious. But the Skipper sat straight and stiff between them, her face a mask and her eyes straight ahead. Finally Michael raised his head.

"Is that all?" he said in a muffled voice.

The Skipper's smile was twisted. "That's all. If you like, Jim, you can send Jack Blinshop out here to me. I suppose it's poetic justice that I should be the person to tell him."

Blindly I groped for words, found none, and choked out, "I'm telling him."

Gay got suddenly to her feet, dropped one swift kiss on the top of the Skipper's head, and went noiselessly from the room. I wanted to follow her, but my feet seemed riveted to the spot.

"I suppose," the Skipper's voice went on, "there's a moral somewhere in this, although at the moment it eludes me. Something about the wages of sin, no doubt."

"Only, Mickie, I—" Her voice caught and stopped. One instant there was silence; the next the room was filled with dry, hard sobbing. Michael crashed to his knees.

I slipped through the game-room and out the side entrance to the lawn, barely feeling the sting of the cold, salt air. I needed a coat, but not badly enough to go back for one. The foot of the drive confronted me before I was really aware that I was walking. Pausing, I stared out across the water toward the mainland. A motor dory was headed straight for the spot where I stood. In another minute the leathery old face of Andie Darrel was staring up at me from under his sou'wester.

"Hi there!" he trumpeted nasally.

About the Author

Esther Tyler (1911-1985) was twenty-five years old and living in Noroton Heights, Connecticut, when this mystery novel was published. *Murder on the Bluff* was the first manuscript she completed. Simon and Schuster was the first house that saw it. And immediately took it. In her own words:

"Ever since I can remember I've had a big itch to write. While I was still smashing windows and falling out of apple trees, I used to fill every desk in the house with my 'authing'. In Junior High School I won the inevitable Lincoln Essay Medal, and in High School I amused myself with writing and producing unpretentious little skits. Supposedly, I was sent to college to study for the teaching profession but I'm afraid it never particularly interested me. During my freshman year I was appointed to the editorial staff of the literary magazine to which I stuck—and to the daily paper, to which I didn't stick. I wrote the freshman pageant—which centered around the history of New London and was pretty foul. Somewhere along the line I also got involved in amateur theatricals, and stayed involved until the present time. I contributed frantically to all the school publications, fussed around directing, acting in, and doing the dirty work for most of the plays. My only masterpiece—the class prophecy—will never see the light of day. Some cautious soul disposed of it. And now here I am under the paternal roof, occupying myself with the dish pan, writing, and the Cobweb Players.

"The background of *Murder on the Bluff* naturally comes from the locality with which I am familiar—Southern Connecticut along the shores of Long Island Sound. Farrington Bluff and its characters are real insofar as I have seen fragments of them about me all my life; imaginary in that I have never seen just such a place or just such people. If some portly soul pops up one day to sue me for maligning his ancestral roof and the ancestral tree on his front lawn, my amazement will equal my embarrassment."

Murder on the Bluff was Esther's sole mystery (published in the UK as *The Family Skeleton*), but she also wrote short stories for *Good Housekeeping Magazine* and radio scripts for CBS Radio. She worked as a copy editor for the Greenwich, CT, *Time,* and as a writer and editor for several businesses. For a number of years she was the executive director of the Connecticut chapter of the National Multiple Sclerosis Society.

MURDER
AT THE
KENTUCKY
DERBY
CHARLES PARMER

Scarecrow
EATON K. GOLDTHWAITE

THE
13th
GUEST
by
ARMITAGE
TRAIL

Details at
CoachwhipBooks.com

Available from your favorite online retailers

Cry Murder
EDITH HOWIE

www.ingramcontent.com/pod-product-compliance
Lightning Source LLC
LaVergne TN
LVHW091039080826
845145LV00002B/553

* 9 7 8 1 6 1 6 4 6 5 5 3 7 *